KILLER CANDY

by Jason Murphy

Beaumont and Crane

Published by Beaumont and Crane, Inc.

ISBN-13: 978-1-735-9761-2-9

Cover design by: Todd Gimbeltaube

Printed in the United States of America

For Kevin and Cody

CONTENTS

ACKNOWLEDGEMENTS

Big thanks to my advance reading team! You signed up without hesitation, and I wasn't sure how this ridiculous adventure would be received. I'm so glad you're on board for the ride.

A belated thank you to the fine folks at Sinister Grin Press. With my first book, *the Black Goat Motorcycle Club*, you introduced me to the publishing world. Giving someone their first shot at this is a real gift and for that, I'm grateful.

Rod, I can always count on you to read whatever nonsense I drop into your inbox. I'm sincerely thankful for that commitment, for your feedback, and for your friendship.

Jeff, I've said this before, but your critiques of my work are invaluable. With your input, I was able to sharpen this story in ways I didn't know it needed, and it helped bring Clark to life. By the time you read this, book three is probably already sitting in your inbox. *checks watch* No hurry.

Allison, some people are lucky enough to have a partner who encourages them when they need it, who tells them to keep going, and that they've got what it takes. That's just where your support begins. You demanded excellence from me at every turn and never let me say 'good enough'. Thanks for being by my side.

CHAPTER ONE

"Zero. That's how many people have been killed or even harmed by ghosts. Zero. Since the history of time. Ever. You know how many possessions there have been? Zero. How many poltergeists? Also zero. How many documented encounters with demons? Zero. And do you want to know why? Because they don't exist. As bad as we want them to exist, so maybe we can make sense of this horrible cesspit of a planet, we don't get that luxury. We don't get to say, 'But ghosts!', because there is no such thing. They are not real."

I stare at the rain falling in great splats across the windshield as Alan's mouth gapes and closes. He can't find the words. His oversized, Jeffery Dahmer-edition glasses are about to slip off the end of his nose.

"Clark," he says. "Man, what happened to you? Are you kidding me? We've been doing this for what? Two years now and—"

"Yeah. Two years. With how many results? Again, let me re-direct you to my favorite number– zero!"

"We're seeking to understand."

"Oh, I understand," I say, sinking deeper into the passenger seat. "I understand that I'm a grown man who runs around abandoned buildings in the middle of the night with a flashlight and a tape recorder."

"Science isn't as glamorous as it looks on TV, Clark. You of all people should know that."

"Science? We're not scientists, Alan. I'm a college dropout with a spotty work history who has already been arrested for fraud. Twice! You're in customer service for a mattress company. The distance between us and science can be measured in light years."

Alan hangs his head. He's a sensitive little nerd. I should apologize. I should get out of the car and dive right into this ridiculous bit of make believe, but I don't. We sit in the heavy silence.

The rain picks up and blots out the view through the windshield of Alan's car. I can't see the others waiting in the SUV across the vacant parking lot. They're probably holding their breath or bitching about me. They'd be right to. I should have done this earlier in the week, when Alan was trying to pitch this dumb idea. Now, sitting in the car with the rain rattling on the roof, it feels like a break-up. In a way, I guess it is. I'm done with this. I'm wasting my time. There's very little money to be had here and it isn't clean. It isn't right. I should know. I've pocketed enough dirty cash.

"That doesn't bother you?" I ask him as he sulks. "We're no better than professional psychics, Alan. I should know. I *was* one. They're all cheats and liars and we're just like them."

"I have never lied to a client. I—"

"We're lying to *ourselves*," I say, and the sad reality of it hits me. Again. I'm tempted to walk out into the rain and just keep walking, but someone is filming. Someone is always filming. They'll get my dramatic exit on video. Then it's on the internet. Then it's perverted into something like *C-List Ghost Hunter Gets Scared and Quits*. I wonder how many likes *that* would get on YouTube. The internet loves failure. Maybe that's what I'll do.

"We're not frauds, Clark. We're not charlatans."

"We're worse. We're idiots."

"All this time, all of the things we've seen and heard—"

"Nothing. We chase noises and shadows. There's no science here."

"Clark, this is our chance," Alan says, wagging his spindly little fingers at me. "Like you said, every major haunting location that's worth a damn has already been documented and explored. All of them. Except this one!"

"How many times have we thought that, though? That maybe *this* dusty building is the one that's going to reveal the secrets to the afterlife? I'm gonna let you in on a little secret– those noises we're going to hear? The shadows we're going to chase? It's either a raccoon or a bum. Maybe it's a bunch of raccoons. Maybe it's a bunch of bums. Maybe it's two bums fucking, like that one time. But it's not ghosts."

Alan sighs. The way his reedy body seems to curl in on itself makes me feel guilty. He wants to believe. He wants to believe *so bad*. I did, too. I wanted that for a long time, back when I thought *maybe*. Maybe there's something to this and if we keep poking around, we'll at least get a peek. Maybe we'll find something that will make me feel better about myself, that I haven't been lying to everyone and convincing myself that all the bizarre nonsense I've picked up over the years wasn't a waste of time, a long con. The grimoires translated, the meaning behind the occult symbology, the names of Solomon's seventy-two demons. One ghost would justify all of that. One documented encounter would justify not getting a degree in business and a mortgage and kids or whatever the hell else was expected of me.

But no. It's all just theater and grifting. When I wasn't scamming people out of cash, I was just hanging out with friends and goofing around on camera and hoping we got a lot of views when we posted the video. And that's all it was– just trying to convince people to watch some adults pretend to say science things about shadows and cobwebs and bums fucking.

"Okay, but—" Alan starts.

"All right. Fine," I say, just to shut him up.

He perks up. "You'll come?"

"You drove me here. I can't sit in your car all night listening to NPR. There aren't even snacks in here and it smells like beef stew. But after tonight…"

I let that hang there, but he takes it. He nods his head, glad for the reprieve.

I turn to him and raise a stern finger. "But if we catch some kind of raccoon/bum orgy on camera, we're posting it. You hear me? *We are posting that video.*"

***

It's a small office park on the fringe of East Austin, where the roads become highways and the corner stores become truck stops. I say 'office park', but it's really just a single, non-descript building in a sea of pavement. The thicket of trees that masks it from the burger joint down the road has started to reclaim the area. Tufts of weeds crawl up from cracks in the asphalt. Shattered windows gape like wounds. With its beige bricks, it could have been a dentist office or an insurance agency, a banal and rotting thing in a field. Across the side of this nothing-building, a spray-painted message reads LIGHT A CANDLE FOR THE WEEPING KING, because graffiti in Austin is a new level of odd.

A few cars pass by on the road, but we're far back, ensconced in the cedar trees. Plastic bags cling to branches and catch in the tall grass next to faded and weather-worn beer cans. It won't be better inside.

Everyone unloads their bags from their cars and scurries out of the rain toward the awning over the entrance. They shoot me sidelong glances, so I know they're all wondering about the outcome of Alan's chat with me.

"You gonna find some ghosts tonight, Clark, or are you gonna sit in the car and be a pussy?" Melissa asks as she makes a point of carrying the heaviest bag with one arm.

"Seriously, Melissa?" I ask.

"Oh my God, language please," Travis says, as he obsesses over every bag. He's one missing tripod away from a crying fit.

The awning sags and spills rain from its lip as we huddle beneath it. I wonder how much weight it will hold before it crushes us all. I wonder if I would care.

"All right, everyone," Alan says, using his best man-of-action voice. "This is virgin territory. We don't know what to expect in here."

"Asbestos," I say. "That's what I expect."

"Oh my God, I didn't pack the respirators," Travis says, his head in his hands.

"*Oh my God*, thanks for cancer, Travis," I say.

"Are you seriously making fun of me right now, Clark?" Travis asks.

He looks like a wet bird in a hot pink polo. Like a sad flamingo who just really wants to go to brunch.

DJ clasps her hands together and her eyes twinkle as she bounces on her toes. "This is so exciting. We're the first. We're explorers! There's going to be so much magic in here!"

With her squeaky voice and gigantic eyes, she is a living anime character wrapped in a drenched orange hoody and oversized club-kid boots.

Melissa is standing in the rain, away from our huddle, making sure we notice how it doesn't bother her. It doesn't bother her purple hair or her tatted biceps. In case the message isn't clear enough, the angry black cat on her forearm hisses at me. *MEAN* is stamped beneath it in florid script. She waves her flashlight through some of the open windows next to us. "And you say one of the Wanderers found this, Alan?"

"Yes! But they didn't want to go in because the place gave off some bad energy," Alan says with a grin. His gangly arms and legs jitter with anticipation.

"Energy? Like chi? What the hell does that even mean?" I ask.

"Bad energy," DJ says with her unbreakable smile. "You know the Wanderers, they're sensitive to that kind of thing. I wonder if I'm going to feel anything. Maybe I could be sensitive, too!"

"Is the place full of gluten?" I ask.

Travis looks back at the cars as if he's considering a retreat. His hands hover near his lips. "The Wanderers were too scared of this place? I thought they didn't get scared."

"Everyone gets scared," Melissa says, her body halfway through the closest window.

"I'm not scared! I'm excited!" DJ says with a bounce. "Okay. Maybe I'm a tiny bit scared… but it's super exciting!"

"Great!" Alan says. "We've got some good energy tonight."

"Which is different from *bad* energy," I say, and smooth out my red brocade tux jacket for the cameras.

"You're so fancy," DJ says, and her pixie grin cracks my shell, if only a little. "Always dressed like such a dapper gentleman in your shiny jacket."

"If you think thrift store jackets are nice," Melissa says. She turns to me. "We know you were on the TV show, dude. You don't have to wear the jacket all the time. With your jeans and Converse, it just makes you look homeless."

I plaster on my most diffident smile. The tux jacket is the only jacket I have. It's all I can afford. And sometimes people recognize me when I wear it.

4

I shrug. "If this gig ever pays me, I'm going to start dressing like the Monopoly guy just for you, Melissa."

"Okay team," Alan interrupts, so giddy he hasn't even wiped the beads of water from his goofy glasses. "Let's get in there and set up base camp!"

We worm in through the window left of the door, careful to avoid the teeth of broken glass lining the frame. The place smells exactly as I thought. Mold. Dust. Rats. The ammonia of animal piss. At least there's nothing dead.

The building has been ransacked. It's been empty for years. The ceiling tiles, having rotted away, leave rectangular shadows lurking above us. The floor is thick with chunks of drywall. Animals have chewed through it. Vagrants smashed the rest. There's graffiti, but not as much as I expected. In one corner is a bunch of beer bottles where squatters or kids camped out to have a good time. Over the reception area, a faded logo greets us. The paint is chipping away, but the image of a lighthouse is still discernible. At the top of it is the all-seeing Eye of Providence, emitting a golden beam.

Everyone stops. There it is. It's that moment in the ghost-hunting show when the resident psychic gets all hot and bothered. *There's something here,* they whisper.

My friends stand at attention, eyes open and breath held. I don't want to say anything. I don't want to acknowledge it. I just keep arranging the bags, sorting cameras, thermometers, and sensors like nothing's happening. Everyone else is transfixed. They look around, their mouths hanging open. It's not the debris they're looking at. It's not the broken glass or the chunks of moldering plaster. It's what they *can't* see.

"What is that?" Travis says, his voice barely a whisper.

Alan snaps out of it. "Oh man. Oh boy. You feel that? That's what Violet was telling me about when I went to talk to the Wanderers Guild."

"Violet?" I ask. "The weird homeless girl with the tarot cards? We're getting intel from her now?"

"Violet knows this town like the back of her hand, Clark," Alan says, his face glowing in the dim light. "She knows more about its secret nooks and crannies than—"

Alan freezes. His face goes slack. He takes a step back.

"What? Oh no. Alan, what?" Travis says.

Melissa shushes him and steps in front of us.

There's someone here.

Inches from the wall, someone sits motionless in a ragged office chair, staring up in reverence at the lighthouse logo. My stomach drops and Travis makes a quiet bird noise.

"Hello?" Alan asks.

They don't move. Long hair clotted with dust and debris spills over the back of the chair, left hand raised in a frozen gesture. The severed right arm rests at their feet next to a used condom and a fast-food wrapper. My stomach goes into freefall.

"Are you… are you okay?" Alan asks.

The arm on the ground is stiff. The skin uniform and slick, unnatural. *Wait…*

I step forward and spin the chair around.

A chipped and faded face looks back at me with lifeless eyes.

A mannequin.

She's got a disconnected office phone in her lap and the plastic wig hangs askew.

Everyone exhales. Travis puts his head between his knees as Melissa bellows with laughter to let us know she was never scared.

"Looks like Debbie's putting in some overtime," I say, and hope my voice doesn't sound as shaky as my hands feel.

"There's another one over here!" DJ shouts from the corner of the room.

This one is poised at his desk. His yellow polo is chewed through and something has nested in his head.

"They're everywhere…" Alan says. He points to Travis. "Get this. All of this. Start filming. Film!"

Travis fumbles with the camera and starts capturing it.

The mannequins litter the place, tipped over in doorways, slumped over desks, or toppled to the floor in undignified poses. A graveyard of business casual Pinnochios.

"This couldn't have been a department store or anything, right?" Melissa says as she sweeps her flashlight across the room.

It was clearly an office building, now just a diorama of corporate life turned to rot.

"I don't understand—" Alan starts.

"What's to understand?" I ask. "It's like when we found that trash bag full of dildos in the abandoned Burger King. People do weird shit all the time."

Alan brushes me off. He looks into the camera, speaking in a hushed tone to let the viewer know this is serious. "Here we have a strange scene, a facsimile of office life. Someone set this up with purpose. What was its purpose? Why do these lifeless sentinels stand watch over their sinister domain?"

"Sinister domain? Seriously?" I ask.

He ignores me. They all do that these days.

We go deeper. There's just enough ambient light to navigate by. Everyone has flashlights, but they use their phones anyway. It's more of the same. Only broken cubicles remain, just offices that open up all around us like rotting cavities. And more mannequins. Mannequins with their heads knocked off. Mannequins repositioned in lewd poses or with dicks drawn onto their fiberglass skin. Mannequins pretending to answer phones. It's the shittiest museum ever.

Alan looks around to make sure no one can see us from the road. "Here. Yeah. This should work."

The mannequins offer no protest to the interruption of their eternal workday. We turn on the lamps and start dragging around tables, arranging base camp. No one is completely focused on what we're doing, though. They're all looking out into the darkness, waiting to experience its mystery. I focus on getting set up. This sensation they're giving themselves over to is poison. It's the poison of unreason, the tingle that makes you susceptible to believe whatever you think you see. If you get that electricity crackling beneath your skin, you'll buy anything. My friends will attribute the vibes to something paranormal. They'll say that we can feel the 'other side' or that it's the disruption in the local electromagnetic field that tells us we're on the right track.

But no.

No, it's not that. It's never that. It's just the chills you get when you're in the dark in an unfamiliar and decidedly unsafe place. It's the rush of adrenaline, the one that erodes your common sense and makes it easy for you to say *Oh, yes. Definitely ghosts.* I'm not going to open myself up to that. When you feel that thrill, you'll believe anything. Alan and the rest of these dumbasses, they welcome it, gleefully blind to the truth.

"Guys," I say, "Get your shit together, okay? This is an abandoned office building. What are we going to encounter? The ghost of Cheryl from marketing?"

So that's how I piss all over everything.

Their shoulders sag, and they hide their scowls as they get to work. I slapped that Spielbergian wonder right off their gullible faces. To tell the truth, I feel kind of gross about it. There they were, finally experiencing something that brought some fireworks to their lives of push notifications and low-carb diets and streaming services. And I couldn't help myself. If I was going to be miserable, I guess I just had to take them down with me.

"We've got to come up with a cool name for it," Alan says, and he gazes into the darkness with wonder, waiting for the mystery to inspire him.

"Undisclosed location," I say.

"What? Boring! Ugh," Travis says. "Use your imagination. Think about SEO."

"The Forbidden…" Melissa starts.

"Forsaken!" Alan says. "The Forsaken... umm... the forsaken... the forgotten..."

"The Forsaken Texas Department of Transportation Annex, oooooooh!" I say, pulling cameras from the bag.

Melissa snickers, but the moment Travis sees me unloading this bag, he has a fit. "No! Wait! There's a system. At least let me get the check list. Oh my God."

"No, seriously," Alan says, "we've got to figure out what this place is so we can document its history."

"We don't have any idea?" Melissa asks. "You didn't do the background research?"

"There was nothing to find," Alan says, replacing the battery and card in the camera. His hands shake. He thinks he's going to miss something. "Records with the county were incomplete. Lots of dead ends. Tax records were missing. Super suspicious."

"Yes, lackadaisical bookkeeping is the cornerstone to any good mystery," I say, but no one bites.

"I still like 'forsaken!'" DJ says. "Or 'doomed'! Or 'profane'! We've never called anything 'profane' before."

"I've been called profane a few times," I say. "But no, seriously, we just need to call this an 'undisclosed location.'"

"Why?" Alan asks.

"Because we're trespassing, Alan. We're trespassing and documenting it on camera."

Alan nods as it settles in. He shakes it off and narrows his eyes, looking cool and determined for the camera in his hand. He speaks into it with soap opera gravitas.

"We're here. We made it in. This is an undisclosed location in Central Texas. Its past is an enigma. We can't give you too many details about the building, certainly not until we've ascertained that it's safe. This place has been largely undisturbed for years and you can feel the energy here, like something is... wrong. This may be Occult Technologies, Incorporated's most dangerous investigation yet."

Alan shuts off the camera and stands there, posing like a ghost-fighting Captain America. I see a soaking wet, balding nerd, standing in an abandoned office building. He's also afraid of spiders.

Travis, the nervous and featherless bird, is flitting around basecamp. Everything has to be just so. He sets up the foldout tables, placing them in a 'V'. Laptops go on the left table, gear on the right. His fold-out chair is *his* fold-out chair, and God help you if you sit in it.

I sit in it.

"Are we going to milk this? Is this going to be one of those all-night things?" I ask, thinking of the video games I'd rather be playing.

"We'll be here as long as it takes, I guess," Alan says. "Have you seen anything? I want to be really thorough, and if there's anything strange here that could be a part of the narrative, tell me."

"So, it *is* going to be one of those all-night things," I say and prop my feet up on the table. "Whelp. As Occultex's founder and resident occultist, I can certify that this particular square footage of rubble and trash exhibits no signs of occult activity."

A low, gravelly sound comes from the darkness. We all stop, frozen in a tableau of tangled wires and cold fear, staring into the pitch-black corridor. The sound is warbling and alive. It's a thing, a discontented mewl, and I'm suddenly aware of how close the shadows are, and how thick.

"Oh my God…" Travis whispers.

A feral cat emerges from the black. You can see its bones as it moves, its milky eyes and its patchy hair. It pauses to yowl at us, a guttural warning, before it slinks back off down a hallway.

"Kitty!" Melissa says and chases after it.

"Melissa!" I call out. "Don't touch that thing. It's all claws and disease."

It won't respond to any language spoken by the living or the holy. That cat only answers to the infernal tongues. And it's going to claw the shit out of her. She vanishes down another dark corridor, calling for the creature until her voice fades into muted echoes.

"We should go get her, guys!" DJ says.

"Yeah, she could get rabies or fall into a pit or something," Travis says, his hands hovering over his face with delicate horror.

"Yes," I say, "a pit. Most office buildings built before 2000 had pits. Just big holes right there in the middle of the hallway."

"All right," Alan says. "Cameras ready. We'll finish setting up when we get back. Travis, you rolling?"

Travis hoists his camera and gives a thumbs up.

"DJ?" Alan asks.

"We're great, chief! Cameras, motion detectors, radios, audio, emf readers, and thermal sensors are all in order."

"Thermometers," I say. "You can call them thermometers."

DJ, her arms loaded with gadgets, says, "*Thermal sensors* sounds so cool, though!"

The room branches out into a web of hallways, quiet and black as catacombs. Our flashlights throw everything into stark relief, turning the faces of the mannequins into alien grimaces.

Alan sets his jaw and nods. "Okay, Occultex team. On me. Once more into the breach."

CHAPTER TWO

"Once more into the breach?" I say with a snort.

Everyone gives me side-eye. Alan's every step is heavy with gravitas, like a py in enemy territory. He's stone-faced and ready for action. His dumbass heatrics have become my favorite part of any ghost hunt.

"Let's watch for signs of the occult, people. Any animal remains, candles, or demonic symbolism, I want it documented. We don't know what we're walking into," Alan says, cheating to the cameras.

"I'm expecting a spray-painted pentagram or swastika, or some misspelled acial slurs. Maybe an anthropomorphic penis, if we're lucky," I say.

The mannequins watch us as we pass and the hairs on the back of my neck tand up. It's nothing I'm proud of. I avoid looking at them. I can't have these diots thinking this place is getting to me.

"Melissa, can you hear us?" Alan calls out into the darkness. He turns to)J. "You getting anything?"

She fumbles with the assortment of toys hanging from her arms and around er neck. "Nothing yet, Chief."

She switches from the thermometer to another EMF reader and stares at its notionless needle before finally shrugging and continuing down the hall. If we ould afford Bluetooth mics and drones and ghost-detecting lasers, Alan would uy it all and go forth like we were about to use it to save lives. I take a look ack in the direction of the front door. Once they're distracted, maybe I will go it in Alan's car. I might even be able to find a video online that'll teach me ow to hotwire stuff. Then I can hit up a strip club or a Whataburger and be ack in time for them to wrap up their silly bullshit.

"Melissa, are you safe?" Alan yells, then speaks in a hushed tone over his houlder. "No word from Melissa yet. I don't want to alarm anyone, but we ave to assume the worst."

"Oh, Melissa, no!" Travis whispers.

Another cat pads past me. It doesn't care about us, not stopping for petting r a rub against my leg. Like the one Melissa chased, the thing looks like a evenant, all bones and patchy fur.

"Another cat," Alan announces. "This must mean something."

"Why can't we ever investigate a place that's infested with puppies?" I ask.

"Aw. I love puppies!" DJ says.

The cat disappears into a stretch of hallway and before Alan can narrate for he cameras, another appears, and then two more. They're heading in the same direction and in a hurry. Everyone's breath catches in their throats. This place has my friends in its grip. I see a herd of feral cats. They see an omen.

The cats mewl with deep, yearning sounds as they pass, but it's not the sounds of hunger or anger or contentment. They yowl with the need for sex, that almost-human moan that only a cat in heat can make. More pour forth, slipping from cracks in the wall and from under desks. Each of them mewls, and their chorus starts to sound like a dirge. Alan and the others are slack-jawed. He mimes for Travis and DJ to keep filming, and I'm worried he might get all weepy with excitement.

The beams of light from the cameras bounce around the jagged hallways. Motes of dust make ghostly shapes as the white shafts cut through darkness. More thick chunks of plaster litter the path. Exposed wiring and studs. Door after door of rooms filled with only rotting, industrial carpet. The cats run in a sickly column, gathering speed and numbers, herding us along with them. We take turn after turn, each twist exposing another decayed corridor that looks just like the last. Fifteen to twenty of the cats crowd the hallway now and follow a winding trail only they can see.

"I'm not a cat person, so someone help me out here," I say. "Is this normal?"

When Alan responds, it's both to me and the audience he hopes to have. "It's well documented that cats are extraordinarily perceptive of supernatural activity. I don't want to jump to conclusions, but I can't shake the feeling that they're leading us to the dark heart of this structure."

We round a corner and the hallway opens up to a flight of stairs leading down to double doors, cracked open. Two more corridors intersect and end here. The cats stop. They whine and slink around our ankles. Alan turns to face the cameras.

"It all leads here," he says. "The cats seem compelled, drawn to this chamber and we don't—"

I step past him, down the steps, and open the door.

The cats recoil. Some of them hiss. They won't go inside. I nudge one out of the way with my foot and step through.

"Clark…" Alan says with his disappointed whine.

This room is much bigger than the lobby or any other rooms we passed. Where the others had drop ceilings with water-damaged or missing tiles, this one stretches up into darkness. It's all concrete floors and steel girders, an industrial cathedral. In the center is a lone door. My stomach goes sour when I see it, and there's a moment of vertigo, my mind unhinging as I see something that doesn't make sense, something that just seems *wrong*. It stands alone. It's not floating or anything, but anchored in its frame, bolted to the concrete floor. There's nothing past it, like a tornado ripped the house away, but left this one door standing. It's nondescript, plain white with basic inlay and a sturdy, silver knob. The frame is made of unpainted 2 x 4's set into what look like some iron braces. Someone didn't want this thing going anywhere.

Melissa is standing in front of it. I can only see her back and her shock of purple hair. She doesn't move. I look at Alan and the others, but they're focused on Melissa. Alan opens his mouth to speak, but reconsiders.

"Melissa?" I ask.

She turns as if she didn't know we were standing right there behind her. The original feral cat is in her arms, ears laid back like it's about to flay her face open.

"Oh, hey!" Melissa says.

Everyone breathes.

Travis walks in a panicked circle. "Oh my God, girl, what are you doing to us?"

"Yeah, I thought you were going to turn around and not have eyes! Like maybe the cats ate them!" DJ says with unnecessary glee.

"Do you guys see this? What the hell is it?" Melissa steps aside to give us a better look.

No one wants to get too close to the door. Its placement makes it feel like an altar, only there are no mannequins in here to worship at it. Just us. Scrawled onto its white surface is a red symbol.

Alan points at it, nearly vibrating out of his shoes, as if we all didn't notice the markings. "Clark! Clark! The symbol. Look! What is that?"

I take a step closer. It's drawn in red chalk, a scrawled intersection of lines and curves, almost like a warped triangle with stars at each vertex. "Hmm. It's primitive, but deliberate. I don't recognize it, but—"

"Wait! Wait wait wait!" Alan says and waves Travis to frame up a shot.

Alan stands next to me and assumes his grim superhero face. It takes everything I've got not to start laughing again. Alan says, "We've found something unprecedented. It's not often that we find direct evidence that the people – the real, living humans that inhabited a place – were involved in occult activity. When we do, it's usually candles or pentagrams or an animal carcass used for nefarious purposes."

I roll my eyes.

"But we have found something that defies our past experiences," he says. "This is new. It is clearly some sort of occult doorway. Is it meant to transport practitioners to some other location? To another plane? Or is it meant for something far more diabolical?"

"Is it meant for letting something through?" Travis asks before throwing a hand over his own mouth. "I'm really sorry I said that out loud."

"Keep filming," Alan tells Travis before stepping aside with a florid gesture. "Alright everyone, I want every possible reading on this thing. I want measurements, vibrations, thermal, the works."

The team swarms around it, but Melissa shouts. "Wait!"

Travis wilts. "Is there danger? Are we in danger?"

Melissa sets the cat down on the concrete. "Careful," she says.

The cat bolts for the door to join its friends. They hover just outside, eddying about, but never taking a step into the room. Melissa walks around to the back of the chamber, scooting past stacks of half-collapsed boxes and old photocopiers lined up along the wall. Desks. A coffee maker. A vacuum cleaner. The remains of the American office.

Behind all of it, almost invisible in the shadows, is a massive pit.

"Holy shit," I say. "Offices do have pits."

At twenty feet by ten, it dominates the back of the room. At first, I thought it was just a staircase, but there are no stairs. Just a deep, black well, a crack running along the back wall. My imagination fills that darkness with tentacles and teeth. The guardrails would keep me from falling in, but I'm careful as I approach and peer over the edge. The pitch black beneath is absolute, gobbling up every breath, every shuffle of our feet. It could descend for ten feet or a hundred. The edges are smooth, indicating that the concrete floor was poured around the cavity. This wasn't some sinkhole that opened up in their basement. It was something they structured the building around. I kick a piece of plaster over the precipice. It's immediately swallowed by the black. It doesn't make a sound, falling forever.

"Whoa," is all DJ can manage to say.

Above is an array of microphones, nearly twenty of them, suspended from cables and boom arms with a lacework of cobwebs festooning them. They all focus on the pit. Wires snake across the floor, all intersecting at a giant, dusty console. It's an antique beast, looking like a piece of equipment that helped us land on the moon. The knobs and dials are all dark.

"This isn't right. This isn't right at all," Melissa says.

In 1989, one of those Christian nut-job TV channels started pushing some real *Weekly World News* insanity. They reported the Russians had dug a hole so deep they were able to lower a microphone in and record audio from Hell itself. It always sounded a little geologically questionable, not to mention theologically stupid, but here in the darkness, in the bowels of this rotting maze, I can almost make myself believe it. Instead, I grab a random box from the stack. This one is full of office phones, all wrapped in their cables. I chuck it over the edge. It disappears. I wait, holding my breath and listening. There is only silence.

"Clark…" Alan says, like an exhausted father.

"Juvenile," Melissa says.

"Travis? Are you getting this?" Alan asks.

Travis nods. Alan clears his throat and straightens up for the camera.

"We've found something unprecedented. A mysterious hole, surrounded by some sort of recording equipment. What were they trying to record? What sounds came from this abyss? I can't quite find the words."

"Sounds like you found plenty," I say, and grab more stuff.

A bulky, beige CRT monitor. Staplers. A coffee maker. The inky black swallows it all. After the first few, Melissa and DJ join in, giggling while chucking stuff over the rail and listening for the crash that never comes.

Then the fun is over. Alan has his arms crossed and watches us with pursed lips. That's fair. We're not even pretending to science. We're just throwing stuff into a hole.

"Can we take some readings, please?" Alan asks.

The others get back to work, but I rummage through more boxes, hoping to find something cool, something that I can carry out of here to hock on eBay. There are technical manuals for fax machines, more phones, a million stray paperclips, more CRTs, and old dot-matrix printers.

"Clark. Do your thing," Alan says.

I keep searching through the pile of junk. "There's no *thing* to do here, Alan."

"What does the symbol mean?"

"I don't know. I can't place it. Probably nothing."

Melissa exchanges a smirk with Travis. My face flushes hot as I catch on.

I wrinkle my nose and try to look studious and authoritative. "It's definitely pre-Christian, but… the closest thing I can compare it to is Sumerian cuneiform. Maybe alchemical symbols? But none that I recognize, it's nothing."

I return to my looting, hoping they'll leave me alone.

"Wow! Ancient magics!" DJ says, and starts moving around the pit, taking readings.

I grab another box. This one rattles. It's full of cassette tapes. My heart skips a beat. Maybe they have some 90s hip-hop. Arrested Development? PM Dawn? Hell, I'll take Colour Me Badd. My collection was long ago snatched up by hipsters after an unfortunate but necessary trip to the pawn shop.

The cassettes are all labeled with tiny, serial killer script.

Durweze, Turkmenistan– 6-19-65

Arecibo, Puerto Rico– 9-8-82

Stull, Kansas– 12-4-77

Dozens of them, spanning decades and locations all across the globe. No Young MC. No MC Hammer. Some of the cases have their own hand-written arcane symbol. Turkmenistan's is the same as the one on the door. It could mean anything. *Evil? Satan? My neighbor owns three goats?* I still don't recognize it.

"Tapes?" Alan asks and rushes over. He reaches for them, but I pull away. "Don't be all grabby!"

"Oh wow. What a find! We need to catalog all of these!" Alan says. "This is a major discovery, guys."

He bounces so much that Travis struggles to keep him in frame.

Across from the pit, the audio console looms, a stoic audience to our jackassery. I cross over to it to take a closer look and blow the dust from its surface. Spiders skitter through the stirred-up clouds. There's a slot for cassette tapes in the front panel.

"The symbols, Clark," he says, pointing at the tapes. "This has to mean something!"

"They're just doodles, Alan. Relax."

Alan puts a dramatic finger to his chin. "In the middle of the door? In the middle of this room? And on these tapes? Doodles? That sounds unlikely."

More smirks. Alan's right, but I don't want to admit it. This was all done deliberately.

"That doesn't mean they knew what they were doing," I say.

"This is an intentional attempt to meddle with the forces of darkness. This isn't something someone just made up," Alan says, circling the door.

"Truth time," I tell him as I try to find the power button on the console, "All attempts to meddle with the forces of darkness are something some weird loser just made up."

Alan says, "Clark. Come on. Please. You've got to be excited about this, right? We've never experienced anything even close to this, and you're still going to be like that? All this time, chasing shadows and noises, like you were saying, and now we find something like this. And you just don't care?" He calls out to the shadows, "To those souls not at rest, who have found they cannot leave this place, my name is Alan. We mean you no harm."

He nods back to DJ to make sure she's getting this. She holds up the audio recorder and smiles.

"Not this shit…" I say. "Who do you think you're talking to exactly?"

"Clark…" Alan starts.

Travis joins in. "We've had lots of promising EVP. You've heard it. I don't understand why you—"

"I haven't heard shit, but if we can get this thing working, maybe we can rock out to some sweet jams."

I look at the tapes again. Dates and locations. "Probably a stack of live shows. Bootlegs. You think we could get anything for these?"

"I don't think now is the time for this, Clark," Alan says.

"No? Is it time for EVP, Alan? Where you listen to stray sounds and try to turn them into words that mean something? I've got news for you, asshole, those noises aren't ghosts. I mean, who thought of that? Who says, 'There's static in this audio. Must be a ghost!'? I'll tell you who– *crazy people!*"

I pop *Turkmenistan* into the tape slot.

"I don't have time for this," Alan says, and turns away. "If anyone here can hear me – and I know you're there – I want you to know it's safe to come out. I'm going to open the door now. Please let me know if this offends you."

I snort again. The snort turns to laughter. The laughter turns delirious. "Are you serious? 'Let me know if this offends you?'"

"Hey, you've made your point, dude," Melissa says with a snarl. "Let it go."

"Let it go? I've broken into a building on the outskirts of town at three AM so my friends can play make believe with some rabid cats and a random door."

"Sounds like a good friend," DJ says, then retreats back into her hoody.

"You want to see a good friend? I'll be a good friend," I say, and my blood runs hot and quick. Everything starts to spill over. I give in to it. "Hey, Alan. Consider this an intervention from a good friend. If you're in an abandoned building in the middle of nowhere, trying to talk to ghosts in the middle of the night, then maybe you need professional help. There's some advice from a good friend."

"Oh my God. *You* need professional help," Travis says as if he's not sure he wants me to hear.

"*Oh my God.* Fuck you, Travis."

I flip random switches and push all the buttons. Massive speakers suspended from the wall crackle to life. Lights flicker across the board. I didn't expect that. This building is dark, the power long ago cut off, but somehow, it works.

"Ooooh, we have liftoff!" I say.

Alan takes a few steps back, so that we're not sharing the frame on camera. He calls out to the darkness again. "We only have a few questions, spirits. If we open this door, will we be safe?"

I'm drowning in the absurdity of this. This can't be real. This is not the life I would have picked for myself. If my mom were here, there would be an *I told you so* about my choices.

"Would you just move, Clark?" Travis says, and nudges me aside to get a better shot.

I slap the camera out of Travis' hands. "Stop this shit!"

The camera cracks on the concrete floor and goes dark. Travis gasps, his mouth hanging open.

"Whoa!" Melissa says, and barrels forward with all her roller-derby girth. "That's enough."

She tries to grab me.

I press *Play*.

The speakers pop and hiss. Everyone stops. They look up at the speakers, then past that, into the darkness above, and down into the darkness below. A knot in my stomach blossoms into something cold and sour in a way I can't explain. I take a wobbly step back on my heels. A primal, lacerating sound tears out of the massive speakers. The volume is set to *KILL*. My fingers fumble for the knob, but everything is worn away or occluded with dust. I flip more switches and turn random dials as the piercing wail attacks us. *Have to stop it make it stop make it stop!*

What comes out isn't music. The tones claw their way through the air, over and on top of each other in a tumbling rhythm that vaguely resembles *the Itsy-Bitsy Spider*. I cover my ears and grit my teeth. The noise sneaks into my bone and fills them with ice. It's in the back of my throat, in the base of my skull.

Travis's eyes roll back in his head. Melissa rakes her fingernails across her face. DJ drops backward onto her ass. I can't tell if she's laughing or sobbing.

I'm on my knees.

I don't remember falling.

I crawl for the door. An army of cats waits at the threshold. Their hackles raised, they bare their teeth, not at me, but past me.

They hiss at the lone door.

"Alan! Get away!" is all I can say as vomit slides out of my mouth.

But no one can hear me.

My vision blurs. I drag myself across the concrete floor, fighting to get away, to escape into the hall.

Someone shouts through the noise, "It's open! My God, it's open!"

Then the screaming starts.

I pull myself closer to the hallway, sliding through puke and blood.

Where did the blood come from?

Am I bleeding?

***

My mouth is full of pennies. My head is full of smoke and thorns. Vision comes back slowly, a soggy kaleidoscope. Something brushes against my face I try to swat it away, but my arms don't want to work. I just fumble, clumsily pushing a stray cat from my chest. Its friends lap at my face, their muzzles slick with blood.

I drag the back of my sleeve across my face and gag, hocking up red-tinged spit. My nose. It's stopped bleeding, but the front of my shirt is soaked.

I'm on my back in the doorway, halfway in the hall, my head resting on the first step. The cats scatter as I rouse. They hide behind toppled filing cabinets and in tunnels burrowed into the plaster. But they watch.

"Guys?" I ask.

My voice echoes across the concrete. When I sit up, the white door is there to greet me. It's closed. And my friends are gone.

I wince as the memory of the song comes flooding back. The screams. The vertigo. I lean against the doorframe and like the cats, I don't want to go inside.

"Guys?"

Across the chamber, the stereo is dark again. I step inside but keep my eye on its switches and dials.

"Alan? Melissa?"

The only signs of them are streaks of vomit and a light spattering of blood. Only some of it is mine.

Past that, the pit awaits. It swallows every sound I make. There's no way to get to it without passing by the door or the stereo, so I keep my distance.

"I want to go home now. I think maybe I had an aneurysm. Or the guy at the taco truck spiked my fajitas with PCP."

Maybe they're hiding behind the door. Maybe they're in the pile of boxes, waiting to jump out and scare me. Maybe they jumped into the goddamn hole.

A mad thought tells me to open the door.

Try the knob. You know there's nothing on the other side, so why won't you try it? Just open it to relieve the pressure of that scream boiling in the back of your mind, the one that wants to get out, the one that will bring you to your knees again. Just open the door. It's nothing. Right?

"I'm sorry about the tape. That sucked real bad."

No snickers. No furtive footsteps. Just my voice, echoing off the stone.

I skirt by the stereo system without touching it. If I bump it, it may scream at me. It might crawl back into my brain and break something that can't be fixed.

They're not behind the door. They're not hiding among the ransacked boxes.

A sound drifts up from the cavity in the floor. Looking over the edge, there is only darkness, but I'm holding my breath, waiting for the noise to come again or for some Lovecraftian nightmare to slither out of the black. Instead, I hear beeping. The beeps are choked and erratic, like a robot sinking into the ocean. At first, it's just one strangled series of tones. Then more join in, a soft cacophony. The office phones I pitched into the hole have started to ring.

I back away.

"Guys?" I say again, but it's only a wheeze.

My heart flutters in my chest, trying to escape.

I run. Cats scatter as I blast through the doors into the moldy hallway, and I keep running. Blindly, I sprint, tripping over stray cables and ricocheting from wall to wall.

Turn left. Run straight. Dead end. Double back. Left again. Straight.

I pass our gear. It's still there, half-packed, right where we left it. I spin around and look back into the hallways, certain I'll find something following me.

"Alan! Melissa!"

I stumble into the lobby. Outside, the rain pours, and I'm grateful for the roar. I'm glad to hear something else, something normal. Not my screams or my panicked footsteps or… the shrieking song as it banshees about in my head.

"Hello?!"

A phone rings. It's a sickly sound, the same drowning digital chime from the pit. The sound of an office phone.

My legs quiver, wanting to keep sprinting or just melt right there into the floor. I bite my lip and search for the source. The flashlight beam jerks and dances across the room.

The phone in the mannequin's lap.

With her blank stare, she offers it as a single red light blinks on its console. The frayed cable, connected to nothing, dangles next to her loose arm. Behind her, the lighthouse and its all-seeing eye glow under the flashlight.

"Guys? Travis? Are you guys messing with me right now? Real talk – I'm scared out of my goddamned mind."

The ringing continues, undulating and feeble, like a digital death rattle.

My hands are shaking and numb. I almost don't recognize them as my own when I reach out to pick up the phone. I operate on autopilot, as if there's no other choice but to answer it. I hold it to my ear, my mouth open to speak, but I don't utter a sound.

"The King weeps for you," the voice says.

The voice is shattered walls. The voice is things abandoned. The voice is a decayed carcass of a building left to rot.

I run.

CHAPTER THREE

I am floating, preserved in amber. There's hot sauce on my jeans. I've been wearing the same clothes for three days. My jacket is a mess of plaster, vomit, blood, and cat hair. That's how I know the cats were real, so I keep it this way. *The Addams Family* is on, but all I hear is canned laughter and the occasional *bon mot*. The coffee table is littered with empty ramen cups and cans of diet soda. The couch is littered with *me*.

I close my eyes and I see the door. The symbol is seared into my brain. The eye of the Lighthouse stares back.

My phone buzzes again, that constant refrain. I've turned the ringer off. I don't want to hear ringers. I don't want to talk on the phone. It's reporters. It's creditors. It's someone's girlfriend or family, asking me again exactly where their loved one went.

I told them everything. I told them about the cats and the cassettes. I told them about the door with the symbol and the phones in the pit, chirping up at me from the darkness. I told them about the strange, shrieking song that raked across my bones. I even told them how I ran. I ran until my lungs burned and my legs cramped, and I collapsed into a muddy puddle on the side of the interstate. I sat there until dawn.

I don't understand any of it, but I told them all of it.

The King weeps for you.

Well, almost all of it.

***

Every time I tell the story, it loses more of its meaning. It becomes something that happened to someone else, something I read about on the internet.

"You just sat there in the rain?" the detective asks as she chews on her pen.

She looks like if Sonic the Hedgehog were a no-nonsense cop whose best weapon is wearing you down with inappropriately long eye contact.

"Yeah," I say.

"Didn't go back inside."

"No. I called a rideshare and—"

"Right. Went home and slept all day. Yeah. We got that part. Where do you think they would have gone?"

"I don't know. I was hoping you could tell me that. Do you... I don't know, have any leads or whatever?"

"You didn't go back and check? See if their cars were still there?"

"No. I... I couldn't."

I can't do anything but call. I can't do anything. Do something. Help me. Help them!

"But you think something bad happened to them."

"Yeah."

"Like... you think they're dead?"

"I don't know."

The second cop is a slab of pale meat and sweat. He's been watching, scrunching up his nose as he looks at me. "Were you on TV?" he asks and there's a smile, a hint of recognition.

The ice in my stomach hasn't gone away.

"Yeah," I say.

"Yeah! I thought so," he says, elbowing Detective Sonic the Hedgehog. "It was a ghost show, right? I saw some of that."

"Yeah."

Sonic sits back while Detective Meat bounces in his chair the way people do when they think you might be famous. I'm not.

"You were only on a few of them, though. Then it was just that other guy, that one 'dude'."

"Kyle Foxwell," I say, and hope that my voice doesn't sound like motive.

"Yeah! That's him. Is that show still on? What was it called?"

"Spirit Squad," I say, and realize that yes, I've sunk into hell. "It got two seasons. I was only on like three episodes."

"What happened? Why'd you leave?"

I was fired and almost sued for fraud.

"It didn't work out," I say.

He nods and takes a note on his legal pad. I can see what he's writing. It just says *Spirit Squad*. Detective Meat leans forward, eyes gleaming for the story he hopes is coming. "You were their occult expert, right? You're the guy who knew about all of the spooky books and demons and stuff."

"That's me."

He bounces again. "And you had that crazy jacket!"

I gesture to the filthy jacket, tossed over a chair.

"Wow! That's the one!" He elbows Detective Sonic again. "That's the jacket he wore in the show. Same one?"

"Same one."

"Maybe we can get a picture later," he says, eliciting a slight snarl from Detective Sonic.

"Sure. For twenty bucks," I say.

This is my favorite part. Whenever someone asks for a picture and you tell hem the price, you can usually see the moment when they change their mind. His mouth moves as he tries to find the words. He's not sure if I'm kidding or ot.

I'm not kidding.

Detective Sonic checks her own notes. "You didn't recover any of your quipment from the site?"

"No."

Detective Meat looks genuinely concerned. "You don't need all that for our work? You're still a working paranormal investigator, right?"

"I don't know. I guess."

"What are you doing for money?"

I straighten in my seat, like this is a job interview.

"I appear at conventions and other... celebrity things."

"Posing for twenty-dollar pictures," she says, looking me right in the eye.

"And autographs," I say, but it's barely a mumble.

"Anything else?" she asks.

"I was... I run a consulting business. Occult Technologies, Incorporated. Ve help people with things outside of your normal, day-to-day whatever."

She just arches an eyebrow in a way that makes me want to keep talking ntil she's happy.

I'm a con man. Just say it.

"Ghosts, demons, possessions, conducting seances, researching potential aranormal hotspots. That kind of thing."

"How's business?" she asks.

They follow my gaze to the detritus of my depression. Trash. Dirty clothes. itacks of bills. More trash.

"Great," I say. "Business is great."

"And you're in no way affiliated with the owners of the building you were n?" Detective Sonic asks again. The pen now looks like a mangled rawhide trip.

"No. I have no idea who they are."

"So, you didn't know they were going to bulldoze the place?" Detective Meat asks.

I sit up straight. "Wait. What?"

"Oh yeah," he says. "The day you called we sent a few units. I went out here myself. Nothing left. They tore it down that day."

I waited almost a day to call. I didn't know what to tell the 911 operator. iverything I could think of sounded like *Hi, I killed my friends!*

"Work was halted via court order," Sonic says. "It was a third-party contractor hired through an intermediary and… it's complicated. We tried to stop them, but…"

"But the pit…" I say, trying to keep the words together in an order that makes sense. "There was a giant hole there. Was that—"

"Filled it all in with concrete," Meat says and shrugs. "There's nothing left but a slab."

"Now, Mr. Vandermeer, after your alleged seizure—"

I stand up. The scream starts boiling again. It cuts off my oxygen and wrap its hands around my throat. "What? They just… my friends were in there. There's a pit! A giant hole. A big fucking hole and they filled everything with concrete? They buried my friends alive?"

***

I'm pointing at the TV above the bar, and I think my voice is at a completely reasonable volume.

"Just change the channel, man. Please. Come on. Seriously."

For the first time, I've got his attention. He glares. "Yeah, I'll get it in a second, bro."

Kyle Foxwell is on TV. The Spirit Squad is investigating the Fisher Davis State Prison. It's a location I secured. It's a narrative I created – a lot of bullsh about cruel prison guards and unsolved murders. I was kind of proud of it. It was sensational, but believable, with just the right amount of truth to make everyone want to go along for the ride.

Kyle strides around in a tight black t-shirt. His hair product shines under the camera lights.

I hoist my leg up onto the bar and crawl on top. My foot knocks over a container of cherries and sliced limes. Up on my knees, the sticky surface clinging to my pants, I reach for the television.

The world spins for a second. There's a lot of yelling and grabbing.

Now I'm on my hands and knees, staring at a half-eaten taco tossed aside i the parking lot. Two young girls film me with their phones as I struggle to my feet. I hope they don't recognize me. Kyle would love that video.

***

The days and nights are a fog of body odor and gameshows, junk food and infomercials.

A revolutionary new way to spiralize zucchini.

A Burrito Supreme.
Lightning rounds.
Nightmares.
More on that story at eleven.
And then the Lazlos.
It's the same commercial I've been seeing since I was a kid. Generic
spooky music plays as a family huddles together on the couch. Doors open and
slam on their own. A framed photo leaps from the wall. The dad, with his 80s
feathered hair and cop mustache, pleads into the camera, "We're haunted!
What do we do?"
My lips move along with the hammy dialog.
Enter Rupert and Kitty Lazlo, all decked out in cartoonish Western wear,
like they got called away from their square dance.
As they pray and thrust a crucifix into the dark corners of the house, the
announcer tells us everything is going to be okay.
*Is your family under assault from the forces of darkness? The Lazlos are a
brother and sister team of paranormal experts with decades of experience.
They can bring peace back to your life. Call now.*
1-800-77-LAZLO flashes across the screen.
We'd call it at sleepovers or whenever we were bored, hoping that one day
the famous ghost fighters we saw on TV would call us back and tell us about
their lifelong war against evil. No one ever called.
I dial the number. Kitty Lazlo answers with a soothing Southern drawl. "Do
you need help? My brother Rupert and I are here for you. Leave your
information and the nature of your paranormal troubles and a member of our
team will contact you right away. *BEEP.*"
I almost hang up. My hands shake. My voice cracks.
"I think something bad happened to my friends. Something supernatural…"

***

A single package of noodles can last me all day. With a little bit of discount
ground beef and some pepper, I can eat off of less than two bucks a day. The
only question is, do I want creamy chicken ramen or picante chicken?
The guy behind the counter knows my name. He calls me 'Mr. Clark,' and
he used to be friendly. Now he just looks at me like he's worried.
The electronic bell over the glass door dings as someone else comes in. The
sound mingles with whatever is playing over the speakers, and the notes are
close enough to trigger something in my brain. It's the song that's not a song,
the sounds from the Turkmenistan tape.

I hear it all the time now. I hear it in TV jingles. I hear it in my sleep.

The refrain plays over and over, drowning out everything else except for the roaring of my blood. Somewhere in there, buried in static and jangly notes, I can hear the screams, too.

Shhh.

Creamy or picante?

***

I call Alan. The phone rings and rings before heading to voicemail. The mailbox is full. Most of it is me. Angry messages. Scared messages. Pleading messages.

I call DJ.

I call Travis.

I call Melissa.

I check their social media accounts. Travis would post three or four times a day, at least. Now he's quiet.

I call Alan again.

***

The knock is feeble at first, and I ignore it. It comes again, more insistent. Then again and again, each time louder than the last. By the time I get to the door, there's crying and screaming and *Clark where is my husband?*

Selena's bellowing is cut short with a sharp gasp when she sees me. Is it the beard? Is it the smell? She doesn't look much better with droopy sweatpants and ghoulish bags under her eyes. The last few days have been hell for her, and it might be my fault. I can't pinpoint exactly how, but I feel that guilt, and I let it inside. Maybe she'll shoot me.

"Clark? I…" she says, and looks me up and down to make sure she's getting it all. "Where's Alan? What happened?"

"I don't know, Selena."

She waits for more, but there isn't any. "You… what? What do you mean? Where did he go? Where's DJ and Travis and… what happened to them, Clark? The police won't tell me anything."

Her voice warbles like a dead phone ringing from the bottom of a pit.

"The police don't know anything. I don't know what happened."

"What do you mean? You were there. Did he… did he say anything?"

No, he just screamed like I've never heard another person scream, Selena.

26

"No. We were working. I had a seizure or something and… then they were all just gone. I… I can't explain it."

She cries, shattering to pieces on the front steps of my condo.

I should let her inside. I should sit with her on the couch and console her and try to go over every detail with her. She deserves that.

Instead I just watch her cry and wish that I could cry too.

***

I'm not sure what day it is. It doesn't matter, really. Tuesday night will smell the same as Wednesday night– a mix of stale food, spilled booze, and sour clothes. I lay there, staring up at the ceiling. Outside, the night is quiet. No crickets. No passing cars or barking dogs. *Ancient Aliens* is on TV, but the volume is off. My phone has died. Thank God. I'm hungry, but I don't have food. I have to pee, but I don't want to move. I shift on the couch, trying to find the best position to spend the next six-to-seven years, but something is off. The all-too-familiar geography of the living room is interrupted by something new and quiet in the corner.

There's someone in the room.

Ice races through my veins, and I scramble backwards on the couch, making undignified noises. The man just stands there and watches from the foot of the couch, his pale face glowing under a fedora. A cop? A fed? Is the SWAT team here?

"What the hell? Who are you? What do you want?"

His smile is polite and unrelenting. His cheap suit looks like a costume. He steps forward, and my hand finds the neck of a half-empty bottle of bourbon on the floor. In his white-as-bone hand is an envelope. When I don't immediately take it, he nods again. His smile widens, and I get a look at his lifeless gray eyes. There's nothing going on in there, like he just drifted off in mid-conversation, but the smile and posture are insistent. He leans in closer to make sure I take the envelope.

I take it. It's got my name on it. Before I can open it, he touches the brim of his hat and exits through the front door.

"Hey! Wait!"

By the time I get to the door, he's gone. The parking lot of my complex is empty. No cars drive away. No doors close or lights go out. He's just gone.

I step out into the night, bourbon bottle in one hand, envelope in the other. I half expect him to leap out from behind the holly bushes and try to drink my blood.

"Hello?" I say, but of course no one responds.

I take a few more steps down the sidewalk. Nothing moves. He's either *really* fast, or he just disappeared. With his strange mannerisms and the pallor of his skin, teleportation isn't out of the question. Hell, after what just happened, I wouldn't be surprised to see him flying away on batwings, silhouetted by the moon.

Instead, all I find is a pile of laundry. Right there in the parking lot, cast aside like a used diaper, are the clothes he was wearing. The cheap suit, the hat– everything. Even his shoes are a few feet away, like he just stepped out of them as he walked. I reach down to snatch up and inspect the suit, but it's glistening in the moonlight. It looks... sticky.

I jerk back. Nope. No thank you.

The entire thing is covered in milky goo. It's thick, soaking everything and spreading out in a viscous pool on the asphalt, like marshmallows melting in the sun.

"The hell?" I mutter.

The envelope in my hand is sealed with wax. My name is written in ornate calligraphy.

I don't want to open it. The amber is comfortable. The amber is the same. It's a steady flow of nothing at all. If I open this envelope, the amber will crack, and I will have to do things. I will have to move and face things. I'll have to *be*. I want to just leave this missive on top of the slimy clothes and walk away. Whoever wrote this is prying at the edges of my reality with a crowbar. They're about to crack it open. My precious amber will spill out and it will flood all the things I'm not supposed to know – mysterious cassettes and pale men who turn into white goo.

Dear Master Vandermeer...

CHAPTER FOUR

Candle House is a fluorescent aberration atop a hill in an otherwise beige
uburbia. It's not just one house. Not really. It's several smaller houses, all
bsorbed into one creeping chimera, painted shades of neon– pinks and greens
nd blues. The nuclear colors once popped. Neighbors complained that it was
o loud it glowed in the dark, that it kept them from sleeping. It was a blister on
quiet subdivision of '80s tract housing. Those respectable homes are all in
isrepair now– duplexes with cracked driveways and barred windows. The
uburbs have deteriorated under the vivid shadow of Candle House.

Kitty and Rupert Lazlo once lived on the corner of the block in a modest
hirteen hundred square foot home. They painted it a shade of green that
loesn't exist in nature, immediately putting them at odds with the families that
ived all around. Five years later, they bought the house next door. They
ainted that house an alien turquoise. Construction bridging the two homes
asted a few months, birthing some bizarre amalgam of the two.

Over the years, they bought more, joining all the surrounding homes into a
urid, postmodern Winchester House. Soon, the Lazlos owned the block. From
he street, it looked unreal, a sprawling and inexplicable warren of colors, alive
n the middle of the little brown boxes. Kids loved to come and stare. They
oved the vibrant colors, and the Lazlos watched and smiled at them from the
nany mismatched windows. But the children would never come too close.
:ven when the Lazlo twins invited them up the winding sidewalk for a soda or
ome candy, the kids giggled and ran.

Eventually, Candle House's paint faded and chipped. The wood rotted. The
awn grew tall and died. The kids stopped coming to gawk. They passed by on
he other side of the street and regarded the house as some sort of perpetually
ick thing they had to live with. It was like the junked Buick in the lot next to
he Quik-Pik Mart or the twitchy pit bull that roamed St. Johns Avenue.

I've driven by it since I was a kid. I still do sometimes. The Lazlos haven't
een seen in years. I heard that behind the veneer of noble spiritual warriors,
hey were into 'weird stuff'. Sex cults. New Age suicide pacts. Devil worship.
Now they've invited me inside.

***

"Hello and welcome to the Lazlo Paranormal Museum at Candle House!
<itty and Rupert Lazlo have been reaching out to the Other Side and proudly

29

helping people explore and experience paranormal encounters for over thirty years!"

More like fifty years. A hundred? The old TV is mounted in the corner of the makeshift lobby, and the promotional tape has the feel of a training video for new hires at a retail outlet. Like their infomercial, it was obviously shot in the '80s. The tracking skips and warps, but the voice continues with bravado a the Lazlo twins– in matching, gaudy Roy Rogers Western shirts– perform thei so-called investigations. They smile like marionettes under heavy pancake makeup. It's like watching a Halloween version of Jim and Tammy Faye Bake talk to ghosts.

The lobby itself is a time capsule furnished with brown floral-print couches on worn burgundy carpet. If my grandmother were a dentist and also insane, this is what her house would look like.

"Together, Kitty and Rupert have used their talents and knowledge to help thousands of people all over the world."

They walk through a park, all glassy-eyed and smiling.

With genteel zeal, they chat on some regional daytime talk show.

Carrying only candles, they enter a dark room and grow deadly serious.

Rupert performs an exorcism on a kid in a trailer park. His voice is the drawl of an old Baptist preacher.

In a séance, Kitty links hands with D-list celebrities from 1978.

Their biographies are packed with overwrought half-truths and outright fabrications. When I was nine, they were superheroes, but this is all kind of sac and gross, like going to Chuck E. Cheese as an adult.

The tape stops, noisily rewinds, and starts again. I imagine it's been doing that for decades, playing on a constant loop to an empty lobby. After the propaganda plays for the eighth time, I'm ready to bust through the door just to get away from the video's Casio synth score.

The card in my hand doesn't offer much. It's handwritten in ornate but unsteady calligraphy.

"Rupert and Kitty Lazlo cordially invite you to discuss your current troubles."

One of the two doors leading deeper into the house opens. A butler enters the room. He's dressed to the nines in a uniform that's fraying at the edges, jus like the lobby furniture. His skin is hairless and pale. There's not a single defining feature and my words – *What the hell is going on? Why am I still sitting here?* – catch in my throat. Everything about him is unremarkable. Normal nose. Normal chin. No blemishes or scars. No tattoos. No crow's feet. His smile is toothy and unwavering as he touches an invisible hat he's not eve wearing and motions me into the hallway. He's the man from last night.

"You," I say. "How'd you get into my house last night? You couldn't have knocked? Or, I don't know, just left your note in the mailbox? Or emailed me?"

Again, he only directs me to the hall.

"Do they not allow you to talk, or are you just weird?"

His smile doesn't flinch.

"So just weird then. Great. You left your shit in my parking lot last night. Clothes and… your mucous."

He acts like he doesn't hear me.

The hallway is cramped and dusty. The burgundy carpet underneath has been flattened and grayed by decades of traffic. Every few feet, there's a glass case recessed into the wall, displaying some sort of oddity. The voice from the video continues over an old, crackly intercom.

"The Lazlos have lived a life of adventure, all in the service of the greater good!"

The first display is just photos of them in an old house in Galveston. Everyone has heard the story– the most haunted home in the history of Texas, the Galveston Ghoul House. In the late '80s, the Lazlos made the news as the team that broke the case and cleansed the home of malevolent spirits. The bad TV movie based on these "true events" glossed over the owners' history of mental illness and profound use of narcotics, of course. The place is a bed & breakfast now that leans hard into the myth. The stories didn't add up (including whatever flourishes the Lazlos added), but by the time the discrepancies were uncovered it was too late. The Lazlos were pushed into the national spotlight for a few weeks. They made their bones.

Past that, an insectoid mandible rests under a spotlight on a velvet mat. The voice claims it's a piece of the 'Roach Man of Baton Rouge', a beast that Rupert himself fought to a standstill in an abandoned church.

They built a legend out of nonsense, a small fortune predicated on lies. It's pretty brilliant, even if now they're clinging to the fable. With the internet, we don't have to take their claims at face value. We don't have to assume some campfire tale is true. Stories can be verified. Witnesses can be tracked down and interviewed without ever leaving your house. Hell, I could probably debunk any one of these while I'm standing here with my phone. A lifetime of bilking gullible people. In the '80s, the Lazlos just got to make shit up and everyone believed they were monster-fighting heroes. People *paid* them for it. And I'm walking right into it, ready to hand over the last of my cash, because *maybe…*

I can see the allure of their comic book lifestyle. It's all a shrine to their exploits, crammed into a retrofitted 80s tract home. Each display holds something outrageous– a finger bone from the world's most-possessed man, a vampire hunting kit, a haunted pencil...

The tour ends with the butler, ever present and ever silent, steering me into a small parlor filled with sunlight and a daybed with a bright, floral comforter. The TV in the corner plays some daytime talk show that hasn't aired in two decades. Next to the daybed is a tray of sandwiches, all cut into polite triangles. The butler closes the door behind me.

A set of French doors opens and Rupert Lazlo pokes his head in. His smile is so big and friendly under all the makeup that I'm sure he intends to eat me.

"Howdy, friend!" he says, extending a cold, wrinkled hand. "I'm Rupert Lazlo, and we are just so pleased to have you visit with us today."

"Wow. Yeah. Rupert Lazlo. Nice to meet you. Clark Vandermeer."

"It is just such a pleasure, Clark," he says, shaking my hand for way too long. "We've been following your work for a while now."

Oh shit. That's not good.

"Wait. You've heard of me?"

"Oh yes," he says, and his breath is a cloud of old soup. "Kitty just thinks you're the cat's pajamas!"

He looks like a corpse wearing a black toupee and a novelty cowboy shirt. The pearl snaps and bolo tie gleam like the unnerving sparkle in his eye. A motorized cart carrying Kitty comes through the doors. She's grinning from ear to ear under a bad wig and suddenly, I'm worried that this is some 'Baby Jane' shit that I really don't want to be involved in.

"Oh, my goodness! It's so nice to meet you, young man!" She says, taking my hand.

I shuffle awkwardly so that there's enough space for all of us. It's crowded, and the motorized cart takes up most of the room.

"Pleasure to meet you, Ms. Lazlo. I've read several of your books."

"Oh, it's Kitty! Please! My friends all call me Kitty! This is my brother, Rupert. Please, sit! Sit!"

The only place to sit is the daybed. I sit. Rupert sits next to me, and I'm already regretting all of this.

"Would you like a sandwich?" he asks, motioning to the spread.

"No, I just ate. Thank you."

"But they're real good. Kitty made them herself."

"Oh no. That's very kind of you, but I'm good."

"Are you sure?" she asks, trying to hand me one. "There's bologna and ham and cheese."

"No, thank you. I appreciate it."

"But they're so good!" Kitty says.

"They look great, but I'm stuffed. If I eat one more thing, I'm going to have to take a nap right here on this bed."

Rupert howls with laughter and slaps Kitty on the leg. "Sandwiches so good they'll make you take a nap! How 'bout that, Kitty?!"

They laugh again, and I immediately wish I knew someone who could call in an airstrike on this very room.

"Tell us about yourself, you handsome young man," Kitty says. She purses her lips and nods with exaggerated sympathy. "We understand you're having some real tough times, mister."

I nod and force a polite smile. The door is close. I could run and they could never catch me. We could all just pretend that this never happened, that I never called that stupid number.

"Well, I've been a professional occult consultant for about seven years now. I'm well-versed in a broad selection of grimoires and ancient texts. Translated a few of them. I—"

"Oh!" Rupert says as he remembers something. "You know, I've got a case that I think you might be interested in. Kitty and I discovered the Tome of The Maltese Moon when we were in Spain on a mission back in the '80s, isn't that right, Kitty?"

"Oh yes! That book has some wickedness in it, let me tell you."

"You know what, if you give me a few minutes, I bet I can find it for us. We'd love to get your take on it, Clark!" Rupert says, and starts to rise. I don't know how to tell him 'no'.

Kitty saves me. "Now Rupert, let's not bother the gentleman with our old hoopla. He's an important individual. He was on the TV!"

"That's right!" Rupert says, and all I can focus on is how his makeup collects in gooey troughs in the lines on his face. "We saw you in those tunnels beneath Seattle! Wow! What a humdinger!"

"Yeah. That's right," I say as they smile and nod. Are they waiting for a story? "Seattle was something. Those tunnels were… really cool."

"You know, we hear from a reliable source that there are real live vampires that hide down there," Rupert says.

"Don't you mean real *dead* vampires, Rupie?" Kitty asks, setting off another chain of cackles.

"You are such a cut-up, Sister. I swear."

"Now let's quit wasting so much of this young man's time. Besides, you know I've got a hair appointment," she says.

Rupert nods and leans in close. His face says *Let's get down to brass tacks.* Everything they do feels artificial, like they're trying to remember how humans behave. I wonder how long it's been since they saw anyone aside from their eerie, hairless butler.

"Tell us about your troubles, son," he says.

I tell them the story. Once the thread is pulled, I can't stop. I unravel. My voice shakes, words tumbling over each other. Tears I can't explain slip down my cheeks. I tell them everything.

When I stop, the energy bleeds out of me onto the old carpet. I can't look at them. I can feel them staring. The pity is too much and my face looks like it did when the sun rose over that muddy patch of interstate. Pale. Scared.

Kitty reaches out and pats my leg. The smallest kindness brings the biggest tears.

"I don't... I don't have much money. I just want to know if... I don't know... if you've heard of anything like this. I just want to find my friends. 'Cause I did it, you know? I played the tape. I pressed *play*."

My voice trails off again as Rupert and Kitty exchange solemn nods.

"I'll shoot you straight, Clark," Rupert says. "That's a real crackerjack."

"Clark, honey," Kitty says, "You heard these tapes? You listened to them?"

"Yeah. Just the one."

Turkmenistan. Now at the top of my *Places to Never Visit* list.

"And you're feeling alright? No lingering effects?" Rupert asks.

"Like tinnitus? I mean, I only wake up screaming every few hours, but other than that, I'm peachy keen."

Rupert chuckles and claps his hands together, "Even after all that, he's got a heck of a sense of humor, sister. Can you believe that?"

"Praise be to Jesus, brother. Praise be."

Rupert leans in again, deadly serious. "Now Clark, you'd tell me if you walked out of there with any of those tapes, wouldn't you?"

"Yeah. No. I didn't. Hell no. Pardon my language, but... no."

Rupert nods. "Good. That's good. 'Cause they unquestionably sound like cursed artifacts. We've come across a number of those, haven't we, sister?"

"Oh, yes we have, brother. That's nothing you want to play with. No, sir."

Kitty and Rupert hold hands and stare into each other's eyes, a pensive and silent exchange.

This was a mistake. My face flushes read. I wipe away the tears and snot and start to get up.

"I'm sorry. I'm sorry to bother you. I need to get out of here. I've got to... yeah. Thanks. Have a good day."

"Now hang on there, fella," Rupert says. "We're going to look into this for you."

If I were naked in the middle of this room, I couldn't be any more uncomfortable.

"You think this is something in your... area of expertise?" I ask. "I mean, I don't even know. Maybe a drifter got them. Or they fell into the hole. Or some ind of weird mass psychosis made them run off to God knows where. I don't now. None of this makes sense and I might have a brain tumor or something nd… I just need to know. Am I crazy? Is it real? All of this – the ghosts and emons and all that – is it all real?"

Rupert raises his hand to stop me. "Son, you've come up against the aranormal. And it's crazy all right, but you're not the crazy one. This defies he known laws of man and God. You're darn skippy, it does," he says.

"And we could never turn away a soul in need, honey," Kitty says.

Rupert rubs his chin. Makeup smears across his fingertips. "We've got a etwork of specialists across the globe. We've been at this a while. Somebody n our international task force has got to know something. Since I'm older than Methuselah, I may have lost a step, but I can tell you this whole tape-and-door usiness rings a bell."

"It does. It does," Kitty says. "Surely one of our experts can tell us more. And maybe we can find out what happened to your poor friends."

The words won't click together. They just bounce around on my tongue as I ry to form a sentence. I want to say *thank you* and leave. Here's where they get ne. When I played at being a psychic, this was the moment. The mark was raw with tears and their belly was exposed. Now you ask for a credit card number r a down payment, the first of many.

"I just hoped maybe you had some information. I can't afford to hire you."

Rupert waves it off. "This one is *pro bono*, son. On the house."

"We don't turn the less fortunate away, Clark," Kitty says.

"But there's something you can do for us."

Please don't be creepy sex stuff. Please please please.

I also can't afford to be picky right now, so maybe with enough whisky…

"Clark, Kitty and I are funding a new big investigation, and we want you nd your team to be a part of it.".

"Wait. What?"

"That's right," Kitty says. "This is going to be legendary. We need your eam to join our network of specialists."

"My team? Well—"

Kitty pats my knee. "Now we know you've had some trouble lately with our business, but we believe in what you're doing and want to help you get ack on your feet."

"Trouble is one way to put it, Ms. Lazlo. My team – Occultex – it's done. hey're… there is no team anymore."

"Well, son," Rupert says, "What you think of as an 'end', we in the usiness see as a 'beginning'. We're gonna help you get back up on that orse."

"Rupie and I want to hire you to assemble a small group to join a few other teams we've put together. It will be the biggest paranormal investigation most people have ever seen!"

"Like in the old days when Kitty and I were doing it with our coterie of ne'er-do-wells. You ever hear of the Specter Society?" Rupert says, remembering some other story he really wants to tell.

"I was a Specter Scout!" I say.

"You were in our fan club? A genuine Specter Scout among us?" Kitty asks.

"I was! I read the comics and everything!"

"Well I'm just tickled!" Rupert says. "Ain't that something? Buddy, let me tell you, this new investigation is gonna be a real whopper. No more kids running around with their cell phones. No sir!"

"Nuh-uh," Kitty adds.

"Nope," Rupert continues. "We are doing this up right!"

Kitty leans in even more, and now I'm having trouble breathing. She speaks in a hushed tone, as if this is *super serious*. "Five teams lead by one of our top fellas, at what has to be one of the single most haunted places Rupert and I have ever encountered."

"Where?" I ask.

They put their fingers to their lips as if to shush me. Their faces light up. "It's confidential," Rupert says. "We'll have to get you to sign an NDA, but w think this could be big."

"And we want to protect the general public, so secrecy is a must," Kitty says.

"Protect the general... Wait. So, you want me to assemble a new team to investigate this... haunted wherever... with five other teams... and you won't tell me where it is?"

"That's right, Clark," Rupert says. "Now this place could be dangerous, but we just know you're the man for the job. While we're busy tracking down these mysterious tapes, we want you to be a part of this historic event."

Kitty bats her fake lashes. "We're only inviting the best of the best, Clark."

"So, you want me to just investigate and provide my findings?"

"Oh no. It's much bigger than that," Kitty says.

"Much bigger, Clark. Real big," Rupert says.

"We want you and the team to finally provide proof," Kitty says and this time she takes Rupert's hand.

"We know what we've experienced all of these years, Clark. We've seen it We've documented it, but still, the non-believers—" Rupert starts to say.

"They call us liars!" Kitty squeezes the color out of Rupert's hand. "Charlatans! The things they say about us on these internet web boards and their social medias!"

"We want to show the world – once and for all – that there is something out there," Rupert says.

I can hear the song. I can hear its shrieks and whistles in the back of my mind. It says *yes, there is indeed something out there*.

"There's something I should tell you," I say. "I'm not really sure if I'm going to continue investigating—"

"Oh! And it will be so much fun!" Kitty says. "Three days on location with a whole bunch of other specialists like yourself. Like a campout!"

Rupert claps his hands. "And you'll walk away ten thousand dollars richer!"

All my excuses crumble to dust. The song is quiet.

"I can start right away. Whatever you need."

Kitty reaches out and pats my hand. "Oh, that's so good. That makes us both just so gosh darn happy!"

Kitty wears a charm bracelet. It's jangly and overstuffed with tiny metal ornaments and ceramic tiles. On the tiles are symbols.

I recognize the symbols and feel the blood drain from my face. I don't say anything. I focus on the bracelet, all decked out with the strange sigils, the same ones on the tapes. Kitty strokes the back of my hand and smiles with her thin, yellow teeth.

"And I promise you, honey, we're going to do everything we can to help you reunite with your friends."

"That's great to hear, Clark," Rupert says, like he just sold me a car. "When our study is over, my friend, so many of your questions will be answered."

CHAPTER FIVE

"I'm a werewolf," she says, and lets it hang in the air like a challenge.

"Like… right now?" I ask.

It's the middle of the day and a girl with a Misfits tattoo on her neck is sitting on my couch.

"No," she says. "When the moon is full. You know… a werewolf."

I set my clipboard aside for a second.

"So, when the moon is full," I say, "You get all hairy and *rawr* and like… eat people? Or whatever?"

"It's not like that," she says, as if it's something basic she's trying to explain to me. "I'm a *psychic* werewolf."

"Like… you're a werewolf, but… you're also in the X-Men?"

Her eyes light up. It's a conversation she's had at bars a hundred times. She loves the look on people's faces. It's all well-rehearsed. "No, it's not like that," she says. "When the moon is full, my wolf spirit takes over."

"Your… you have a wolf spirit?"

"We all do. Everyone does. Even you. I was born with the ability to access mine. I can't control it around the full moon, though. The lycanthropy is too intense, and sometimes I just have to… give in."

"This is a lot to unpack. So, when you give in, is that when you eat people?"

"No, most psychic werewolves don't hurt anyone. Some do, but they're ostracized. If we went around hurting people, we'd be hunted to extinction."

"Okay. If you don't hunt and eat people, how does your lycanthropy manifest exactly?"

"I get angry. And it's harder to resist my passions."

"Your passions?"

"I eat voraciously. I yell at people. I have a lot of sex. I take what I want. The wolf spirit is raw, animal urge."

"So… every full moon, you transform into… an asshole?"

I'm interviewing people to assemble my team for the investigation. It's not going well.

***

38

I don't know what Marianne Reznicek is doing here. She looks like a real estate agent, sitting on my couch as she looks at her phone. *I'm* interviewing *her,* but she doesn't seem to have time for my bullshit.

"Your resume is… there's not a lot of paranormal investigating."

"Yeah, I haven't really done much of that. Those people are… no offense, but they're usually kind of *off*, you know?"

"Oh yeah. Well aware."

"I've got a day job. I'm in sales at Balefire. Cubicle job. Client visits. That kind of thing. That's not flexible. Monday through Friday. I can take the odd day off every now and then, but I'll need notice."

"You don't see much use in paranormal investigation?"

Her phone buzzes again. She checks it as she talks. "Eh. Maybe. I guess? I just never thought it was necessary."

"No? I mean, I get that, but—"

"I don't need your little toys and gadgets. They're fun to play with or whatever, but… I don't need that."

"Really? Are you sensitive or psychic or…?"

"Yeah, you could say that."

"So, you're a medium?"

"Medium implies that I let spirits talk through me and… well, fuck that. I'm not letting some dead weirdo just run around in my meat tube."

"Do you just…"

"I just talk to them. Whenever I can see them. Which is pretty regularly. Like all the time."

Great. That's just great.

"You just see ghosts, huh?"

"And talk to them. I know it sounds crazy, but you've seen people do this before, right? I mean, I'm not the only one."

"No. No, I've never… is there anyone here? I mean, in here with us right now?" I ask, and get comfortable, waiting for some theatrical bit of crazy.

She just smiles and nods.

I look around. "Where?"

"Well, there's the guy next to you." I look to my left. She points to my right. "Nope. Right there," she says.

I scoot away from the empty spot in the room. "Umm. Hi."

Jesus Christ. How do I get her out of here?

I pretend to make a note on my clipboard. "That's fascinating! You've got some real talent, Ms. Reznicek. We'll be making our decision in the next twenty-four hours, so—"

"Wait. What? Really?" she says.

"Yeah, the investigation is this weekend and—"

"Not you," she says, cutting me off and turning back to the empty space next to me. "Under the couch?"

She smiles and nods at nothing, then gets on her hands and knees to reach under my couch.

"Umm," I say. "You probably don't want to do that."

She pulls out my cell phone. I haven't seen it in about a day. She hands it to me with a smirk on her face.

"He said you were looking for it," she says, and then pauses to listen. "And that your neighbors can hear when you sing *Mambo Number Five* in the shower."

"Get out. Both of you."

***

Sister Miranda Divine looks at me with the zeal of a cult leader. I don't trust anyone who gets that excited about *anything*, and she looks like she's ready to pounce with a glossy-eyed rendition of *kumbaya*. Her robes aren't helping with the whole 'white-Nikes-and-arsenic' vibe. They're hand-embroidered with stick figures crossing a bridge and entering a glowing gate. There's a lot going on.

"So, tell me about the…" I check my notes. "Church of the Holy Passage?"

"The once-living are still among us, Mr. Vandermeer, and even they are in need of spiritual guidance."

"Wait. You run a church… for ghosts?"

She smiles and tucks her graying hair behind her ear. "Oh yes. Think about it. Most of us prepare for the afterlife while we're living, but the bell has already tolled for them. They missed the call. Just like we, the living, need that sense of community and fellowship, so do the once-living. We have to help them find their eternal reward."

I look through her resume. There's not much there. "You don't really mention any experience in paranormal investigations here."

"No, but that would be a tremendous opportunity. Each of the spirits we meet at an investigation needs guidance. They need the word of God. We don't need to exorcise them or threaten them. We need to offer them a chance at salvation," she says, with twin globs of spittle collecting in the corners of her mouth.

She gets agitated as she explains and waves her hands, rising off the couch to clutch at her chest. Sobbing might come next. Or maybe a knife. If she touches me, I'm going to kick her right in the face.

"Just to make sure I understand, Sister, you want to become a paranormal investigator so you can spread the word of God to ghosts? Like a Jehovah's witness to the dead?"

"We prefer to call them the 'once-living'."

"Thanks for your time."

***

"Can I get a picture?" Greg says, and he's already got his arm around me before I can protest.

I motion for him to sit, but he's looking around my condo like it's the Sistine Chapel. "This is it, huh?" he says. "Weird."

"Weird?" I ask.

"Yeah, I mean, I don't know. I just thought your place would be bigger. Because of the TV money."

"I was on three episodes of a 'reality' show on basic cable. That doesn't pay much."

"Dude!" he says. "Is Kyle here? Do you guys still hang out?"

Okay. He's definitely not getting the job.

"No, we don't hang out."

"What happened with that? Are you ever going to do more episodes?"

"No. The show was cancelled."

"Cool. Why weren't you on the rest of the show?"

"They decided to go in a different direction. Can you tell me about your interest in paranormal investigating?"

"Well, my mom says I need to get a job."

He's wearing cargo shorts and a Slipknot t-shirt. That's reason enough to call the police, right?

***

"Wait," I say, unsure if I heard him right. "Your name is Zeke and you punch ghosts?"

He nods and slouches into the chair, throwing his leg over one of the arms. This guy looks like he stepped out of *the Warriors* with his shredded Black Flag t-shirt, gaudy rings, and mohawk. It's not a polite, 'Mr. T' mohawk, either. He's got his afro cut into a tall, wide blade, right down the center of his skull. It says *Say something. I dare you.*

"Yeah," he says, all languid and careless. "Punch them. Kick them. Nunchucks. Whatever it takes."

"Nunchucks? You've fought a ghost with nunchucks?"

He points to a bright red gym bag next to him.

"What's that?" I ask. "Is there a ghost in there?"

"This is my red bag. I keep this with me at all times."

"Okay?"

"Take a look," he says, nodding to the bag.

Please don't be a severed head.

It's all weapons. Swords, daggers, nunchucks, throwing stars, eskrima sticks, brass knuckles. I don't know what to say and I'm a little frightened.

"I'm prepared," he says.

"You've fought ghosts before? Like actually fought them?"

"Many times. I don't put up with that shit."

There's a flicker that tells me I'm in real danger, that this is a dangerous person who has brought dangerous things into my home and maybe I'm going to get murdered right now.

"But ghosts are incorporeal. They're… intangible. You can't touch them."

"I know what incorporeal means," he says.

"Sorry. I didn't mean… it's just hard to imagine. I've never seen anything like that."

"Most people haven't," he says. "I don't know what to tell you, my man."

"Can you use all of these weapons?"

He nods. "I'm a black belt in seven different martial arts, as well."

"So… you can fight…?"

"Anything. Put me in front of a ghost, a normal person, or a… Dracula or something? I'll whip his ass."

My palms are damp and the buzz of nerves keeps everything all twitchy. I swallow. If I make a run for it, I'll have to get past him to get out the front door.

"Cool," I say. "Well, we're reviewing all of the applications and—"

"Is that Mario Kart?" he says, nodding to the Nintendo beneath my TV.

"Hell yes, it is," I tell him.

"And how much does this pay?"

"Umm. Five hundred. Cash."

Shut up. He doesn't need to know.

"For three days?" he asks.

"That's right. Room and board included, but we're really not sure what direction we're going to go with—"

"Best two out of three," he says and levels his gaze at me.

"What?"

"Mario Kart," he says, and crosses the room to turn on the TV. "Two out of three. You beat me, I go away. I beat you – and I *will* beat you – you hire me."

I'm about to tell him to leave. This room has seen too much crazy for one day. Besides, if I were to humiliate him on Bowser's Castle, he might just draw one of his swords. I'll die the stupidest damned death – a grown man, stabbed with a sword over a game of Mario Kart.

Instead I say, "Deal."

CHAPTER SIX

The sun rises at seven AM on Friday. In the pre-dawn glow, our cars idle in the parking lot of the Fellowship Baptist Church in South Austin. It sits between a tire shop and a skating rink. The sign out front says *NEED A LIFEGUARD? OURS WALKS ON WATER.* My eyes glaze over as I picture Jesus in board shorts with a stripe of zinc oxide down his nose.

Outside, everyone mills about in their various cliques. I recognize most of them. The science nerds from the Scientific Anomalies team sit in their Camry, staring at their phones. They're so far down the rabbit hole of fringe 'sciences' I don't even know how to talk to them.

The Wanderers – also a bunch of misfits – are in their van with the side door open, smoking cloves and casting what looks like chicken bones into a Spice Girls lunchbox. They're probably doing it for attention.

The occultists, who I'm sure spent a lot of money on their Anne Rice costumes, stand quietly off to the side like a pack of Siamese cats. They're the Phantom League, always watching, always scrutinizing, always looking ridiculous in their mascara and layered black velvet. Marianne Reznicek is with them, but she's eschewed the *Bauhaus* schtick. While they're ready for an absinthe ceremony, she's off to the side, happy to sip her latte and check social media. I guess they liked her *Hey, there's a ghost that watches you poop* thing.

The more people that show up, the more it seems unreal, like it's going to get out of control. The science team is going to start screaming at the Wanderers, and the Phantom League will act like entitled pricks, and everyone is going to get real stabby, especially if we're all locked up in the Fellowship Baptist Church of South Austin. It's a single-story, brown brick building and has room for *maybe* two teams. Are we supposed to hang out in the parking lot and do our investigating in shifts?

Another car arrives, this one a Cadillac Escalade that announces its arrival with AC/DC blasting from an open window. It pulls up right into the middle of the lot, ignoring the lines and lanes, and throws its doors open. My breakfast taco rises in the back of my throat.

Kyle.

Fucking Kyle.

Black-on-black, with sculpted hair and a spray-on tan, Kyle hops out of the Caddy's shotgun seat and presents himself. He takes off aviators and scans the parking lot. When his eyes land on the church, he sets his jaw and nods. He's accepted its challenge.

"Fuck you, Kyle!" I scream into my windshield. "Fuck you!"

No one can hear me. Probably.

The rest of his lackeys – all in matching black – join him for a pose by the side of the gleaming vehicle. The last one out makes sure the moment is caught on her phone and posted to social media. Kyle holds the pose, arms akimbo, the captain of Mount Badass.

Someone raps on my window, and I nearly dump coffee into my lap. Zeke climbs into the passenger seat with his red bag in tow and glowers at Kyle.

Finally, he sighs and says, "You ever take a look at someone you've never met and think 'I want to kick that guy in the teeth'?"

"I think you're my new best friend," I tell him.

He didn't win the bet, by the way. Okay, so he won a few matches, but it didn't end up being best two out of three. It was three out of five. Then it was best of ten. Then we moved on to Mario Kart 64. Then the neighbors started interrupting.

Is everything okay over here? It's after midnight and you keep shouting the f-word. A lot.

Or…

Please stop screaming 'Burn in hell, Yoshi'. My children are trying to sleep.

Then it was the cops, so we had to wrap it up.

I don't think Zeke is a certified 'ghost-puncher', but I think he might actually be crazy enough to kick Kyle in the face, so I'm glad I hired him.

"You think this is going to be one of those church lock-in things?" he asks. "Like where we're promised pizza, but we're really gonna talk about Jesus?"

"I could go for some pizza."

"Same."

"That dude right there," Zeke asks, pointing to Kyle. "He stole your TV show?"

"Something like that."

Zeke stares at me with his drowsy-eyed look that says, "Well?"

"We developed a ghost hunting show for television," I say. "Seems like everyone was getting them. They were just handing them out. About three episodes in, the producers tell me they've decided to 'go in another direction', which meant, 'we want to replace you with a hot girl'. Kyle was all for it. He helped them push me out. We were friends and… whatever. The show got cancelled after the second season. Now he's famous on YouTube. The asshole can't lose."

Zeke watches me, waiting for more. He's the type of guy to use silence to get you to keep talking. I try not to squirm and manufacture a convincing smile.

That's it. That's all. That's the whole reason I was fired. No other reason. Nope.

Zeke thinks on it for a second as he watches Kyle peacock around the parking lot. Some of the other investigators are coming up to get a selfie with them. Kyle eats it up.

Zeke says, "I got a feeling you're really good at getting under his skin, right?"

"Yeah."

"Yeah, you're probably good at doing that to a lot of people. So... you poke at him and get him to take a swing at you."

"Okay?"

"And then I subdue him."

"Subdue him? What does that mean?"

"I beat his ass."

"Oh shit. You *are* my new best friend! But I don't need you to kick his ass for me."

"I think by the end of the weekend," Zeke says, "I'm going to kick his ass for *me*."

As the parking lot wakes up, the Wanderers flit around their beat-up van. They watch everyone from beneath their ragged hoodies, whispering in their odd *patois*. Inside the van, it's her eyes I see first– one lavender and one pale green. She's spreading tarot cards onto the back of a tattered briefcase.

It's her. It's Violet, the one who told Alan about the place, the undisclosed location.

I'm out of the car and crossing the parking lot before I realize it. A flock of whispers flies through the crowd as I'm recognized. It's never the good kind of whispering anymore, but I pretend not to notice. Something in my stride makes the other Wanderers scurry aside like Jawas. Violet pauses when she sees me, the next card hovering in the air. Her eyes cut right through me, so pale they almost glow. Her smile is warm, mysterious, and feels older than it should. She's only nineteen, but everything she does carries the weight of secrets, like she's holding onto something that *you and only you* can understand.

"I need to talk to you, Violet," I say.

Jojo, another gremlin from the Wanderers Guild, hovers just over her shoulder, shuffling about like a raven. They're never far from each other, always staring and whispering like some gutter punk children from the Village of the Damned.

"Ooh, Violet," Jojo says, flashing a gold tooth as he smiles, "he needs to talk to you."

"Good morning, Clark. Would you like a reading?" she says and continues to lay out the cards in a Celtic cross.

The cards are hand-painted, one of a kind, and not from any tarot I've ever seen. Jojo whispers their names as Violet displays them. This is the bit of theater they do to seem more mysterious. It helps bilk tourists and drunks downtown out of a bit of cash.

"The Dark Sailor, The Void Guardian, The Two of Sickles."

"You know I think that shit is stupid," I say. "Why haven't you called me back? I've been losing my damned mind here."

"He's losing his mind," Jojo says.

"Please stop that. I know you're trying to be mysterious, but it's just annoying," I say.

Violet smiles and her compassion feels like someone lit a candle. "I don't have a phone right now, Clark. I'm sorry."

"But you knew I was looking for you."

"She knew."

"I did. But I don't have the answers you're looking for," she says.

"The Locust, The Mandala, The Five of Songs."

"What was that building, Violet?"

A shadow falls over her face, and she studies her cards for a moment. "I don't know. I... I'm sorry, Clark. I tried to warn Alan. I warned him not to go. The cards even said—"

"The hell with the cards. What was that place?"

"The Sea of Mon, The Rotting Tree, Danse Macabre."

"The Lighthouse," she says. "I don't know, but it was poison…"

Jojo shifts and bounces behind her. "So poisonous."

"Yeah, no shit."

"It was a foul place, Clark. I tried to tell Alan not to go, but he wouldn't listen," she says, and I believe her.

The tone of her voice is hypnotic, almost unreal. If she were an elf, she might give me a side quest.

"How did you find it?"

"The Wanderers find places all the time. This city, it's full of them. Sometimes we explore them. Other times, we mark them."

"Mark them?"

"To stay away. Some places are tainted, Clark. They're rotten," she says and knits her brow as some horrible realization grips her. "Like this one."

"The Garden of the Goat, inverted."

I look over at the church. In the morning sun, the only threats it poses are pot-lucks and gossip. "This place?" I ask.

"No," she says, and scoops up her cards. "Where we're going."

On cue, a yellow school bus rolls up into the parking lot. It pulls off to the side, bucking and rocking across the jagged asphalt. Its windows have all been blacked out. The name of the school, too. Everyone stops to stare. Our ride is here.

When John Elder gets off the bus, we all take a step back and whisper. He's built from leather and oak, with a dangerous amount of stubble. Under his army jacket, you know there's a patchwork of knife scars and serious tattoos. He's the kind of old man who only smiles right before a bar fight. If you were to drop him in the middle of a remote jungle, he'd come back with panther gristle between his teeth. I've only heard rumors. Before now, I wasn't even sure if he was real. He's the Chuck Norris of paranormal investigations, only he doesn't have a Twitter or a YouTube show. All he has is his legend.

He appraises everyone and nods. "All right everyone, gather 'round."

We obey.

"My name is John Elder. I work for the Lazlos, and I'll be heading up this operation. I want to be loaded up and on the road before 0730, so we've got to hustle. Does anyone have any questions?"

One of the occultists raises her hand. She's not wearing the Anne Rice get-up, opting for a Nosferatu t-shirt and some combat boots. Andromeda Thorn. I didn't know she would be here. I catch myself grinning at her and immediately swallow it down.

"John, dear, where is this little adventure going to take us?" she asks.

"Miss Thorn, unfortunately I am not at liberty to say. The Lazlos have instructed that the location be kept under wraps for the foreseeable future. It's safety issue."

Belinda, one of the science nerds, raises her hands. "Are we looking at environmental hazards?"

"I'll cover the safety protocols once we arrive at the site. From this moment on, you're to do everything I say," he says, prowling back and forth like a drill instructor. His eyes, the color of a cold morning, look over all of us. He's looking for fear and respect, so I start checking my phone.

"If you do not follow instructions, you will be ejected from the investigation. You will be taken back to this parking lot. You will be left here. You will not be paid," he says as everyone withers under his gaze.

No one can look at him, no one but Andi Thorn. She raises her hand. "Will there be gluten free and vegan options with the provided meals?"

He stops and tries to break her will with his sheer presence. "No," he says in a rusted-metal voice. She arches an eyebrow, but her smirk doesn't falter. My insides turn to baby oil and Pop Rocks.

He continues, making sure to pause and make eye contact with everyone as he passes. "There may be danger involved, for you or the general public. This isn't some house where Mom heard something in the attic. This is the real deal. This is a live-haunting situation, and if you do not respect my expertise and my authority on this, you may be harmed. You may be killed. Some of you may not make it home."

Zeke's face lights up. He's paying attention now. "Cool," he whispers.

"While it is not my job to keep you safe, it is my goal to bring all of you home. In my thirty years of experience, I have lost men. I have had to visit families and tell them that their loved ones were killed by forces I cannot explain. I have no intention of making any of those phone calls about you this weekend. Are we clear?"

"Yes, sir," everyone says in low, chastised tones.

Kyle steps forward and shakes hands with Elder. "Good morning. Kyle Foxwell with the ParaSquad. Sir, your word is inviolate law. That's crystal clear. If there's anything I can do to make this operation run smoothly, I'm your man."

Zeke and I exchange glances. He whispers to me. "I'll kick his head clean off."

I snicker, and when I look up Elder's iron stare is leveled at us. Everyone is watching.

"You ladies finished?" Elder says. Kyle stands behind him and apes the man's disapproving frown.

"We were just taking bets on how long it would be until you tell us you love the smell of ectoplasm in the morning," I say, and feel the group tense up around me.

Elder cuts through the crowd with a lazy stroll. Here it comes.

"Clark Vandermeer," he says, leaning close enough that I can smell the coffee on his breath. "In my experience, when only one man walks out of an operation, that man is at fault for it going sideways. He's got blood on his hands."

He punctuates it with a sneer. My words catch in my throat, and my face flushes as the group begins to whisper again. They all know the hows and whys of me getting kicked off the show and apparently, word has traveled fast about the Lighthouse.

"If it wasn't just some gimmick for publicity. Gotta get those clicks," Kyle says, kicking off another wave of conspiratorial whispers.

"All right, everybody load up!" Elder says as he walks away.

"You ever use your karate on a crazy old man?" I ask Zeke.

"No, but I'm looking forward to it."

***

Zeke and I sit at the back of the bus. For most of the morning, it rattles down the road, and as it gets up past fifty miles per hour it threatens to shake itself apart. The blacked-out windows give it a preternatural darkness. The world outside has gone away. We're barreling along with no idea what direction we're heading. East? West? Straight down? We could watch through the front windshield, but everyone is too busy getting to know each other. Some of Kyle's 'bros' sit with the science team. One of the occultists in the Phantom League purrs and offers a Wanderer some chocolate. This is a bottle of tequila and a cheap motel away from turning into Spring Break at South Padre.

I watch Elder as he drives, guiding the bus onto a dirt road. With each mile, the assembled teams get more restless. They joke. They sing. They swap seats and trade war stories. But John Elder sees none of it. He watches the road. His movements are precise and robotic. He doesn't flinch. Doesn't smile. He just focuses. I know how this is going to go, my relationship with him. There aren't a lot of outcomes that don't end with him losing his mind and kicking my ass. Zeke's watching him, too, as he listens to some aggressive punk music from an old Walkman. The look on his face says that he's not impressed with John Elder. Not at all. I realize that Zeke's not just stewing. He's taking the man's measure.

Marianne Reznicek plops down in the empty seat across from us. "What's up, nerds?"

"Oh. Hi. Marianne, right?" I ask.

"Yeah. We spoke yesterday, and you got all weirded out and didn't hire me."

"I wasn't… I wasn't weirded out. We just—"

She interrupts me, extending her hand to Zeke. "Hey, I'm Marianne. You can call me Rez."

Zeke takes off his headphones and shakes her hand. "What's up? Zeke. I punch ghosts."

She looks at him. Back at me. Then back at him. "I don't know what to say to that."

Zeke shrugs.

I don't know what her angle is or how she pulled that stunt with my phone. I've seen games like that. I've *run cons* like that, I just can't figure out how she did it. Probably some parlor trick. She just wants to get at the ten grand like everyone else. When I didn't bite, she tried it with the Phantom League. They fell for it. But she doesn't look like a grifter. She doesn't try to push her 'gift'. Instead of luring you with a dazzling opportunity, her attitude is more matter of fact. You either accept that she can speak to ghosts or you don't. It's not her problem.

"Looks like you got on with the fruitcakes," I say.

"Yeah. I am now a member of the Phantom League, which sounds even stupider when I say it out loud."

"You don't like them?" I ask.

Up front, Dominic, the leader of the Phantom League, is holding court. It's probably a story about him having sex with the ghost of an eighteenth-century duchess or something else completely absurd. Every word he says is emphasized with a flourish of his hands.

"They're fine, I guess," she says. "I work in sales. I do yoga. I don't have the bandwidth to run around telling people I drink blood."

"So why are you hanging out with them?" Zeke asks.

"Money, dude. Mama's got bills, and I want to get my boobs lifted."

"Same," Zeke says. "I mean, not the boob part, but... why are *they* hanging out with *you?*"

"Rez here claims to see ghosts."

"You can see ghosts? I *fight* ghosts," Zeke says, paying full attention now.

Rez says, "About that... You just... fight them? Just like any ghosts?"

"Yeah. Ghosts are for punching. I don't tolerate poltergeist foolishness or possessions or whatever. Your unfinished business in this life is not my problem," Zeke says, then nods to me. "My man here doesn't even believe in ghosts—"

"I didn't say—"

He doesn't let me finish. "So, when we get to this place, and you see a ghost, tell me."

Zeke grins and cracks his knuckles.

"So, you can punch it?" Rez asks.

"Damn right."

"That's kind of psychotic," she says.

Zeke points to Dominic, whose story is reaching a dramatic conclusion. "You're the one hanging out with Type O Negative," Zeke says.

"He's got a point," I say. "Not to start a rivalry, but your friends look stupid."

"Yeah, they're dickheads. Hey!" she says, changing the topic. "Scuttlebutt is that your team just vanished a few days ago, but no one thinks it's real. They think it's a hoax, that you're doing it for attention because you lost your TV show or something. I don't know. Something like that. I wasn't really listening," she says.

"Oh…" is all I can muster.

They wait for me to add more, but I can't make the words work. If they weren't all gossiping before, Elder's little jab fanned the flames.

He got kicked off that TV show.

He's under suspicion of murdering his team.
He's a skeptic. Why is he even here?
Everything slows down and goes quiet for me. The only thing I hear is the blood rushing in my ears and behind that, the piercing cry from the cassette tape, haunting me with its horrible non-melody. They think I'm a fraud. They think I'm just a clown, like Kyle.

The bus slows and the conversations are hushed, their eyes drawn to the front window. At first, I see only weeds and trash. Tall grass, gone crispy and yellow in the sun, waves in the breeze. Wildflowers erupt from cracks in the pavement. The bus cuts through into a dome of giant oak trees. Overhead, a wrought-iron sign reads *The Oswald Academy*.

It's a campus. Six buildings, all institutional and brown, are situated around a courtyard under the canopy of green. Some of the windows are smashed. There's graffiti, but not a lot. An old bell that now houses a bird's nest sits on a post in the center of it all, like it's the pin that nails this place to the earth.

No one gets off the bus. As Elder kills the engine, everyone crowds around the front to get a better look at their home for the next three days. I stay in my seat and feel myself sinking into the world. It's just a bunch of empty buildings. I've been into dozens of them, maybe hundreds. This one is no different. This one isn't going to swallow my new friends. This one isn't going to make me look behind the curtain. It's not going to take my reality and shatter it with a hammer. It's just a bunch of empty buildings. The worst we have to worry about are spiders and exposed wiring. It's fine. It's all completely fine.

We climb off the bus, and our silence follows us. Kyle steps forward, his camera operator following him. "We're here at the mysterious Oswald Academy, located somewhere in the Hill Country of Central Texas. My team and I—"

Elder walks over and swats the camera out of the operator's hands. It shatters on the pavement and everyone stops dead.

"What is this?" Elder says. "What do you think you're doing?"

Kyle stammers, all his *look-at-my-perfect-hair* bravado gone out the window. "We were just... I was just trying to begin my investigation."

"Your investigation? *Your* investigation, Foxwell?" Elder says, then pauses. The cold anger in his eyes fades. He swallows it. "Listen, Son. This place is dangerous. We have to be careful. You don't know what you're dealing with here. I don't want any of your TV horseshit, okay? We're not making things for YouTube. We're not entertaining our fans. This is research. This is important, and I need you to listen to me, savvy?"

"Copy that, sir," Kyle says.

Rez raises her hand while looking at her phone. "I'm not getting a signal. Is anyone getting a signal?"

Others wave their phones through the air, but all shake their heads 'no'.

"There's no signal out here," Elder says as he unloads the bus.

Discontented mutters ripple through the group.

"So…" Rez says, "what's the Wi-Fi password?"

Everyone snickers, but Elder doesn't bother answering.

I stand in the brisk morning and try to focus on the chill as it enters my lungs. I focus on my breath. I control it, trying to get my hands around the electric panic boiling beneath my skin. I ignore the things that are piling up around me.

There is no cell signal. I ignore that.

My peers think I'm a joke or maybe a murderer. I ignore that.

I try to ignore the sound lurking in the back of my brain, whispering to me from the bottom of a black pit, but I can't. It's a constant refrain, reminding me that everything I know is wrong, and that I have seen the hidden fangs of the world.

Rez grabs my arm, her nails digging in. She's looking at the tree line, where the edge of the property turns into miles of nothing but cedar and oak. "Did you see that?" she asks.

"What?" I ask and try to ignore the feeling of the bottom falling out from under me.

She raises her sunglasses up and points out at the trees. "There. There was someone there. A kid."

"In a tree? Like an Ewok?" Zeke asks.

"No, dude, not *in* the tree," she says.

"Was he a ghost?" Zeke asks.

"Calm down," she says. "Don't go punching ghost children. He was far away. It was a little boy with dark hair. He was watching us."

Zeke, Rez, and I scan the trees. There's no kid there now. There's no sign of anyone, just an impenetrable thicket dappled in morning sunlight.

Zeke looks at Rez. "Don't mess with me right now. For real."

"I saw it. He just stepped into the trees and… yeah."

"Hey Elder," I ask, and he looks up with a snarl on his face. "Anyone live out here? Like nearby?"

"No," Elder says. "We've got the place to ourselves."

"So, no neighbors?" Zeke asks him.

"No neighbors. Not for fifty miles."

"You got your red bag, right?" I ask Zeke.

He hefts it up so I can see it. "Damn right I do."

"Good. I have a feeling we're going to need it."

Zeke nods. "No cell service. Isolated building. Crazy ex-military guy and now ghost kids? This is the opening act to a horror movie. I'm ready."

CHAPTER SEVEN

As the gymnasium lights warm up, they bathe everyone in a sickly half-light, caught between day and night as reality struggles to catch up. The gym smells like the undisclosed location, the scent of decay, and it triggers another surge of anxiety. One basketball goal remains, hanging askew. Collapsible bleachers are pushed off to the side. Insulation hangs from the ceiling, sloughing off in lazy flaps where pigeons roost.

The center of the gym is filled with cots and fold-out tables, all lined up like we're refugees on the run from a hurricane. In a frenzy, everyone rushes to their preferred cot, staking claims and marking territories. The Wanderers spread out among the bleachers, probably setting up a little warren beneath it like the spooky bastards they are. The science team focuses on their equipment, claiming the tables for workspaces. The Phantom League, of course, start to set up curtained partitions. Not just any curtains, mind you. These are lush, dark velvet. There are also pillows and candles. It takes them all of fifteen minutes to turn their section of the gym into an opium den. Kyle and his team just change clothes. Black shoes are exchanged for black boots. Black tees are swapped with… more black tees.

Zeke and I don't care. We just look at each other, shrug, and grab the closest cots. Rez is standing there, stupefied.

"Ohhhh shit. Are you serious?"

"What's wrong? You were expecting an Air BNB?" I ask.

"No, but… are you kidding me? Cots? I don't know where these cots have been. Ugh. Bedbugs, dude. Bedbugs."

"Bedbugs," Zeke says, "If that's what's worrying you about this trip, you're really not going to like what's crawling around in these other buildings."

"Spiders are… whatever," she says, rolling her eyes. "I can handle spiders. I can smash a spider. But bedbugs? And butts? People's butts have been all over these. All over. Just butts. Over every one of these."

Dominic calls out across the gym. "Marianne, would you like to join us so that you can select your bedding?"

"Yes, Marianne," Zeke says. "Go select your bedding."

She smiles at Dominic. "Be right there!" And then under her breath, "So creepy."

"Go be a vampire," I say.

She sighs, plasters on a fake smile, and runs off to join the dorks.

I get comfortable on the cot. Despite the flurry of anxieties and all the bustle, I could go right to sleep. Elder walks by with slow deliberation. As he makes his way to the center of the floor, every bootstep announces him. Everyone pauses, silenced by his presence. He expects it, and you can tell by the self-satisfied gleam in his eye, so I stay reclined.

He hands Kyle a stack of papers. "Pass these out," he says, and Kyle begins with the eager efficiency of a hall monitor.

"My name is John Elder," he says, and crosses his arms. In spite of his age, they're ropey with muscle and marked with tattoos that look vaguely military. "I've worked with the Lazlo family off and on for twenty years. I've led over three hundred paranormal investigations and expeditions in my lifetime, and I still cannot say that I've seen it all. Some of you may believe that you yourself have seen it all. I'm here to tell you unequivocally that you have not.

I am optimistic that we will have a number of encounters here. Some of these may alarm you. Some of them may affect the way you perceive your world. Some of them may harm your sanity or even your physical person. It is not my job to keep you safe. You're all adults with experience in these situations. Use common sense. If you're in danger, remove yourself from the situation and alert me immediately. Don't be an idiot.

As you can tell, this is the Oswald Academy and it was a school for children ages five through twelve. It operated primarily in the 1960s before closing its doors in 1973."

Ariel, one of Kyle's black-clad minions, raises her hand. "Will we have access to their records? I'd like to do some research on the property."

"I'm providing you with all of the background you need, Ms. Kwan," Elder says. "The day to day operations of the facility were not unlike any private elementary school. Its history and the details of its closure have been investigated privately by myself and the Lazlos. I will personally be handling that aspect of the investigation."

"Yeah, sounds legit. Sure. Right," Zeke says to me.

I see the same suspicion slither through the crowd. Elder ignores it. It's his word, his law.

He continues, "Breakfast will be at ten AM to accommodate late-night investigations. Dinner is at eight. There will be provisions for you to snack on throughout the day or if you choose to take a lunch. Behind the gymnasium is a generator that powers this building alone. The other buildings are without power, so exercise caution."

"Horror. Movie," Zeke says to me.

"While this location is isolated," Elder says, "It has not been completely unmolested. There is evidence that there have been a variety of trespassers over the years – bums, kids, and probably some ghost hunters like yourselves. I have performed reconnaissance on all the buildings and have verified that we are currently squatter-free. If you encounter a squatter or anyone who is not a part of our group, notify me immediately. Do not engage. Use your common sense."

Somehow, through the course of the speech, Kyle has inched closer and closer to Elder. He's standing close enough to give the illusion that he's *with* Elder. Kyle keeps nodding along, like he's co-leading the gathering.

"Mr. Elder," he says, "Can you go over the building assignments for each of the teams?"

"There will be no assignments. You will all be able to work as you please. I don't want to interfere with your methods. If you want to spend all day in the chapel, then do that. If you feel your time is better spent in the library or the dormitories, then do that. Building six, however, is off limits."

His steely eyes bore into the crowd to make sure they understand, and suddenly I feel like I'm held captive by my seventh-grade football coach.

"Building six is off limits," he says again. "Building six. Is. Off. Limits. That place is loaded with asbestos. These documents ensure that you will not sue us for being stupid, for not using your common sense and getting hurt. We do not want you to get hurt. We do not want you to get cancer. So, stay out of building six."

I sit up and lean close to Zeke, "We're going into building six."

We bump fists. "Bring it, cancer."

"You got something in your red bag to fight cancer?"

"I'll punch cancer, too. I'll punch cancer right in its dick."

"Cancer has a dick?"

"How else is it going to fuck you?" he asks, and I snort loud enough to get Elder's attention.

The meeting grinds to a halt, and his gray eyes lance right through me. I brace myself for the tough guy admonishment, but it doesn't come. It doesn't have to. The look says it all.

Elder clears his throat and continues. "This also applies to the surrounding area. Stay on campus. There's no reason for you to leave here. The wilderness surrounding the school can be treacherous for even experienced outdoorsmen. I'm reasonably certain that none of you are that."

Well, that's one thing we can agree on.

"Now," Elder says. "I do expect all of you to play nice. You don't have to be friends, but we're all working toward the same goal. In that spirit, I want one person to stand and give an introduction to their organization." He nods to Kyle. "You first, Mr. Foxwell."

Kyle steps in front of Elder and postures before the group. He's sucking in his gut. "I'm Kyle Foxwell, founder and host of the Paranormal Response Squad. 'We stand against the night'. That's our motto. We've been fighting supernatural evil for over two years now. I also hosted two seasons of Spirit

Squad on the World Experience Network, so I think it's safe to say you will not find a more professional group of investigators than my team."

The other members stand upright with their arms crossed and their eyes narrow. They can probably hear triumphant music playing. Or Drowning Pool. It's probably Drowning Pool.

Zeke raises his hand. Kyle nods to him as if it's the question and answer period of this bullshit. "Hi. Zeke Silver. Occult Technologies, Incorporated. I have a question about your TV show."

Kyle smiles that reality-tv smile. His teeth look like gleaming plastic. "Hi Zeke. Glad to be working with you, sir. What's your question?"

"Your show was called Spirit Squad," Zeke says. "Was that the one with the cheerleaders? Like they all lived together in the same house?"

Kyle's smile wilts. He immediately looks at me. I smile back, and someone in the crowd chuckles.

"No," Kyle says. "It wasn't about cheerleaders."

"No," I say, nodding. "Zeke's right. They were all from different schools and at the end of the season, they had to perform their routine for the judges! I loved that show!"

"Right! Right! And Brienne…" Zeke starts, jumping up and down like a giddy little girl.

"You were *on the show,* Clark," Kyle says and looks to the others for help.

"Brienne was my favorite!" I say over Kyle's grumbling.

"But she was such a bitch!" Zeke says.

"I know, but she was real, right? She kept it so real! But I still can't believe what she did to Neveah!"

"I know! That was so messed up!"

"Kyle," I ask. "Is there going to be a third season? Because I really—"

"Shut the fuck up!" Elder screams.

Everyone wilts. Shamed, they avert their eyes. Even Zeke takes a step back. The man's voice is sharp and loud enough that it feels like the lights flicker. His gaze lands on me again, but I can't let myself look away. I want to. I want to climb under the cot and maybe become invisible. But I can't. I can't give him the satisfaction, so I just and smile. He holds that look long enough for everyone to notice. They look away, they can't witness it. They know I'm sealing my fate.

Finally, he relents, and I can breathe. There was recognition there. The terms were all laid out, and we both understood them. He was in charge, but I was not going to play along. I should, of course. I should smile and make notes and present my findings and just cash the damned check. But I can't. I know it, and he knows it.

"Vandermeer," he says with a snarl. "Go."

I stand and smooth out my jacket, noticing a Chef Boyardee stain on my lapel. Oh well. "Hi. I know a lot of you. I'm Clark Vandermeer, head of Occultex, Occult Technologies, Incorporated. I was kicked off of a cheerleading show after a few episodes."

Kyle and his team hiss and turn to Elder, expecting him to intervene. He just watches me.

"You can often find me at various comic book conventions, sitting between a washed-up professional wrestler and that one girl who played an alien in season four of StarGate."

I say it because they're all thinking it. No matter how I announce myself, they're all thinking, *But he's not* really *an occult expert. He's a fraud. It was all over Reddit.*

"We don't have a cool motto," I say, and then motion to Zeke. "This is Zeke. He punches ghosts, apparently."

Zeke nods to everyone.

I shrug. "That's all I got."

Kyle raises his hand. Here's where he tries to be funny. I can't wait. "Are you actually incorporated? Or are you lying about that, too?" he asks and looks to his friends for approval.

"Do I look like a lawyer?" I ask.

Everyone watches.

Are you lying about that, too?

They wait for my reaction. I hope they believe the devil-may-care grin I'm struggling to maintain.

"All right," Elder says with a growl. "You two work this shit out on your own time. Wanderers, you're up."

It's not Violet that steps forward. She's the *de facto* leader of these little goblin people, but she's nowhere to be seen. I imagine she's already crawled into a storm grate or is building a nest inside a utility closet. Instead, it's Jojo, looking desperately uncomfortable since he's not perched over Violet's shoulder. Without her, he wiggles his fingers when he speaks and rocks on his heels.

"They call me Jojo," he says, avoiding eye contact. "Violet is… she's not here… right now… But we're the Wanderers Guild. Or just Wanderers, I guess."

Her nervously rubs the ankh tattoo beneath his eye. Two other Wanderers cloaked in threadbare hoodies lurk behind him. They could be kids. They could be geriatric. Their jewelry is cannibalized from machine parts or bits of trash. Their clothes are all things they've found or repurposed – stitched together t-shirts, mis-matched shoelaces, and fingerless gloves. I can't tell them apart. Perched on the bleachers, a loud noise would scatter them like ravens.

Wanderers are usually friendly when you try to talk to them, but it's like talking to a pixie you meet in the forest. They speak in riddles, and at any moment they could vanish in a cloud of fairy dust. Some say they've got a gift that they know how things really work, that they see the patterns in all things.

Mid-sentence, Jojo sits down, indicating his introduction is over. After an awkward pause, Elder points at Belinda, of the science team. Tablet in hand, Belinda stands with a backdrop of her cadre of nerds, all surrounded by gadgets and monitors.

Belinda waves to everyone before hiding her hands behind her back. She's ashamed of the scars. Apparently, Belinda's brand of science tends to get a little explode-y. "Hi everyone. I'm Belinda Grant of Scientific Anomaly Investigations. We're just going to focus on readings and try to stay out of everyone's way. Anyone is welcome to review our results if it would help you in your aspect of the investigation." She gives a half-hearted curtsy as she step aside to show the rest of her team. "We'll be putting up lots of equipment… lots of little devices to take every possible measurement we can… so if you se one, just please don't mess with it. Some of it can be finicky and also very expensive. And if you find something that's broken or whatever, just notify us and we'll take care of it."

The woman behind her, a spiky Hispanic lady I recognize as Cris, Belinda' girlfriend, says, "You break it, you buy it. And I will cut you."

"You heard them," Elder says, straddling a foldout chair. "Don't touch other people's things. We're adults here. It's not hard."

Dominic swaggers forward as if he's approaching the stage. He smooths ou his velvet coat and takes a deep bow. "Good morning, fellow seekers of the unknown…"

Just as he starts, I catch Rez roll her eyes and start looking at her phone.

"I am Dominic Rose of the Phantom Paranormal League. As I'm sure many of you know, the Phantom League, as we call it, has a long and storied tradition dating back to the late nineteenth century. We are one of the oldest operating paranormal groups in the world, with members as far away as Pakistan. We do not see ourselves as paranormal investigators, per se, but as scholars of the occult. *Figura Ac Tenebras.* 'Shape the darkness.' That's our motto, and that's what we intend to do. Some of us have unusual sensitivities and abilities that you may not understand. We possess knowledge of the dark arts that may frighten you. But I assure you, we are all working toward the same goal – we want to find truth in the darkness. We want to coexist with it. We want to invite its mysteries into our lives and embrace the night."

Zeke leans over with his face scrunched up like he's constipated. The agony of holding back the laughter is about to make him burst. "Is he for real?" he whispers to me.

"So that's everyone," Elder says, standing up again. "If you need anything, showers are working. The kitchen is stocked. Everyone just play nice together. I don't want to have to deal with any junior high bullshit. You hear me? So, go out and get started. Do whatever you need to do. I'll need full reports this evening."

Elder walks away, leaving everyone holding their things and staring at each other.

Kyle claps his hands and grabs a bag. "Let's go! Come on! Let's do this, people! Let's go!"

He herds his team toward the door.

"It's not a race," I tell Kyle. He gives me the finger and leaves.

I look to Zeke. "I can't believe I'm getting paid for this."

"Don't cash that check just yet, boss," Zeke says.

"What do you mean?"

"Was I not clear? We're at a mysterious, abandoned location with no cell service and no way to leave unless we get a bus ride from some crazy old dude with anger issues and probably PTSD. That generator? When it goes out... and it will... people are going to lose their minds."

"Eh. It will be fine."

"I'm just saying, I'm doing some pretty basic math here, and it all adds up to some bad shit going down by the time this whole thing is over," he says, and stands with purpose. "Now. You want to go break into building six?"

"Yes."

We turn to leave, only to be blocked by Jojo. Jojo is a tiny coil of nerves, and if I pull his string, he might come completely unwound, spinning around the room like a dervish until there's nothing left but his crusty hoodie and mismatched tennis shoes.

"Hey, Jojo," I say, unsure if he's about to start sobbing or maybe just scream and run away.

"Clark Vandermeer."

"You need something, buddy?"

"I do. Yes. Yes. I have a need. Well... it's about Violet."

"What's wrong with Violet?"

"She's disappeared," Jojo says, and splays open his fingers when he adds, "*Poof.*"

"Maybe she had to pee?" I ask.

"She was afraid, Clark. Violet is rarely afraid."

Was there a door? I want to ask. *And cassette tapes? Did you hear the screams? Did dead phones start ringing?*

"What scared her?" Zeke asks.

Jojo looks at his hands and kneads his tattooed fingers. "This place. The school. It has a stink to it."

I look to his gang of weirdos watching from the bleachers. It's probably *them* he smells, but I don't say anything.

"So, she left?" I ask.

"No, she…" he says, trying to find the right words. "She went underground."

"Ha!" I say. "I knew it! Did she crawl into a storm grate?"

"Yes."

That's what Wanderers do. They squat in abandoned buildings. They pick locks and take all the secret paths. They hide in walls or crawl around in ceilings. They watch. They listen.

"Listen, Jojo," I say, patting him on the shoulder. "Violet does this, right? I thought that was kind of your whole thing. I'm sure she's already discovering some fascinating things about this place. She'll be fine. In a few hours, she'll show up, and take us all to some hidden chamber she found. Don't worry."

He starts again, "Help me find her? She trusts you, Clark Vandermeer. And we worry."

"I'm sure she's okay. But yeah, man, we'll help you find her," I say, but Jojo hesitates. He paces back and forth, like he wants to return to the conversation, but can't decide if he should. "Jojo. What is it?"

He pauses. "This place," he says, "She said it isn't what it seems."

CHAPTER EIGHT

"Your friends are weird," Zeke says as we stroll through the courtyard.
"Friends? Colleagues. We just work together. Kind of."
"Don't have a lot of friends?"
"Not anymore," I say, and watch the teams spread throughout the campus like ants. They write in notebooks and affix cameras to perches. They document everything, filming every surface and peeking through every window.

Violet could be anywhere. In any one of the buildings, she could be rooting through its remains, finding overlooked rooms and service corridors that the other teams would have passed right by. The Wanderers Guild is good at that. If Violet doesn't want to be found, we're not going to find her.

Zeke and I take our time, splitting a bag of chips we swiped from the kitchen. Making a beeline for building six would be way too conspicuous, so we pause near the bell in the center and enjoy the morning. The bell itself is ancient. While the campus is the picture of 70s brown institutionalism with harvest gold chairs and avocado counter tops, the bell looks plucked from the deck of an ancient ship. The metal is dull, dinged and tarnished from sitting exposed to the elements for decades, but if the school were to get hit by an asteroid, the bell would remain. I fondle the chain and consider ringing it, but we're trying to make sure no one is paying attention to us.

The gymnasium is set at the northern end of the school. To the east, it connects to the cafeteria and dormitory which extend south. To the west of the gym is the library and theater. Even those are housed in a non-descript box. Everything is function over form. Looking at the school, it could be an office park or a sanitarium. The building with the classrooms dominates the western section of campus. It's a three-story block with a surprising number of windows still intact. I watch as investigators buzz back and forth inside, taking photographs and measuring the EMF.

And then there's building six. It, too, is three stories of brutalist brick. The windows are all boarded up. The doors out front are bound with thick chains. It looms over everything, an immovable object.

"Those chains are new," Zeke says, noting the shine.
"How likely is it that asbestos is the real reason Elder wants us out of there?"
"Pretty close to zero."
"Right? I mean, all of these buildings were built around the same time, but *they* don't have asbestos, too?"

"Exactly."

"So, what's he hiding?"

"Nothing good. I'll bet it's dead bodies."

"Why do you say that?" I ask.

"'Cause it's always dead bodies."

"This happens to you a lot? Finding dead bodies in abandoned buildings?"

"Creepy dude is up to something. That's all."

'Creepy dude' is watching us. I open my mouth to say *Fuck it, let's go around back* when I see him across the courtyard, staring at us from the front entryway of the dorm. He knows. He knows what we're planning. We look back at him, but don't know what to say. He's definitely onto us.

"Should we wave? We should wave," I say, offering him a feeble wave. Zeke waves, too.

"Hey, Mr. Elder. Sir," Zeke says. "We're just planning our approach." Elder just stares.

"Do you want to check out the classrooms?" I ask Zeke.

"Yeah. Yeah, we can do that."

For the entire walk, I feel Elder's eyes on my back.

***

It's been vacant since the 70s. Leaves and dirt collect in the corners. Lockers hang open, some torn from their hinges by half-hearted vandals. Throughout, we can hear the footsteps and sounds of the investigation – electronic beeps and lots of hushed conversations as everyone makes discoveries and takes notes.

We walk through the halls, snacking on our purloined bag of chips. Zeke doesn't seem to care. He's just here, taking it as it comes. There's a quiet Zen that he carries. I mistook it for laziness at first – and he may in fact be very lazy – but it's not just that. Every motion is easy and slow. Whenever Elder is in the room or one of Kyle's goons passes by, Zeke is watching. He's like a guard dog in the backyard. He's lying in the shade, keeping an eye on things, lazily wagging his tail – until it's time to get up and bite someone. He may or may not be able to punch ghosts. I don't know. But I think he bites.

"This Elder guy, he's not going to tell us anything about this place?" Zeke asks.

"Maybe he doesn't know," I say, poking my head into another musty classroom.

"You believe that?"

"Nope."

Every classroom is a little different. Some still have the tiny chairs, all rranged in rows before a chalkboard. Others have those chairs piled in the orner, a bizarre monument. There are still decorations here and there – anners with *Reading is FUNdamental* or a poster with the anatomy of a artoon cow. One room will be completely gutted, like vandals decided to ocus their efforts on one specific spot, smashing windows and spray-painting icks on the walls. Other rooms, as you get to the upper floors, are snapshots of lassroom life from 1978. Lesson plans are still on the chalkboard. The desks till hold school supplies, like rounded scissors or a rainbow-hued mass of nelted wax where crayons were left to cook over the summer.

I'm reading a book report about Beezus and Ramona that's pinned to the vall when Zeke says, "I'm not a paranormal investigator, right? I don't nvestigate shit."

"Right. That's why I hired you to be a paranormal investigator."

"Because I don't have the required skills?"

"Your skills are way cooler. Continue."

"When you're asked to investigate a location, isn't part of the whole thing ooking into that location's history?" Zeke asks.

"That's what we're doing."

"No, we're not. We're walking around eating Doritos. I mean, shouldn't we o to the county and get the records or check the library or… I don't know, just joogle the place?"

"Sure."

"But we're just supposed to figure out what happened here on our own? I nean, isn't the investigating the history part crucial to the whole process?"

"Yeah, but… there's a method to all of this, right?"

I turn to him as he makes himself comfortable on the teacher's desk. Alright. Truth time," I say. "There's no science to any of this. None. Maybe ne science team is doing something that I'm unfamiliar with. Maybe there's a nethod to their madness, but all I've seen today – all I ever see on these nvestigations – are people running around trying to convince everyone else ney know what they're doing. There's no method. There's nothing tested. Jone of this is proven. None of their experiments and measurements and eadings hold up to even the most basic scientific standards. This is all just a unch of assholes saying, 'Hey! Let's pretend to be scientists because we have ll these gadgets we ordered off the internet!'"

Zeke looks at me, bemused. "You mad, bro?"

"What? No. Maybe. I get a little mad about it. A little."

"'Cause you're still here."

"I need the money."

"Word. But you're just here pretending to investigate something you don't even believe in?"

"I didn't say I don't believe."

"This is about your friends."

A cold spark flutters in my stomach.

"Yeah."

"You expecting to find them here?"

"No. No, I just… I don't know. I need the money."

"Yeah. That again. We all need the money. Sure. Times are hard. But talk to me. Do you know what happened to them?"

"I… it's hard to explain. The short answer is 'no'."

He puts his hand on my shoulder. "But the long answer is… you've got an idea. And it's hard for you to wrap your head around."

"Yeah. If all this is real, then I guess I kind of know. Sort of," I say, my voice fading into a mumble. I kick a bit of trash. "So, you're for real? You believe in all this?"

"I don't have to believe," Zeke says. "Belief is for faith. I don't need faith for this. It's fact. I *know*."

"That must be nice. I don't know much of anything anymore. The Lazlos, they're doing me a favor, trying to help me find out what happened to Alan. I think they sent me here to teach me some kind of lesson."

Zeke frowns. "Don't trust those people. Straight up. Don't trust them."

"You know them?"

"I hear things."

Andromeda Thorn appears in the doorway, her turquoise hair and switchblade smirk making her look like she's going to invite me behind the band hall to smoke. I don't smoke anymore, but if she offered…

"Clark Vandermeer," she says, her voice sly and musical. "Just the gentleman I was looking for. What are you two boys doing, playing around in here? Working hard?"

"Hey, Andi. You know us – working smarter, not harder,"

"Hmm," She says, "I don't think I've known you to do either of those things. Who's this strapping young man with obvious fine taste in music?"

Zeke looks down at his original Melvins t-shirt and grins.

"Andromeda Thorn, meet my newest and only team-member, Ezekiel Silver," I say before turning to Zeke. "Zeke, this is my friend, Andi. Andi's a witch."

"Cool."

"Doesn't bat an eye," she says. "I love it."

"Eh," Zeke says and shrugs. "People tell you who they are when you meet them. They *show* you who they are later."

"I hope I don't disappoint," she says, extending her hand.

Zeke takes it, but rather than shake it, he clutches it to his chest. "I can't imagine how you ever would."

I shoot him a glare before I realize it. He sees it and winks at me.

"While I'd love to stay and be charmed," she says and turns to leave, "We've discovered something of particular interest to you, Clark, in room 313."

The second she disappears, I turn to Zeke. "Did you just Lando Calrissian me?"

"Because I'm black?"

"Umm. No, I mean… I—"

"It's cool," he says with a smile. "I take it as a compliment."

"I've been trying to get to know Andi Thorn for years."

Zeke slides off the desk and dusts off his pants. "I'm working smarter, not harder."

***

The Phantom League is at work in 313. Dominic stands before the chalkboard with his hands clasped behind his back. The rest of his weird coterie, with their ascots and porkpie hats, lurks among the desks next to Andi. Simon, a gangly, sweaty freak in a bespoke wool suit, moves like a daddy longlegs through the classroom, gathering up papers from the desks. Simon speaks with a rich baritone and the heavy accent of British aristocracy. He grew up outside of Houston. Asshole.

When we enter the room, he looks down his beak at us. "Hmm. The dilettantes have arrived."

I ignore him, captivated by the chalkboard. It's filled with gibberish, really evil sounding gibberish.

Shalem kudd Pagru. Missakka Varuk shemt.

Over and over, it fills up the entire blackboard. Dominic and his minions at me like I've interrupted something, but I ignore them and study the writing. Every word crawls across my skin.

At first, I think it's some sort of pidgin speak, mixing vocabulary from a number of different obscure languages, but none of the words are quite right. The syntax is all wrong. It doesn't even really behave like a language, but I feel a familiarity there. It's close, a name on the tip of my tongue.

"All the way creepy," Zeke says.

"Dominic, you didn't write this, did you?" I ask, and his gaze hardens.

"Can I help you with something, Mr. Vandermeer?" he asks.

Andi steps forward. "I asked Clark to come take a look for us. He's something of an expert in occult languages."

She knows about me.

Simon sneers and clucks his tongue.

"I don't recall requesting the assistance of a known fraud. I think the Phantom League has this well in hand," Dominic says.

I bite the inside of my cheek to keep from screaming. Zeke looks at me as if to say *Are you gonna take that?*

"Do you read Latin? Enochian? Sumerian? The Theban alphabet?" I ask him. "Call me a fraud all you want, but I'm probably the only one here who can."

He opens his mouth to speak, but stands there with his breath held, so I continue. "That's what I thought. And those are just the obvious occult tongues. There are any number of infernal languages, some that haven't been spoken in over a thousand years, but if you think you can make heads or tails of this because you've played Dungeons and Dragons or bought a grimoire at Barnes and Noble, then by all means…"

"There are these, too," Andi says, gesturing to the classwork Simon has gathered.

They look like children's worksheets. The top one has a cartoon monkey and the name GARY MARSDEN scrawled across the top. Instead of basic multiplication or a book report, it's line after line of this ancient or maybe made-up dialect, written in the wobbly script of a ten-year-old. My stomach flutters.

"The hell?" I say, and pinpricks of icy sweat dribble down my spine for reasons I can't explain.

I start to reach for the stack in Simon's hand when Dominic says, "Okay. We'll revisit this later."

He starts to erase the blackboard.

"Whoa! Whoa! Whoa!" I say, moving to stop him.

He keeps going, faster now, his lips pursed into a tight knot.

"Are you serious right now?" I ask him.

As he finishes, he turns to me, "Please, Mr. Vandermeer. Allow us to conduct our work. This is our specialty. We'll share our results with you when everyone reconvenes at dinner."

He plucks the stack of homework from Simon's hand. Andi shakes her head and steps away as Zeke comes forward, wiping the Doritos off his fingers. "Hey, dork," he says to Dominic. "Hand them over."

Dominic, for all his magisterial posturing, wilts as Zeke squares up to him. He clutches the papers to his chest and sputters as Zeke steps closer. Zeke's slow and sure demeanor is gone. He's a hard and cold pillar in the center of the room.

"Sir…" Dominic says, but can't make any other words come out.

Silence descends. The air feels fragile and sharp. Any movement could erupt into something horrible.

Through the window, a faint movement catches my eye. It's a flicker, really, like thinking you see something right as you turn around. Across the courtyard, in the window of one of the dormitories, was someone in a hoody. She was watching us from the second floor before ducking out of sight.

"Violet?"

***

"The dude was about to give me those papers," Zeke says as we cross the courtyard.

We hurry as dead leaves scrape across the bricks.

"We'll get them," I say. "Those assholes don't know what to do with that language. It could be in modern Spanish and they still wouldn't have a clue."

"Why are we chasing this lady?" he asks.

"Always watch the Wanderers. They're freaks, but they're good at this. Based on what Jojo told us, I've got a hunch Violet knows what's going on."

We burst onto the first floor of the dormitories, and it immediately feels different. It's darker. There aren't as many windows here, just dozens of narrow dorm rooms, all lined up and down three stories of concrete corridors. The silence is heavy. Once you step across the threshold, it wraps around you, suffocating the sounds outside.

We pause in the first hallway and listen. There's not so much as a whisper.

"Should I get something ready?" he asks, holding up his red bag.

"Nah. We're good."

"You feel that, though, right?"

"It's quiet. You're in a dark, unfamiliar building. That's what you feel," I tell him.

"Bro, it's not that. It's something else. You don't feel that?"

I do. It's the feeling of someone standing just over your shoulder, so close you can feel their breath down your neck.

"Just nerves," I say, motioning for him to follow me up the steps.

The second floor is identical to the first. Only a little ambient light gets into the main hall. The sunlight that does get through feels stained as it makes its way through the dirty windows and the dust-choked air. If not for the decay of decades, it would feel like a hospital, austere and simple. Each room is crowded with two single beds and minimal furniture. The beds lay eviscerated, torn to the springs by nesting rodents. Resting among the guts of one of them is what looks like a nude GI Joe figure. He's been stripped to the waist and impaled with multiple screwdrivers. Above it, a faded poster peels from the wall. It's a cartoon of the Lazlo siblings. They're fighting a spooky, green ghost.

Do you want to fight the forces of darkness? Join the Specter Scouts today!

"Say what you will about the lack of science going on around here," Zeke says, "but there's no way this place ain't haunted."

"She was up here," I say, my voice barely a whisper, and the way it reverberates across the stone walls sounds like scampering rats.

"The kid with the crazy eyes?" Zeke asks.

"Yeah."

"Umm. She's right there," he says.

She's at the far end of the hall, standing still in the intersection.

"Violet?" I ask, but I'm afraid to put any volume to my words.

We're whispering and there's no reason to whisper. There's rarely *any* reason to whisper on a ghost hunt. But we all do it, like we're afraid our voices might stir something awake or worse, draw its attention to us.

She doesn't move and we can't make out her face, always hidden beneath her worn gray hood. "Violet?" I ask. "You okay?"

She runs, disappearing down a corridor.

"Wait!" I say, but Zeke grabs me by the shoulder.

He shakes his head and clicks his tongue as he opens up his red bag. "Huh-uh. Nope. Nope."

"What are you doing?"

He pulls out a black nightstick. Its surface is chipped and chewed. It's been used. A lot. "That right there? With that little goblin not saying anything and running around? That shit ain't right. So, if we're going to go chasing that – which is not going to end well, by the way – I'm gonna have my stick ready."

"Fair enough."

Nightstick in hand, he slings the bag over his shoulder, and we jog down the hall in Violet's tracks. I don't run. That would be pointless. We won't catch a Wanderer unless they want to be caught. She probably already has at least two ways to get out of here that we'll never know about.

When we get to the end of the hallway, we enter another. It looks just like the last– dozens of dorm rooms lined up on either side. Most of the doors in this passage are closed, their tiny windows giving a small peek into the cramped rooms. Add some bars and you've got Shawshank for ten-year-olds.

But there's no Violet. She had just enough time to disappear into any one of them or make it to the end of the hall. It was like she wanted us to see her,

70

hough, to follow. The games are annoying, but if you can get a straight answer from a member of the Wanderers Guild, there's usually some intel there.

I point at the knobs. "Creepy," I say.

"What is it?"

"The doors lock from the outside."

Zeke takes another look. "You don't finish your dinner or miss a homework ssignment, I guess you get put in the hole for an evening. This place doesn't eem real wholesome."

"It was the '70s," I say.

"Why are we so worried about this girl? She a friend?" Zeke asks.

"Not really. Just concerned," I say, swallowing down the truth.

I don't know how to explain to him that if Violet is scared, then *we* should e scared. She and the other Wanderers were too afraid to set foot in the ighthouse. If this place scares her, then I want to know why, and I want to get he hell out of here, maybe not in that order. If I see one stray cat...

The sound of every footfall bounces down the hallway. Sunlight creeps in rom the small windows in the children's rooms. Slim blades of light cut hrough the dusty air. Some rooms offer glimpses of the kids that once lived here. A forgotten jacket hangs on the back of a chair. An Incredible Hulk oster has slid to the floor.

HAPPY HALLOWEEN hangs in cartoonish letters. A missing 'L' and an rrant 'P' has left the message looking gap-toothed. Next to each door is a rayon drawing of the kids that lived there. Sammy was a cowboy. Jennifer vas a vampire.

"Whole lotta 'nope' on these walls," Zeke says.

I want to call for Violet, to yell her name, but I can't bring myself to raise ny voice. We're still sneaking, still trying to slink along without drawing the uilding's attention. A few steps ahead, Zeke looks through a window and reezes. His grip on the nightstick tightens. "Yo," he says, and motions for me ɔ join him.

Through the small and dirty portal in the door, I see her. She's standing vith her back to us, looking out the window.

Zeke takes a step back and shakes his head. "I don't appreciate this Blair Vitch foolishness."

I lightly tap on the door, watching Violet. She doesn't flinch, doesn't espond at all. Zeke and I exchange looks before I knock again, more isistently this time.

"Hey, Vi," I say. "You okay in there? What's going on? Your friend Jojo is vorried about you."

She doesn't so much as tilt her head.

I try the knob. It's locked. She couldn't have locked it, not from the inside and not without a key. There must be another way in. I cup my hands and press my face to the glass to get a better look.

"There's another door," I say. "It might be a closet but…"

I try the next door. This room is littered with fallen drywall and beds that have been upended like the place was picked up and shaken. An *en suite* door connects this room with the one Violet is in.

"Through here," I tell Zeke.

"Hold up," he says. "If she turns around and she's got like devil teeth or something, I want you to be ready for what happens next."

"What happens next?"

"I'm going to beat her monster ass with this damned stick."

"I'm into it," I say, as I navigate the debris.

The side door is cracked. Chunks of plaster and other trash make it hard to open. I put my weight into it. The metal shrieks as the askew door rakes across the floor.

There's no one there.

I stand at the threshold, looking in as though maybe she'll appear, like maybe I just haven't spotted her yet in the nine by twelve room. She's not under the beds. She's not *on* the beds. She's not in the cubbyhole that acts as a closet. It's just us.

"See?" Zeke says as I finally step into the room. "I told you. Didn't feel right."

I look around the room, checking the walls for other passages, like maybe a small trap door beneath the bed. There's nothing. There's the locked door to the hallway and the way we came in.

I look up again at the jagged mess of moldering ceiling tiles. Some hang all swollen and warped. Others have fallen to the floor and turned to powder. She could have gotten up there. Maybe.

"That's like nine feet," Zeke says, reading my mind. "Your friend is what? Maybe five feet?"

"Yeah…" I say.

The ceiling is the only way out. There are no handholds for her to get up there, not that I can see. No dressers or chairs to stand on, either.

Zeke relaxes and sits on one of the beds. "Are we the first to see a ghost? 'Cause I think we should get a prize or something for being the first."

Rez saw one.

I almost say it. Almost. But I don't want any part of that conversation. The truth buzzes right in front of me, demanding that I acknowledge it. It was a ghost. Just say it. Say *Yes, Zeke. That was a fully formed apparition.*

But I can't. I can feel the other thing waiting. I can hear the jagged and unearthly notes from the tape playing softly, waiting for me to recognize them, to hum along. I can hear the voice on the phone. Every horrible thing that might be true presses against the door, a flood of realizations that I don't want to deal with right now. If I admit that what we saw wasn't Violet, then I have to admit so many other things.

"I don't want to be insensitive about this," Zeke says as he stands and brushes himself off, "But maybe that was your friend *and* she was a ghost."

"Like maybe that's Violet, and she's been turned into a ghost?" I ask.

"'Turned into a ghost'. That's a fun way to say 'murdered'."

"Whoa," I say. "That's… let's not go there yet."

"Do the math," he says. "We're looking for ghosts. We see one. It's trying to tell us something. Maybe that was your friend trying to get us to solve her murder. I mean, it's not a leap, right? You've seen movies before."

"Not a leap? You're saying we were brought out here, and she was murdered in… what? The last few hours? Now she's already haunting us and passing on messages from the beyond? Yeah, it's a bit of a leap."

"We're gonna see her again," Zeke says, and tucks his nightstick into his belt. "I guarantee it. We're gonna see her again, but next time, there's gonna be blood everywhere. Bodies. Heinous things. Count on it."

"Jesus, dude. What kind of ghost hunts do *you* go on?"

"The real question is," Zeke says, nodding to the view out the window, "What was your friend looking at?"

The window overlooks the courtyard. Directly across from us is the old theater. Elder stands on the front steps, looking up at us.

CHAPTER NINE

Stepping out into the daylight feels like a jailbreak. The noon sun is overhead, but sprawling oak trees shut out most of the light in the courtyard. Only sparkles filter through the leaves to dapple the bricks. Across the way, Rez is peeking into the chapel. The front doors to the squat, single story building are propped open. It looks like it could be a mattress store or an insurance office in a strip mall. There's no steeple. There are no markers of any faiths.

Rez sees us and waves us over. Her eyes are as wide as her grin.

"Come here! Come here!" she says, keeping her voice low.

"What's up?" I ask.

"You've got to see this," she says, motioning to what's going on inside.

The pews have been knocked over like dominos, pressed up against the dark, plywood wall or lying on the green shag carpet. Kyle is standing in the center of the room with his arms outstretched. The rest of his team hovers around him with video cameras, like they're capturing the second coming.

"Come at me then!" Kyle yells into the air. "If you're so scary and powerful, show me what you've got!"

He's like Alan, but with more testosterone and better hair.

We're leaning into the doorway like the Three Stooges when Zeke asks, "Who in the hell is he talking to?"

"That's his signature move," I tell Zeke. "As part of the narrative they're shaping, Kyle challenges the ghost or the demon or whatever that inhabits this place. He's very manly and is going to save us all by beating his chest and scaring them off."

"Looks like TV horseshit to me. Can he punch ghosts, too?" Zeke asks.

"We will not let you terrorize people!" Kyle says and puts his hands on his hips. "We will not allow you to run unchecked through this holy place, spirit!"

"I'm going to go with 'no'," Rez says.

Zeke walks into the church and waves for us to follow. "Come on. I've got to see this."

"You really don't," I say, but Rez is already chasing after him.

We sit in the back pew. A few of Kyle's lackeys scowl but ignore us.

"If you'd like to parlay, spirit, you talk to me. We want to help you find peace," Kyle says. "But if it's war you want, it's war you'll get."

We burst into laughter. Rez laughs so hard she has to rest her head on the pew in front of her. The ParaSquad stops, lowers the camera, and looks at us, their faces sharp and cold.

"I'm sorry," I say between gasps. "I'm sorry. That's just… that's a new personal best for you. When you say that in the video, you could kick in some sweet ACDC jams. Like maybe the opening to *Thunderstruck*."

Kyle tries to stare me down.

"It's war you'll get!" Rez says, projecting with a 'tough guy' voice. "That's the best! Was that from a movie? Like John Wick or something?"

Again, the laughter overtakes us. I can barely breathe.

"Oh my God!" I say. "Kyle, you're like the John Wick of ghost hunting!"

Zeke produces our Doritos and passes them to me and Rez. "Please!" he says to Kyle with a mouthful of chips. "Keep going! This is great!"

Kyle drops the act. He storms over to us, so I prop my feet up on the pew in front of me.

"Don't you have work to do?" he asks. "Or are you getting paid to piss me off?"

"I am the most qualified in that field," I say. "And isn't this a flagrant disregard of the old man's orders? No TV horseshit?"

Kyle ignores the question.

Zeke looks at me. "So, this is what the Spirit Squad does? I was expecting there to be more cheers."

"It's ParaSquad now," one of Kyle's goons says. Blake. Blake is Kyle's quiet giant, a hulking idiot with a chili bowl haircut.

"ParaSquad?" Zeke asks. "Like… Paralympics?"

Kyle stops in his tracks, stumped. Somehow, he hadn't thought of that. "Uh. No. Not like that. Not at all."

Rez says, "So you're the ParaSquad, but you don't have any disabled people on your team? Not a good look."

"Maybe you should go back to Spirit Squad," I say, struggling to get the words out through the laughter.

Rez stands and strikes a cheerleader pose, not two feet from Kyle. She blasts him with the cheer. "Two bits, four bits, six bits, a dollar! All for the Spirit Squad, stand up and holler!"

Kyle shoves her.

Surprised, Rez falls back onto the pew. Someone in the chapel gasps.

Before I can react, Zeke's on his feet, moving for Kyle. Blake intercepts him. He hits Zeke with a hard push, knocking him off balance. I start to say *oh shit*, but Zeke is already up and flying at Blake. Zeke's eyes spark with a frenzy, but his face is cold and implacable as he leaps to take the big man down. They tumble into the rows. Someone on the ParaSquad screams. Everyone backs up, trying not to get caught by toppling pews.

Zeke whips his head forward and Blake's nose erupts with blood. Before the first drop has touched Blake's shirt, Zeke pivots, slides behind him, and wraps him in a chokehold. Immediately, Blake claws at Zeke's arms. There's no escaping. As he squeezes, the look on Zeke's face is vacant. The light in his eyes dims and he stares at Kyle. His training takes over, and I wonder just how far it will go as Blake's face turns the color of bruised fruit. This isn't a fight.

"Now," Zeke says, whispering into Blake's ear. "I'm sorry it came to this. I am. I'm going to let you go in a second, and we're going to be cool, okay? We're going to talk about this peacefully."

Blake nods. His skin begins to soften to angry red as Zeke lets up the pressure.

Rez, with her own steely calm, strolls right back up to Kyle. Kyle takes a cautious step back.

"What the hell was that?" Rez asks him.

"I'm sorry," he says, "that was unacceptable. I'm sorry. I just... you were being intentionally antagonistic. This is important to our team and you..."

Rez's hand slides into her purse and holds it there. "That doesn't sound like an apology."

"Listen, I acknowledge that I should not have put hands on you, but—"

"Oh, you think?" Rez says, taking another step closer. Her hand lingers in her purse.

"Rez?" I ask.

The rest of the ParaSquad clusters together and retreats as one. Every time she takes a step forward, they huddle closer. Zeke releases Blake, who collapses into a pile at his feet, coughing. Zeke helps him up, but all eyes are on Rez.

Kyle is eyeing the purse now. He gets it. His hands float up, and he backs away some more. "I'm really sorry. I am. I'm sorry."

"Rez. Stop," I say, but she ignores me.

"It's cool. It's cool," Kyle says.

She gets right up in his face with only the purse between them. "No. You don't get to say it's cool, Kyle. You don't get to say that. Right now, I'm the one who determines if it's cool or not. And you know what? It's not cool. It's not fucking cool at all."

They stand there, nose to nose. Kyle is backed against a pew. He's holding his breath, and she's got her hand in her purse, letting everyone know.

"This is Texas, asshole," she says. "And I'm a Texas girl, you know what I'm saying?"

Kyle nods.

"Rez..." I say.

Dominic appears in the doorway. Andi, the rest of his witch club, stand behind him. Their faces drop as they recognize the tension. "Marianne,"

Dominic says, swallowing hard. "I'm sorry to interrupt, but we're having a meeting in the library if you could join us."

"Sure!" she says with a smile. From her purse, she pulls out a pack of gum. Without breaking eye contact with Kyle, she unwraps a stick and pops it into her mouth before offering him a piece. "Gum, Kyle?"

Kyle shakes his head. "N-no. No thank you."

In the courtyard, Dominic is clutching a stack of papers to his chest. I wipe Dorito dust onto my jeans and get up. As I pass Rez, she shoots me an apologetic look I don't know what to do with. The electricity in the room ebbs and she feels everyone's unease, their fear of her. I watch her wither. Part of me wants to stay and clean this up, but I want those papers.

"Hold up!" I say and chase after the weirdos. They don't stop.

"Mr. Vandermeer," Andi says with her lilting purr. "How's your investigation going?"

"Oh, you know. Apparitions. A fight. Maybe a gun. It's off to a good start."

"How titillating," she says. "I can't wait to exchange what we've learned." Dominic shoots her a glance.

"About that," I say. "I'd like to just take a quick look at those papers, if you don't mind."

Simon's lip curls in disgust. Dominic sighs and picks up his pace. He flicks his long locks, as if to dismiss me. "We've discussed this, Clark. We'll share the findings with you at the appropriate time."

"Listen, Dominic. I'm the guy who can translate whatever that is, so—"

"I think you'll find we're quite resourceful, Clark, but we appreciate your offer," he says.

I try to follow them into the library, but once everyone is inside, Dominic stands in front of me, blocking the door.

"At least let me see if I can identify the language," I tell him.

He smiles, knowing he's won. "No," he says. "And that's my final answer in the matter."

He closes the glass doors of the library and locks them without giving me another glance. On the other side of the glass, Rez is looking at me, her face downcast.

"I'm sorry," she mouths.

I shrug. "It's okay," I say quietly to her.

She disappears into the shadowed aisles.

"Want to bust it in?" Zeke asks.

It's all glass. The noise would bring Elder running. That probably crosses the line from investigating to vandalism.

"Nah," I say. "We'll get in soon enough."

Both of us look at each other and finally feel like we can exhale.

"You all right?" Zeke asks.

"Me? Yeah, I'm fine. You?"

"I had it under control."

"I know."

"You think she really had a gun?" Zeke asks.

"I think it's a distinct possibility. Everyone here is just crazy enough to pul something like that."

Zeke looks in through the windows. The Phantom League disappeared into the stacks. "You think they're going to let you see those papers?"

"Doesn't matter. I've got a plan."

CHAPTER TEN

It's a grade school cafeteria in purgatory. With the generator, only the necessary lights are running, making everything glow like a gas station bathroom. The tables and chairs are all novelty-sized, meant for nine-year-olds. Twenty black-clad adults, all reviewing footage on laptops and cameras, are squeezed into the chairs and hunched over the long tables. I imagine micro-sized plates and forks.

The Scientific Anomalies team buzzes around each other, passing notes and charts back-and-forth in a fever. They seem to like what they've found. Kyle and his crew talk strategy, which I imagine is mostly Kyle talking about cool stuff he's going to yell into an empty room. The Wanderers, of course, keep to themselves. They're over at their own table, whispering secrets and excitedly rolling dice. Dominic is in his corner with the rest of the Phantom League. Simon rifles through the papers, reading them all with such zeal I wonder if he really didn't find some porn. Rez is with them, but not really paying attention. She's looking at her phone, closed off to the world.

The back doors are wide open where Elder is grilling hot dogs on the patio. Beyond him, the sun is casting the day's last blazing oranges and reds across the rolling hills of central Texas.

Zeke glances over at the Phantom League. "We're just going to swipe those later, right?"

"Yeah," I say, scanning the crowd, "that's the plan."

"That's not a plan. That's a goal. What's the plan?"

Off in the corner, Jojo is in a heated discussion with one of the hoody-wearing imps from the Wanderers Guild. Zeke and I amble over to them and take a seat on the table. Jojo is stuttering and agitated. He's dropped the cryptic stage-whispering.

He sips what's probably his eighth cup of coffee and drags me into his fevered orbit. His eyes twitch, bouncing from me to the floor to Zeke and then off into space. Maybe he's on something. Maybe he'll share.

"Clark. Hello, sir. Hey."

"Jojo," I say, "How'd you like to make some money?"

Zeke raises an eyebrow at me but says nothing. Jojo looks confused.

"I have no use for money, Clark Vandermeer."

"Fair. Okay. Well, I've got an idea for some mischief." I say.

Jojo's smiles. A Wanderer rarely turns down an opportunity for mischief. I whisper my plan to him. Behind me, Zeke begins to chuckle.

"You in?" I finally ask.

Jojo considers and puts a finger to his chin. "I want something, though."

"Name it," I say.

He looks back to his friends. They all nod. "The button from your coat," he says.

"My... a button?" I reach down and take a look. They're cheap black plastic. "Sure. Done."

At one point, they were shiny. The brocade was pristine, and the left pocket wasn't hanging loose, but I guess that was a long time ago.

"Not that one," Jojo says, and points to the bottom of three buttons. "*That* one."

I pluck the button loose and toss it to him. He snatches it out of the air and raises up the hem of his hoody to tuck his payment into a Dora the Explorer fanny pack. It's full of other buttons. Jojo winks at me and slips away through a side door, out into the night. At least he's not pacing, worrying about his friend.

"The old man is gonna lose his damn mind if he figures out what's going on," Zeke says. "Then things will get real unfortunate."

"Don't lie," I say with a smile. "You *want* that to happen."

"Chow time," Elder calls out with a growl. He drops a tray of hotdogs onto a table.

Zeke's eyes narrow at the sound of Elder's voice. "I'm starting to think it's inevitable."

***

Zeke's on maybe his fifth hot dog. After everyone else was done, he carried the tray with him into the gymnasium because eating non-stop from a tray of hot dogs is a totally normal thing to do. He slides them down his gullet, like feeding them into a wood-chipper. It's mesmerizing.

"How are you all ripped and muscular? I don't understand. That's like... five hot dogs, which is at least three too many. Are you okay?" I ask.

"If there was chili, I'd be getting weird with it right now," he says, each bite a slow, deliberate grind.

"I don't know what that means," I say.

Everyone has returned to the gym to prep for the night's investigations. It always has to be at night, because *science*, I guess. The Scientific Anomalies team fiddles with cables and various boxes that make beeps and boops. Kyle's giving an inspirational speech while his team stands at attention. The Phantom League has retreated into the curtained off bordello they've set up in the middle of the gym. In there, Dominic and Simon hoard the homework I want while the rest touch up their mascara. I catch glimpses of them. They're both glazed in a light sheen of sweat. It's cool in the gym with the autumn breeze coming in, but they look gripped with fever. Simon's barely looked up from his notes as he rifles back and forth through the children's worksheets.

Every time I see them flinch, every time I see Dominic's eyes spark with recognition or excitement, the more I want those papers. It could be nothing, but I can't bring myself to ignore it. The words still crawl around in my brain, flirting on the edge of memory. They're familiar. I know the tongue. I've read it before, I'm sure of it. I just can't place it. Every minute they don't let me see them inches me closer to craziness.

Any minute now, Jojo will make his move. He better not have just run off with my damned button.

"What's taking so long?" Zeke asks.

Right on cue, a chime sounds. A red light near one of the science team's computers blinks. They all bustle over to huddle around the laptop.

"No way," Cris says.

Kyle turns his attention to them.

"Science team, you got something?" he asks.

Belinda and her team turn to the rest of us, but they don't speak. Their mouths open and close as they decide if they want to tell everyone. Kyle bullies his way through to get in front of the laptop.

Michael from Scientific Anomalies plants a finger on the screen. "There," he says.

Kyle begins to nod. The air in the gymnasium crystallizes as everyone waits for him to speak. "Ladies and gentlemen, it looks like we've got ourselves a BEK. Let's move!"

The crowd explodes. They stumble over each other, shoving and shouting commands. *En masse*, they rush for the door. Kyle leads the way and carries himself like a Navy SeAL he saw in a movie. Zeke and I can't quite hide our amused smiles as they scramble.

"BEK?" Zeke asks.

"Black-Eyed Kid."

"Black-Eyed Kids are aliens," he says.

"Black-Eyed Kids aren't real."

Once the double doors to the gym close, we take a look at the Scientific Anomalies' workspace. At least twenty cameras all over campus feed video through five different laptops. Standard. Low-light. Infrared. Each one covers a barren area of the courtyard, a cubbyhole behind a building, or a stretch of debris-strewn hallway. The red light draws our attention to a computer with a paused frame. A blurred image, a short, scurrying specter, is caught in mid-flight across the roof of the dorm.

I laugh. "See? And you didn't even have to kick anyone in the face. Keep an eye out."

I stroll over to the Phantom League's curtained lair, take one last look around, and slip inside. A brazier of incense smokes with a thin cloud of sandalwood. There are fold out tables, comfy chairs – where in the hell did they get stuffed, velour chairs?? – and throw pillows. They brought throw pillows. Jesus Christ.

And Andi. Andromeda Thorn is lacing up her combat boots and grinning. The smile lances right through me. "Clark Vandermeer," she says. "To what do I owe this dubious pleasure?"

CHAPTER ELEVEN

Andromeda pins me with those big eyes and everything in me short circuits, everything melts into warm goo. I should run, but my knees don't really work. I should come up with a lie, but my tongue turns into a thick lump.

"Umm. I just… I…"

She arches an eyebrow and winks. Just like that, she's got me on the ropes.

"Clark, darling, do I need to call your pugilistic companion out there to render aid?"

"No. No. I'm good. I'm all good."

Get it together!

"So…" I say, and my voice cracks. "You're not interested in the sighting? Why aren't you out there with everyone else?"

She stands and waves off the suggestion. "Oh no, running around, frolicking through these filthy buildings, chasing shadows isn't something I'm particularly interested in. You know I prefer the more esoteric pursuits."

Her closeness robs me of breath, and she can see it. She doesn't try to hide her self-satisfied smile.

"Walk with me," she says, and of course, I do.

I take one last look around their workspace, searching for any sign of the yellowed sheets of homework, before following her through the velvet curtain. Out in the gym, Zeke's on watch. When Andi emerges from the curtains, he averts his gaze like he's just out there minding his own business.

"Where we headed?" I ask her.

"It's a nice night. Let's have a little stroll," she says in a way that reminds me of Kaa enwrapping Mowgli with a hiss and a purr.

"Yeah. Okay. I mean… yes! Yes, let's do that. I just…" I nod to Zeke, who's trying not to stare at me as I fall apart. "Zeke's gonna go rassle that ghost, so just let me…"

"I'll wait," she says. "But not for long."

Naturally, I trip over someone's cot when I turn. Zeke winces. I hope she's into guys who remind her of Mr. Bean. Zeke bites his lip as I approach. He's trying not to laugh.

"When's the wedding?" he asks, low and quiet.

"Shut-up. She's a witch. I think maybe she cast a spell on me."

"Have you spoken to a woman before? Like a real human woman? 'Cause it kinda seems like you haven't."

"It's been a… you need… I don't…"

"It's cool," he says and grins. "Go on your walk. I'll check for the papers after you two are gone. Just… be yourself. Or maybe a version of yourself that isn't a huge nerd."

"Not helping."

When I return to her, she slithers up next to me and slips her arm through mine. "Maybe you're just a suspicious-looking person, Clark my dear, but you two have the look of a couple of fellows who are up to something."

"And you're not up to something?" I ask.

"I'm in the Phantom League, handsome. We're always up to something."

"What? Like your Ann Rice book club?"

Okay. So, I get a little mean when I'm nervous. She just giggles and rolls her eyes, Audrey Hepburn with Manic Panic and fingerless gloves. "Oh Clark, you're better than childish and trite jabs like that."

We slip out into the night.

***

The air outside is cool and restless. The last bits of purple fade to black on the horizon, snuffed by rolling thunderheads. Trees rattle like bones in the breeze. The teams scramble across campus, shouting commands in their hurry to engage the "ghost".

"Ooh! A storm," Andi says, clapping her hands. "It's going to get spooky around here."

"Are you going to start casting spells? With your witchiness?"

"Maybe. Any requests?"

"I don't know. Kyle? Can you cast a spell on him or something? Maybe turn him into a huge pile of poop like in *Weird Science*?"

"I think someone beat me to that one, but I will indeed protect you with all the dark magics I can muster."

I can still breathe. My legs still work. She doesn't have *that* much of a hold on me, but as we walk, my words all come out tangled and thick. We stroll in no particular direction, and I manage to choke out the worst possible response. "Don't you have a boyfriend?"

She pulls her arm away and smirks. "And what exactly did you think was going to transpire on this little jaunt?"

"No! No assumptions at all. Just… just making conversation."

She grins. A few words form on my lips, only to die before I can speak. Something over my shoulder gets her attention.

"Marianne," Andi says, "sitting all alone?"

Behind me, sitting on a bench with a half-empty bottle of whiskey, is Rez. She barely looks up, only giving a wan smile. "Hey," she says.

"Where'd you get whiskey?" I ask.

"I'm always prepared. I'm like a Boy Scout. But with booze."

"Would you like to join us, dear?" Andi says, and I shake my head 'no' so subtly that I'm hoping only Rez picks up on it.

She doesn't.

"Sure," She says, her voice heavy with obligation.

She swigs from the whiskey and suddenly all I can think about is getting that purse away from her. All we need is an angry drunk with a gun. As she walks with us, she hangs her head.

"Sorry about earlier. That was… extreme," she says to the bricks at her feet. "I just wanted to scare him. He needs to be scared."

"Oh, you scared him. You scared all of us. But it's cool," I say. "I've wanted to shoot him before. With guns bigger than will fit in your purse."

"How are the local spirits, Marianne?" Andi asks.

"The ghosts are pretty quiet, unfortunately," she says.

"But there are ghosts here?" I ask.

Rez looks to Andi for approval. Andi says, "Tell him."

Rez grabs me by the arm like she's got some hot gossip to share. "Dude, this place is hella haunted."

"Hella haunted?"

"Like all the way super haunted."

I look around as if I expect to see ghosts climbing out of the damned windows. "No kidding? Really?"

"Really."

"What… what did they say? Did you talk to them?" I ask.

Andi says, "Our spectral friends have been a bit shy about interacting with us."

"But you've seen them?" I ask.

"Maybe. Not exactly," Rez says, "but they're here. I can feel them. There's no mistaking it."

"Oh…" I say and feel the giddy hope wither. "So, no evidence? Just… a feeling?"

Whatever Zeke and I saw in the dorms, *stays* in the dorms. It's not that I don't want to share, I just don't want to feed into their frenzy of pseudo-science and 'feelings'.

We're standing in front of the library when one of the Phantom League brushes past us and slips inside without saying a word. Andi catches me eyeing the papers clutched to his chest. Inside the building, flashlights cast sharp shadows across the ceiling and shelves.

"What's going on?" I ask Andi.

She smiles and opens the door for me. "Come on," she says. "I'll show you."

Rez smiles, too, and for some reason, my hackles go up. It feels like an ambush. It's not like this posse of crackpots is going to do anything to me, but there's something they're not telling me.

Inside, it's not big. It can barely be considered a library. The books are all there, and all the stacks are intact but for one, its contents vomited up into a pile on the carpet. Andi leads us to the back, toward the bouncing light. I scan the books as we pass. It's a typical YA library from the 70s, shelves packed with Judy Blume and SE Hinton. Part of me was expecting the *Grimoire of Honorius* or the *Malleus Maleficarum*, dark tomes that would fill in some of the gaps in this place's history.

Dominic and his entourage are waiting at the end. They're standing next to a heavy, wooden door that leads to an office enclosed at the back of the building. Their lights are fixed on the knob. Dominic gives me a terse nod.

"Mr. Vandermeer," Dominic says. "So glad you could join us."

I look at Andi and Rez. "What is this?" I ask.

"We've searched the library, and sadly it amounted to nothing. No mysterious spell books or indicators of diabolism. Nothing out of the ordinary. It's a normal library," Andi says and motions to the door. "But we can't get in here. It's the only door in the building that's locked. I've got a feeling there are answers in there."

"Okay," I say.

Dominic steps forward and gestures to me with deference. "Andi has indicated that you're quite capable of picking locks, Clark."

"Ah," I say and my cheeks flush. This wasn't a date. This wasn't some sneaky getaway or sexy intermission. This was me, misreading the cues. And Andi knew it.

She says, "You've got just the unsavory set of skills that we need tonight, Clark. Care to help?"

"Let me get this straight. You won't talk to me. You won't even let me in the building, but now you want me to pick this lock for you?"

Dominic says, "Clark, please understand, we were just trying to conduct an orderly investigation. There's a lot of ground to cover in a library. We had to look over every single shelf. Anything we miss could be a clue vital to unraveling the mystery of Oswald Academy."

I turn to Rez. "Did you know about this?"

"No! I mean, I knew there was a door and…" she starts, but her words trail off, and she looks away, slumping drunkenly against a shelf of children's encyclopedias.

"Well?" Dominic asks.

Andi puts a restraining hand on his arm.

"Well what?" I ask. "You self-important assholes want to keep me out of here and don't want to work together until you need something. I'm not doing that. Nope. I'll just wait until you retreat to your Hot Topic coffin and come in here myself."

Dominic flings his hair. "That would be invasive and disrespectful to our investigation. You need to respect the sanctity of dealing with the paranormal. Ours is a sacred tradition and—"

"Please shut up. Please. Please," I tell him, rubbing my eyes. "I'm not even that good at lock-picking. I mean, I kind of can, but…"

Inside my jacket, is a pouch I keep my picks in. It's kind of for show, really. Bought them off the internet and watched a few tutorials online. But if you carry lock picks, people start to think you actually use them.

"You know what I'm going to ask for next, right?" I say to Dominic.

"Of course. Once the door is open, you'll be allowed to review the papers we recovered from the classroom."

He shrinks, turning away from me as if I'm going to snatch them right out of his hands.

"Nope," I tell him. "Now. I want them now. I put them in my pocket, then I unlock this door for you."

"Clark," Dominic says with a chuckle, "We can't be sure there's anything of merit in here. Andi has a feeling, but as with much…"

"Then you lose. You get nothing. Good day, sir. You want into this room, you give me the papers."

Simon stiffens and refuses to look at me. He's got all of the stoic charm of a Beefeater.

Dominic stammers, "But, Dominic, I can figure this out. It's starting to make sense to me now."

"Dude," I tell him, "All you've done is sweat over them. Literally sweat. You're maybe the sweatiest person I've ever seen. I'm honestly concerned about you, medically. I didn't want to say anything because I thought maybe it was a condition that you can't help, but now I think it's because you're weird and you're wearing way too much velvet, so just give me the damned papers."

Dominic's face tightens, as if he's bracing for impact. He's trembling. His eyes are bloodshot, but he hands them over. He follows my hand as I stuff them into my jacket pocket.

"See?" I say with a big smile. "And to think that everyone always says you're just a bunch of pretentious shit-gibbons. That's not true at all! You're perfectly cooperative and occasionally tolerable shit-gibbons. Now step aside and let papa make some magic."

I don't look at Andi when I say 'shit-gibbon'. I don't want her to think I'm calling *her* a shit-gibbon, even if luring me out here with her amazing cheekbones was a very shit-gibbon thing to do.

I crouch down and go to work on the lock. And by 'go to work', I mean 'try to remember how to do it'. The hooky-thing goes over the bent one? And I rake across it, I think? Or maybe the bendy one goes over the serrated one. After a few minutes, everyone looming over me begins to shuffle. I can feel them exchanging glances.

"How long does this usually take?" Dominic asks.

"As long as it takes. This is an old lock. I'm not familiar with this model. It's jamming me up."

That's a lie.

They lean in, like if they get close enough, they'll notice something on the lock that maybe I missed. Dominic is radiating a feverish heat. His breath is sour over my shoulder, mingling with his perfume that makes my eyes sting, and Rez's breath is boozy, polluting the entire library.

"Hold the light still, please," I say.

They take a step back but start inching in again as the first beads of sweat collect on my brow. I can feel things rattling in the lock, and I'm just going by feeling, hoping that one of the implements will hook something and I'll hear that satisfying *click!*

"I can't go while you watch," I tell them.

"Ooh!" Rez says, her words all emphatic and mushy. "That reminds me! Gotta go potty!"

She stumbles away, using the stacks for support.

"I'm beginning to think your reputation as a lock pick is overblown, Mr. Vandermeer," Simon says.

"Just… give me a second."

"I know that lock shouldn't take this long. I think I'm going to have to ask for our papers back while we explore alternative methods," he says. "It seems that once again, you've overstated your skillset."

Everyone in the room goes still. They were all thinking it. I keep jabbing at the lock, ignoring him.

"Clark, please. You're only embarrassing yourself. Given your history, I guess I shouldn't be surprised," he says. "The papers, please."

"I've got this, Dominic."

"Enough. If you can't fulfill your part of the deal, then…"

"He's just using the wrong tool," Zeke says, appearing in the doorway.

He led the rest of the party over here, so now my failure has a bigger audience. Everyone gawks at the front of the library, like they've stumbled across a car accident. They've forgotten our 'ghost'. Jojo must have ditched

hem to go hide in a drainage pipe. None of these jackasses can resist the lure
f a locked room. If they only knew…

Dominic says, "Regardless, Mr. Vandermeer has failed to uphold the
greement or even demonstrate any value he might be contributing to this
roject so…"

Zeke steps forward with bulletproof cool. He points to Blake, whose nose is
till purple and swollen from their fight. Blake's unibrow lowers, making him
ok like an angry sheepdog.

Zeke rolls his head on his shoulders. "This one goes out to Blake, who
hought he was going to roll up on me in the chapel and put me in my place."

He piston kicks the door. The crack of the wood is ear-splitting. The door
ies open. The impact shakes the books and rattles the glass. Everyone flinches
nd takes a step back.

Dominic, slack-jawed, is still standing there with his hand open, waiting for
he papers. "I… our deal wasn't with you, Mr. Silver, so Clark, I'm going to
ave to…"

"Ask for those papers one more time. Demand them," Zeke says, leaning
gainst the warped door frame. "I dare you. I double dare you. Try to take
hose papers."

Dominic lowers his hand.

"No?" Zeke asks, motioning to the open door. "Then after you."

Dominic starts to step in when he squeals and stumbles back. "Oh my!" he
creams.

I poke my head through the door. A small person is sitting atop a filing
abinet in the back. The dusty hoody hangs over her face like a funeral shroud
s she roots through boxes.

"An apparition," Dominic says, breathlessly. "A specter waiting for us,
urking in this forgotten—"

"Hey Violet," I say.

Violet looks up at me and smiles, as if oblivious to the arguing and the
xploding door. Her lavender and green eyes reflect the flashlights.

"Oh, hello Clark," she says and scampers atop the cabinets to get at more
oxes.

"How did you…" I start, but see the open vent by the ceiling.

"Why didn't you let us in?" Dominic says to her. "Surely you heard us."

"I thought you might be one of them," Violet says without looking up.

"One of them?" I ask.

Zeke says, "Yeah, if there's a *them,* I think I need to know."

"Or her," Violet says. "She's here, too. She's the one you have to worry
bout."

"Who's that, dear?" Andi asks.

89

Violet points to a picture on the wall. A frowning schoolmarm stands next to the bell in the courtyard, her students lined up before her. They all stand at attention, looking more like prisoners than nine-year-olds. She rests one hand on a child's shoulder while the other arm is curled up to her chest like some gnarled tree branch.

"Claw hand lady?" I ask and dust off the frame. "Are we talking about the lady or the *ghost* of the lady?"

But Violet is already gone. We catch a glimpse of her ratty, mismatched tennis shoes as she vanishes back into the vent. The others take that as their cu and descend on the boxes with a Black Friday frenzy. They tear open the desk and filing cabinet like they're looting the place. In seconds, the other nerds car tell there's blood in the water. Cris elbows her way in, trying to take readings with one of her gizmos. Kyle comes barreling through with one of his cronies running the camera. The mounted light blinds us. We hiss and grumble, but Kyle smelled the opportunity for a bit of theater.

"My esteemed associate at the Phantom League, Dominic, has located a hidden room within the bowels of the library," Kyle says, snatching things from the shelves.

I scowl at him over a stack of ledgers. "This isn't the Temple of Doom, jackass."

He ignores me.

"What we find in here could help unlock the secret of this unnamable place," he says, grabbing what he can.

Dominic raises a hand to protest, but his shoulders sag in defeat as he witnesses the fervor of the mob around him. They ransack the place, hoping to be the one who finds something that might be haunted, something they can attach some sort of meaning to. In a dusty corner, I spot a small parcel that's fallen behind the desk. I crawl beneath, grab it, and tuck it into my jacket without looking. If the rest aren't going to share, then I sure as hell won't.

"I'm going to guess it's her ghost," Zeke says, holding up a newspaper.

The headline on the Hill Country Examiner says *Teacher Still Missing, Fo* *Play Suspected.*

"Oh…" Dominic says, his attention captivated by the headline. "Oh my…"

"You know who this is?" I ask.

"Well, that's… that's… No. No, maybe not," he says and waves it off.

"Come on, Dominic. Help us out here," I tell him.

He shakes his head and continues to look through the desk, but the way he avoids looking at the newspaper is all the tell I need.

"Hey, Kyle!" I yell, calling him back into the room. He comes striding bac in with his lips pursed. That's the face he makes when he's trying to be all coo and serious.

"What's up?" he asks.

"Dominic has discovered something," I tell him. "And it sounds like he's got a story to tell us."

Kyle perks up and motions for his idiot brother to follow him with the camera. "Talk to me, Dominic. As an expert on the arcane, we're going to need all of your skills to solve this mystery. Can you help us?"

Dominic immediately buys into Kyle's man-of-action gravitas. None of them can resist the spotlight. Dominic looks around at the gathered investigators. Most of our group is here, waiting for his answer, so he clears his throat and climbs up on the desk. He spreads his arms wide, like he's about to launch into *Julius Caesar*.

"You're good," Zeke says to me, his voice barely a whisper.

"He's wearing velvet and an ascot. *Of course* he wants attention," I tell him under my breath.

"Friends and fellow explorers of the unknown," Dominic starts with the grandiosity of community theater. "There are some stories so heinous, so shocking, they lay hidden for decades, only spoken of in whispers. We hear bits and pieces of them from friends who had cousins it really happened to! Stories told around the campfire! Mysteries that change shapes over the years as they're passed down in the oral tradition. The phantom hitchhiker! The woman in white! But where did they start? What atrocity took place to give birth to such enduring and nightmarish legends?"

I wish I hadn't asked. Everyone else, on the other hand, is a sucker for a good campfire tale. They focus their flashlights on him, putting him center stage.

Dominic paces across the desk, pausing for effect. "And I am here to tell you, friends. We have come across something tonight that may shake us to our cores. For tonight, here at the Oswald Academy, we find ourselves at the epicenter of such a tale. That's right! We are treading upon sour ground. Gather close, friends! Gather close, and I'll tell you the tale of Iris Angel!"

With courtroom authority, he points at the newspaper with Iris's stern face. Even without Dominic's overwrought narration, everything about her says she's a teacher who secretly eats the children that misbehave.

"When Iris was young," Dominic continues, "Her arm was mangled in a farming accident. She carried this with her, this shame, her entire life, choosing to avoid people, to stay inside. You would, too, I would think, if people spat at you – only a child – when you walked down the street. *Freak,* they would call her, as they mocked the withered thing that hung useless at her side. *Monster! Devil!* You see, that arm was too grotesque to be anything holy. It was too obscene to be God's will. No, this ruined appendage was from Satan himself. He must have touched Iris, marked her as his own!

"Now this was just talk, right? These were just the cruel things that children say, but Iris? Well, Iris began to believe them. As a child, she once thought she'd be a nun. It was the only place that would have her, surely. A disfigured thing like that? Who would want her but God? But like water against the stone, the constant mocking Iris endured even eroded her faith in God's love. Maybe the Devil was indeed her patron, she thought.

"Within time, Iris found herself teaching the fine children of the Oswald Academy, this same institution. She was feared, as you can imagine. Her punishments were legendary for their cruelty. Step out of line once, and you'll feel that hateful gaze. Step out of line twice, and you'd get that twisted and horrible hand resting on your shoulder. That's when you knew that Iris Angel had come for you.

"And yet, her students loved her. They worshipped her, and their parents were alarmed by how much they talked about Miss Iris Angel. They drew pictures of her in crayon and sang songs about her. In spite of her draconian methods, one class, Miss Iris's fourth grade class of 1973, was particularly loyal. Each day, Iris would stand in the courtyard and summon them by ringing the bell. She'd ring that bell, and all her little children would come running. She'd reward them with a piece of cinnamon candy.

"But this class was different. You see, they didn't learn about math or history this year. Iris had developed her own curriculum. Feeling like God had turned His back on her, Iris turned her back in kind. Over the years, she'd become fascinated by the dark arts, like many of us. Only Iris wasn't just a student of the occult. She was a participant."

Dominic looks out over the crowd, making dramatic eye contact with each of us before continuing.

"And Iris wanted to pass on what she had learned. As many of you know, the dark arts are not always solitary endeavors. Sometimes, you need confederates. Or in Iris's case, a coven…"

Someone in the crowd gasps. "Ritual satanic abuse," they whisper.

"Not real," I say, but I only get scowls.

"Yes, Iris took this class of innocent boys and girls, and she began to warp them. She pulled them into her world of darkness. There were rumors of animal sacrifice, of unholy rites, and of Iris's connection to an incomprehensible evil from beyond time and space."

"She was into Cthulu?" Zeke asks, leaning in close. "That's cool."

"Also not real," I say.

"As you would imagine, people began to talk. Rumors spread. The locals started to regard Iris and the Oswald Academy itself as something to be feared. Iris was undeterred, fueled by her profound hatred for God and all his creations. She was planning something, some sort of black mass that would either result in the death of these misguided and tainted children… or perhaps usher in a new age of darkness.

"Late one night, a group of angry parents decided they had enough. They stormed the school, searching for their children. But Iris's class, some twenty children now touched by darkness, were missing. The panicked mothers and fathers went building to building, calling out. They searched room to room, but their children were nowhere to be found. At last, the parents caught up to Iris. They bound her, demanding she tell them where she'd hidden their kids, but Iris only laughed. Some who were there say she spoke in forbidden tongues, languages unheard by the ears of men since before the time of Christ. They said there was a shadow present that night, a shroud that loomed over the Oswald Academy, one Iris herself may have summoned from the beyond.

"Well, the worry for their children began to turn. Mob mentality, you might call it. That group fear turned to mania and that mania turned to bloodlust. If Iris wouldn't take them to their children, then they would send Iris and her withered arm back to hell. That night, twelve parents took Iris Angel and hanged her."

Gasps. The crowd whispers excitedly. For all his carnival panache, Dominic is actually pretty good with a ghost story.

"But… she didn't die. Like Rasputin, she kicked and spit and cursed at them. And any good Texas father has a knife, right? So, they stabbed her, again and again, their bloodlust turning into an orgy of murder. Still, Iris fought, swiping out at them with her malformed claw, uttering profane, blasphemous things about them and their children.

"Finally, late into the night, Iris died, but only after they dragged her out into the courtyard and burned her. The police were never called, of course, and Iris Angel's remains were never found. Some say they're hidden, somewhere on the grounds, anchoring her foul spirit to this accursed place. What's more… they never found the children. Twenty of them vanished that night and only Iris Angel knows what happened. Some rumors say they were sold to a cult that took them away in the night. Others say that the children are still here, all grown now, but twisted and evil, lurking in the hills and still holding on to Iris's teachings. I'd heard the story growing up. I never suspected that it was real, even today, while walking these very halls. And yet here we are, on the very grounds where it all took place.

"Late at night, campers in the area will sometimes hear the sound of the bell, ringing in the distance. Some even say that if you hear it and stand still, you might just feel Iris's withered and twisted hand resting on your shoulder."

The crowd is holding its breath. Dominic smiles and takes a deep bow, sparking a rapturous applause. Kyle's got a shit-eating grin. He nudges his brother and says, "Now we've got a story!"

Kyle shakes it off and assumes his cool exterior for the camera. "Now this evil has a name. Now we know what we're up against. Until now, we've been..."

"Wait!" one of the Wanderers yells, silencing the crowd. "Listen!"

Everyone freezes, listening to the wind rustle the dead leaves. This is the part where some asshole, usually me, screams *Boo!*

But then we hear it. The bell is ringing.

CHAPTER TWELVE

The crowd holds its breath, listening to the chimes. I look up at Dominic. Nice touch."

As he holds his hands up to say *It wasn't me,* the dam breaks and everyone pills out of the library. They stumble over each other, boxes and papers tuffed under their arms, while they try to ready their recording devices.

My stomach flutters a bit at the thought of seeing some undead hag floating ear the bell, summoning us to our deaths. But it's probably Jojo. I never told he kid when he could stop and when it comes to mischief, the Wanderers can e tenacious. This could go on all night. He'll be out there perched on top of he bell like some sort of bird or he'll sneak away, timing it so that everyone nly catches a fleeting glimpse of this mysterious Black-Eyed Kid.

But it's only Rez, slumped against the post in the center of the courtyard. he rope for the bell is wrapped around her wrist and she's giving it angry, loppy tugs. The sound reverberates across the courtyard and out over the hill ountry. The turbulent night sky answers with thunder.

Just like that, the crowd turns. They lower their cameras and sneer at Rez, isappointed that she's not some disfigured revenant schoolteacher. Sharp vhispers ripple through the group. They gather around but keep their distance rom the spectacle.

Rez spots us and says, "Hey, I can't find my phone. Have you guys seen .?"

The bottle she's clutching in her free hand is now empty. I'm almost npressed as I try to lift her to her feet.

"Nope. No. There's no walking," she says, and gives the bell's rope a few 1ore good jerks.

"Okay, you can stop with the bell. You've got our attention. Let's get you ɔ bed," I tell her. "Zeke and I will help you. Come on."

Kyle sniffs, and his lips twist with disgust. "Ugh. This is embarrassing. I 1ought we were all professionals here."

"Your mom's a professional," Rez says with a slur.

"You keep real classy company, Clark," he says to me.

Zeke stops and gives him an *oh really?* look. "You and me are about to ave a conversation, son," Zeke says.

Rez waves the empty whiskey bottle at Kyle, "By conversation he means arate. On your face. Hi-ya!"

She karate chops the air and dumps the contents of her purse onto the round. Makeup, wallet, her missing phone, and a black 9mm handgun.

"Oh my God," says someone in the crowd.

"Is that a gun?"

"Are you kidding me?"

Rez shakes loose of my grip and crawls over to scoop everything back into her purse. "Chill-out, nerds. I've got a permit."

"Isn't having a gun on school grounds a felony?" Cris from the science team asks.

"Your mom's a felony," Rez says.

I step between them, trying to shield Rez from the crowd's judgment. I'm all too familiar with getting sloppy because you hate yourself. "Yeah, but it's a *haunted* school. It's totally cool to carry guns at a haunted school. Because Texas."

Zeke puts a hand on my shoulder. "Hold up," he says, looking past me.

I follow his gaze up to a third-floor window in the dorms. There's a face. I raise my hand to wave to Jojo, to let him know that the joke is done. Then I see the pallid skin, the black eyes. It's not Jojo.

It's a kid.

"Oh, holy shit," Cris says and holds up an EMF reader like a talisman.

The kid stares down at us in true spooky ghost fashion. Unmoving. Expressionless. A flash of lightning makes him look like a silent film with missing frames. Each subsequent flash offers a subliminal glimpse of him—

Pressed against the window, screaming

Body contorted into an impossible shape

And hints of something else, some inhuman thing – an insect? – that I'm not sure isn't just a trick of the light.

Then it's gone.

The group erupts into excited chatter. Everyone focuses their devices up at the window.

Kyle gets frantic, bouncing and waving to his crew. "Come on! Come on! We gotta move, people!"

Immediately, they forget Rez and her poor choice of purse accessories. They trip over each other and race to be the first ones into the dormitory. Zeke and I are still standing there.

"Is that for real? Or did Jojo just really commit to the part?" Zeke asks.

"Real ghost," Rez says, swaying in place. "All the way real."

"Okay," I say. It's all I can manage.

"We chasing it?" Zeke asks me.

There it is. More than the doors in the Lighthouse, the sounds from the pit, or the voice on the phone. Proof. A thing. It's a thing I can see, and *they* can see. But I can't chase it. I can't make my legs move, and I can't say to myself, "Okay. Now we have to believe in this."

"Nah," I say with a grin I hope Zeke believes. "We did that. We know how it ends. And chasing children around an abandoned building is a good way to get put on a list."

"Would you rather chase after a ghost kid staring at us from the trees?" Zeke asks.

"Hey, can you call me?" Rez asks as she stuffs everything back into her purse.

We ignore her as Zeke points to the tree line, just past building six. It's the one we were chasing earlier, the one I thought was Violet. This kid is standing there just at the edge of the oak and cedar, watching us. The trees whip and bend in the wind, the changing leaves rattling like bones, but the kid's clothes are unmoved. The gray hoody is pulled back just far enough for me to make out a solemn look and eyes blacker than the darkness beyond him.

The molding walls of the Lighthouse are closing in on me.

"Oh, now just what in the happy hell is this? How many of you bastards are there?" I call out to him.

The kid doesn't move.

"About twenty, I'd guess," Zeke says.

"No, seriously," I say. "What? Why are you just standing there? If you've got something to tell us, just come over here and tell us. I'm not into this horror movie bullshit right now."

Silence.

"Damn it," I say. "He's gonna make us walk all the way over there isn't he?"

"My Spidey-sense is tingling," Zeke says.

"What does that mean? That some shit's about to go down?"

"Some shit's about to go down."

"Where are you at on punching children?"

"Ghost children? I'll kick a ghost kid's ass," Zeke says and adjusts all of his gaudy rings.

"Okay," I say as we start to walk toward the kid. "That's a good defense against charges of assault of a child. We'll just tell the cops we thought he was a ghost. That should work."

The bell starts to ring again. I turn to scowl at Rez.

"You assholes are just going to leave me here?" she asks, so we turn, scoop her up, and start shuffling to the trees.

The kid is still there, motionless, trying to be creepy.

"Hey!" I say to the kid. "I'm Clark. This is Zeke. This sack of booze between us is Marianne Reznicek. She can apparently talk to you people."

Zeke cocks an eyebrow at me. I shrug.

"You people?" Rez says and starts to laugh. "You're racist against ghosts. You're ghost-ist."

"Please stop talking," I say.

Twenty feet away, the kid begins to fade. He doesn't exactly disappear, but with each step, he starts to lose definition. Within a few more steps, he's gone, vanished with such subtlety that I'm not even sure we saw him in the first place.

My stomach drops, and I feel everything begin to spin. Suddenly, I smell cat piss. I smell dust and rotted dry wall. I can feel the walls of the Lighthouse surrounding me. I can almost hear, somewhere deep in the forest, that discordant tone, singing to me like a broken lullaby.

Zeke drops Rez and rushes into the brush. The darkness swallows him, and I want to tell him to stop. He might not come back, vanished along with Alan and the rest. I catch glimpses of him flitting in and out of the shadows, searching for the kid.

"Oh, you little fucker!" Rez yells. "You think you're clever, with your little *boop!* I can still see you, bitch."

"You can still see him?"

"Yes!" She says, stumbling closer to the trees. "He's right there! Laughing. Quit laughing, you little shit! Yes, I'm drunk, but I've had a hard day. So, fuck you!"

"Rez, he's like ten," is the only thing I can think to say.

"I don't give a shit," she says. "I hope Zeke karates his ten-year-old ghost ass."

Believing her isn't a problem. It's an easy step to take, but my mind is coming untethered. It means my friends at the Lighthouse didn't fall into a hole or get abducted by human traffickers. Something took them, something I can't explain.

Zeke steps out of the trees, his eyes wide.

"What's wrong?" I ask, and I can feel my heart beating in my throat.

"Dead body."

"What?"

"Oh shit. For real?" Rez says and turns to the empty place in the brush where she says the kid is standing. "Did you make a dead body, you little bastard?"

I find myself taking involuntary steps away from Rez and whomever she's talking to. My beliefs, forged in bitter disappointment, are dissolving in my hands. My cynicism had protected me. It had been my shield, keeping me away from things that shouldn't be possible, things like this. This is what I get.

My feet are moving, following Zeke into the trees. The lightning casts Expressionist shadows, a kaleidoscope of thrashing branches and glimpses of faces in the darkness. Just twenty feet into the thicket lies the corpse.

It's tangled near the roots of an old oak, the limbs twisted, torso snapped in half. The lightning's blue-white flashes reveal swathes of vivid crimson.

"Jojo," I say, but can't speak loud enough for Rez or Zeke to hear me.

Among the blood and shredded clothes and twisted limbs is a faint patch of skin, the ankh tattoo on his cheek. He wasn't stabbed, burned, beaten, or shot. He was mangled, like someone pulled him from a car crash and dumped him here in the trees.

"Oh shit," Rez says, leaning against a tree for support.

Zeke's standing over the body with a knife in his hand so big that it might be a small sword. His eyes scan the woods.

"This…" I say, my words coming out numb and heavy, "This is a crime scene. We need to wake up Elder."

Zeke reaches down at our feet, and I almost scream *Don't touch it!* He holds up a piece of candy with a red, cellophane wrapper. They're scattered around Jojo's body. Zeke sniffs it.

"Cinnamon," he says.

"Like in the…" I start to say.

Zeke pockets the candy and looks past me. "Stay close to me."

"What? I…"

I see it. In the trees and all around, faces staring at us with empty, bottomless eyes. White faces lurk in the branches or from the shadows. The children.

Zeke tenses. He shifts his stance, but all I can do is feel the ball of ice in the pit of my stomach expand, spreading through my bones and into my blood.

"Who did this?" Rez yells like an angry mom, pointing at the body. "Who did this? Did one of you little fuckers kill this guy? And leave candy?"

"Can you help us?" one of the children asks.

"Please help us," says a girl in the tree.

"Help us."

"I'm hurt."

"We want to come with you."

"Or you can come with us."

They all start speaking at once, from every direction.

"Maybe we should go," I say.

Zeke nods once. "Move slowly, back the way we came. You first."

He raises his giant knife and points it at the kids. "I ain't putting up with this shit, y'all. I'm about to march over there and start cutting off ya damn heads."

Thunder claps so hard it shakes the earth. With the next flash of lightning, the children are gone. I walk faster, tripping over roots while trying to reign in my panic.

"They gone?" Zeke asks Rez.

She looks around. "Yeah. They left."

Zeke frowns and sheathes his knife. "Jibber-jabbering at me with your "I'm so spooky" shenanigans. Nuh uh. No, sir."

Rez digs her nails into my arm as she wobbles along beside me. "This was a warning," she says.

"What do you mean?" I ask.

"They didn't do this."

"Then who did?" I ask.

Rez looks at me, but she doesn't want to say it. I don't want her to say it, either.

CHAPTER THIRTEEN

The only sounds in the cafeteria are sniffles, whispered platitudes, and the patter of rain on the roof.

Everything's going to be okay.

Jojo knows how much you loved him.

He was such a kind soul.

We're staring at the door to the kitchen. Behind it, Elder has Jojo's body laid out like he's on the slab in the morgue. I focus on it, my anchor. My mind tumbles, jumping from thought to thought, trying to come up with all the ways that I saw absolutely could not have been real.

It was a weird reflection, it was just the lightning, someone playing a prank. This is all just a reality show we're being punked but it wasn't a ghost no way nope not a ghost.

"Dude really just picked up the body and moved it?" Zeke asks to me, his voice low.

"Yeah," I say. "Said he was qualified, whatever that means."

"I didn't see a badge," Zeke says.

"Me neither."

At the next tiny table, Violet quietly rocks back and forth, eyes glazed.

"Hey," I whisper to Zeke. "Those things earlier. Were those… you know, real?"

"As opposed to imaginary?"

"You know what I mean."

"You heard what Rez said, right?"

"Yeah, but…" I start to say, realizing he's going to make me put it into words.

"Yeah, bro. Those were ghosts. Or revenants, maybe. Some kind of undead. You freaking out?"

"No! No, I'm fine. It's just…"

"You're freaking out."

"A little bit."

"Wait. Is this your first time?"

I start to speak but can't do much more than move my lips and swallow the words as I reconsider them. I shake my head. "Somebody is messing with us, right? Like this is a reality show, and they're filming us, filming our reactions to all of this… foolishness, as you called it?"

Zeke furrows his brow. "That kid was dead. The blood? That was real, too. Real body. Real murder. Real ghosts, man."

I sit with that for a second. Zeke watches it sink in.

"No," I say. It's the only thing I can think of.

"No?"

"No, it's… I've been doing this a while. A few years, anyway. Years of looking around in buildings and filming things and taking readings and blah blah blah. And… there was nothing. And you want to know something? I don' know if I ever really expected there to be anything. I mean, there was that excitement, right? That 'maybe'. Maybe I'll come across something crazy. Wouldn't that be cool? It's kind of like when you're a kid and you want to believe in Santa Claus, but really, deep down, you know it's just your mom an dad. You know that, but you keep playing along because part of you hopes that… there's something more, I guess. And now maybe Santa Claus is real. And he killed my friends."

"Clark," Zeke says. "Let me tell you, brother. There's something more. Yo saw it."

"I saw *something*."

"You saw ghosts making a bunch of noise around a dead body. I saw it, too Rez is three sheets right now, but she'll tell you the same thing. You saw ghosts. A bunch of them."

"Is it always like that?"

"No, man," Zeke says, reclining. "Never that many. I've heard of situations like that, but I've never seen that many in one place."

"You ever seen a ghost hurt somebody?"

Zeke nods and drifts off for a moment. It's a question I can't believe I asked. Until now, I thought punching ghosts was just his gimmick. Like that was the thing he put on his business card, but he was really just another crackpot like the rest of us.

"Yeah. I've seen it."

I can't decide if I want to ask for more. This might be as much of this worl as I can handle. If he tells me more, I can't come back from that. I might have to accept it and make it part of my life. That's not something my brain can reconcile right now.

Elder steps out of the kitchen and peels off a pair of dish gloves. He looks like he's been crying.

Everyone sits at attention and holds their breath.

"Is Jojo…?" Violet starts to ask but lowers his head before he finishes. We all know the answer.

Elder clears his throat. "This is what happens when protocol isn't followed."

The tone in his voice makes everyone shift in their seats and avert their eyes.

"Considering we're all adults here, I didn't think it would be necessary to set out some written rules. Apparently, I was wrong."

"Rules about not getting murdered in the woods?" I ask, and my voice cracks with something that feels like hysteria.

Elder's stare chills the room. Zeke sits up with the same tension in his shoulders, the same focus on his face as when we were surrounded by the spectral children.

"Don't run your mouth at me, Silver," Elder says.

Ariel Kwan raises her hand but doesn't have the audacity to raise her camera. "Can you tell us what happened?"

"Mountain lion. If you stray into these hills at night, that is a very real possibility. Unfortunately, Jojo came across one that was sick or injured. Usually they're afraid of people, but the wilderness – where you are not to go under any circumstances – is their domain. Jojo was mauled by this animal, an accident that was wholly avoidable. Leaving the Oswald Academy is a violation of protocol. Violating protocol will get you killed. I hoped you all would behave as professionals and respect the parameters of this assignment and that no one would get hurt. Unfortunately, someone had to die so you all could learn this lesson. For those of you who still don't get it, let me be crystal clear – do as I say or you may die. Is that understood?"

Bleary eyed from sobbing, everyone nods, a bunch of scolded children. Zeke and I exchange skeptical looks. Michael is a timid guy on the Scientific Anomalies team who constantly cleans his glasses so he doesn't have to look at you when he speaks.

"Sir?" he asks, rubbing his t-shirt on his lenses. "If we're, you know, not comfortable and would like to leave, would that be possible?"

Elder's gaze is so hard I half expect Michael to melt in his seat. "Speak to me privately if you'd like to abandon your assignment. But note that if you do not complete the assignment, your contract stipulates that your fee, in its entirety, will be withheld. Any more questions?"

He puffs his chest, waiting for dissent. It's all I can do to keep quiet.

"Good. The sheriff will be here tomorrow. Now go sleep it off. If there are any more shenanigans like tonight, you answer to me," Elder says.

He walks through the cafeteria, his head held high, and as he passes, none of us dare raise our heads to look at him. Once he's gone, I turn to everyone else. They're still sluggish with shock, as if they can't decide what to do with themselves. "A violation of protocol? Are you kidding me? And a mountain lion?" I ask. "Does anyone buy that?"

Shrugs. Noncommittal mutters.

"They didn't see him," Zeke says. "We did. We know what happened."

"We really don't."

"Man, I'd bet my favorite knife that boy got all pretzeled by the undead. I hope so, anyway."

"Why do you hope so?" I ask.

"'Cause if not, that means one of these people is legit crazy," he says, motioning to the other investigators. "And we're stuck in a haunted school with a psycho killer."

The rest of the group hobbles back to their cots, heads low and heavy.

Zeke continues, "Either that or a big, pissed off cat. And brother, I do not want to fight a mountain lion."

"There's something else," I say so that no one else can hear.

"'Sup?"

"Did you smell him when he walked by?"

"Elder? Nah, I generally don't try to smell people, especially crazy old people."

"He smelled like cinnamon. Like the candy."

Zeke shakes his head. "Mountain lion, my ass."

***

I wasn't the kid who drew pentagrams on things. There was no mysterious stranger with an evil tome or a tough home life that drove me to reefer and the devil. How did I discover the forces of darkness? Laziness and opportunity. After college, all that waited for me was a series of fly-by-night debt collection jobs run out of abandoned store fronts in derelict strip malls. It was a life of cigarette breaks and preying on the elderly. I learned how to talk, how to say what people needed to hear. I was good at it, too, constructing whatever malleable, but always charming persona was needed on the other end of the line.

Then I became a psychic.

Twenty of us sat in what used to be a Payless Shoe Store just across the parking lot from an abandoned car dealership. For two dollars per minute, you could connect to a video chat with the psychic of your choice, and the first three minutes were free. Each of us, taking names like 'Leilani' or 'Madame Frost', had our own thing. Leilani's real name was Naomi Gonzales. She was a single mother of three with a two-tone Corolla and a thing for Troll dolls. When she was Leilani, though, she decorated herself with luxurious sashes and eyeshadow thick as tar. The vague and completely fake Eastern European accent didn't hurt. All day and night, lonely people would call in to ask about marriage, work, or if the president was actually a reptile.

I just dropped my first name and went by *Vandermeer*. With the red tuxedo jacket I found online, and a healthy dollop of hair product, Horizons Psychic Alliance's most mysterious and powerful mystic was born. Imperious, grave, and enigmatic, Vandermeer had peered into the darkness. Vandermeer trafficked with devils and sorcerers. He read forbidden texts and walked a lonely path. He roamed the world, seeking out its esoteric secrets. And he could share his knowledge with you, over Skype, once you provided your credit card number.

Early on, I learned the tricks. Be vague. Be positive. Say things that people want to hear, that they want to be true. Let them tell you whatever you'll need to use later, so you can repackage, rephrase, and make them think you can see through the veil into the beyond.

The right people believed me. Everyone called for Vandermeer. My shifts were full of people calling in wanting answers or just wanting to experience the pageantry I brought to every call. Then one of them hired me. As my mom used to say, the Cabrera family had more money than sense, so they recruited Vandermeer to be their own personal Rasputin. I was a live-in *consigliere*, consulting them on the dark arts and acquiring various mystical antiquities for the family, many of which I found at thrift stores. And they bought it all. They believed I had an advanced degree in occult studies, that I'd learned from Nepalese mystics, and been trained by South American witches. To preserve the glamour, I actually did end up learning a lot about the occult, enough to fake it anyway. I learned to kind of read Latin, Enochian, and a bunch of Sumerian stuff. Memorizing all the demons in *the Lesser Key of Solomon* was helpful, especially when I needed to rattle off some cryptic trivia at a cocktail party. I started to enjoy it, too. It's nice to be respected for something, even if it's a lie.

And now here I am again, hoping I can fake it long enough to cash the check. I'm the guy who thinks he's a detective because he's watched lots of CSI. The lights have gone out and the snores of my colleagues echo throughout the gym. I'm on my cot, shuffling through the accursed homework and I feel like *I'm* being tested. If I can crack the code and figure out what this all means, maybe they'll all stop looking at me like I just shat my pants. They'll understand that I'm not just some jackass grifter, taking advantage of their abnormal little hobby. And maybe I can figure out what happened to Alan.

I examine the wobbly text and strange runes scrawled across the papers with unsteady, pre-adolescent hands. Lots of rebellious kids get into Satan. Not in a 'let's-summon-the-dark-lord' way, but in a way that makes them think they're more interesting. It's something to scare the jocks and the adults. The kids of Oswald Academy? They skipped Satan and went full *Necronomicon*.

The words seem familiar, like a song I heard once, playing in the background of a commercial. I can't quite place it.

Aggathot virilus. Maxugg zazz.

But it's the symbols I focus on. At the top of each page is a crude pictograph. It's the same one on all the papers, different than the one on the cassette and door, but of the same family. They look more like something you'd find chiseled into a stone in the desert, not some kid's writing assignment. I keep going over them, hoping to unlock the meaning of the alien words. A part of me hopes that it won't ever add up, that maybe I'll realize that no, these aren't the same sigils I saw at the Lighthouse. These are different. Nothing about these doodles or whatever magic I imagined they contain made me hear those noises, or made my friends disappear in the middle of the night. Cold anxiety washes over me.

There's no key, no way to decipher it on the paper, but I'm sure with enough digging, we'll uncover some textbook. By 'textbook', I mean something written in blood and bound in human skin.

I keep hoping against hope that maybe this is just some fun code, that Miss Angel was teaching these kids about Egyptian cuneiform or basic cryptography.

Shalem kudd Pagru. Missakka Varuk shemt.

As I shift on my cot, I feel something poking inside my jacket. I'd forgotten about the small, brown paper parcel I recovered from the office. It's wrapped neatly and bound in twine. There's a postage stamp, and it was sent to Iris Angel's attention, courtesy of the Oswald Academy. It's from the Lazlo Paranormal Museum.

"The hell?" I mutter under my breath and tear open the wrapper.

It's a cassette tape.

Beelitz, Germany– 10-13-1956

My hands shake. I almost drop the cassette. I want to. I want to tear the ribbon from it, smash it on the ground, then light it on fire. Instead, I open the case. The tape inside has a sigil drawn onto it. This one is new. It looks like an upside-down teardrop with an intricate star pattern in its center.

Again, the cats herd me down rotted hallways toward my friends' final destination. The Lazlos knew. *They fucking knew.* I grind my teeth until my jaw aches. For once, my hands aren't shaking out of fear as I imagine their folksy goddamn grins.

On the cot next to me, Zeke is asleep. Right by his bag is his Walkman. Careful not to wake him, I grab the player and eject his tape to swap in this new one. I can't help myself. I have to know.

My finger hovers over the button, and I take a deep breath just before I press *Play*. A moment of silence. The microphone rustles. Then there's a wail.

nstantly, every muscle in my body locks up. My gorge rises and I clench my ists. The sound slithers between my ribs and tickles the back of my neck. nside the wailing are moans. Jabbering nonsense. I imagine a thing with welve suppurating mouths, bellowing. The chorus writhes into a rhythm, nonsters attempting to sing. It's almost a song, not the Itsy-Bitsy Spider, but a 1ew and horrible dirge.

Before the sound ends, I snatch the headphones from my head and toss hem aside. I'm sweating, and I can't catch my breath. The tape has stopped, but the noise won't go away. It plays on a loop in my brain, like the instant before a car crash or the moment a lover broke your heart.

It will be another hour before I sleep.

***

I'm in a mineshaft, the walls, chalk white.

No.

It's drywall.

The ceiling is too low. Extension cords slither about, stapled to the wall to ang work lights up and down the narrow corridor. It seems to go on forever.

There's someone crawling toward me. Their eyes are sunken. Their skin, aundiced. Ragged clothes. Bleeding sores. They're reaching up for me, egging.

Something is behind them, something that carries a shroud of darkness with :, snuffing out the lights as it passes. All I see are teeth.

The crawling man screams. Blood sprays from the darkness, covering me nd decorating the walls.

I turn to run.

There's a man there.

No, two men.

No, there are fifty. All pasty white skin and blank smiles.

They're naked and smooth between the legs. No navel. No genitals.

They smile politely before reaching for me. They swarm.

I'm drowning in them.

As they pull at my clothes and limbs, they begin to shriek.

CHAPTER FOURTEEN

I awaken to my own scream. Still in my clothes, I'm on the floor, face down in the gym. On the cot across from me, Zeke is sharpening a knife. No one else is around.

"You alright there, bro?" he asks with his *what-bullshit-is this?* eyebrow.

The papers are strewn about on the floor. I must have fallen asleep with them. No one bothered to take them. They wouldn't be able to make heads or tails of it either. I scoop them up and tuck them into my coat.

"Where is everyone?" I ask.

"Investigating."

Most of the gym is empty. In the science team's workspace, Cris is scrubbing through footage on her laptop. She glances at me, scowls, and goes back to the video, matching up timecodes and checking the motion sensor logs. The Anomalies team nothing if not thorough.

"That's the look," she says, without facing us.

"What look?" I ask.

"The look when you want something, Clark."

"Just wondering if you found anything."

"Mostly just Kyle trying to be an alpha bro, a few suspicious blurs, and the Reznicek lady throwing a fit this morning because the coffee here is trash."

"You know what I mean," I say, leaning in.

"No. No murder. I've been looking through the footage all morning. I don't even have Jojo going out there."

"Is the sheriff here yet?" I ask.

"Not yet," she says, shrugging. "But I've got about an hour of some orbs that you might find interesting."

"Orbs?" I ask. "Don't give me orbs. You know how I feel about that stupid shit."

"Fair enough," she says.

"Where's the old man?"

Cris turns back to us, smiles, and narrows her eyes.

"Oh," Zeke says. "Oh damn. That's a look. You get him on camera being freaky? Tell me it's something good."

She turns back to the laptop and toggles through a few video clips until she lands on one with Elder, standing in the courtyard.

"Oh no," I say, and can't hide the grin on my face. "This does look like something good. What's he looking at?"

"Just wait," Cris says.

Elder stands perfectly still, staring straight ahead in the liminal darkness before the dawn. From out of his pocket, he pulls something small and red.

"Dude…" Zeke says.

"The candy," I say.

Elder eats it, still staring straight ahead. Instead of savoring it, he chews it like a bitter pill. The lines on his face harden. He takes a deep breath and seems to be steeling himself, like someone about to step into the ring. Finally, he pulls out a tangle of keys and steps forward to unlock thick, coiled chains binding the doors of one of the buildings.

"Is that…" I ask.

"That's building six," Cris says.

Elder scans the courtyard to make sure no one is looking before he slides inside and closes the doors behind him.

"What about all of that asbestos?" I ask.

"Exactly," she says.

"Man," I tell Zeke, "I told you we should have gone in there."

Zeke shrugs. "Sorry, I got distracted by the brutal murder."

"I told you, though!" I say, nearly jumping up and down. "I told you! Iris Angel. What a bunch of horseshit. This is some Scooby Doo business here."

"What are you talking about?" Cris asks.

"Scooby Doo. This. This whole thing!" I say. "Everyone is all scared of ghost-teacher-claw-lady, but it's really just some old dude killing people! Scooby goddamn Doo!"

Zeke and Cris both look at me like I'm crazy.

"Bro, there were ghosts. We talked about this. And that body…" Zeke says.

"You found it! What was it like?" Cris says, dropping her serrated disinterest.

"All messed up," Zeke says, "for real."

"Mountain lion," I say.

"Ain't no damn mountain lion and you know it," Zeke tells me.

"So, you think it actually was Iris? Because we've been getting some seriously curious readings—" Cris starts.

"Don't start with your readings. What? EMF and orbs equals ghosts?" I say, rolling my eyes.

"Hey," she says. "You're the one who saw an old man walk into a building and came up with Scooby Doo."

"That makes more sense than ghosts killing people!"

There's a glint in her eye, a look that says she's got me where she wants me.

"There's something else? Stop being all coy and just tell us. Jesus," I say.

"Yeah, we got shit to do. Stop playing. No one around here wants to work with each other. Everybody is trying to swing their metaphorical dick around," Zeke says.

Cris keeps typing and sighs. "Metaphorical dick? That's rich, coming from the guy with a bag full of swords."

"There are nunchucks in there, too," Zeke says, a little wounded.

"What do you got, Cris? Let's see it," I say.

She pulls up footage of us all in the courtyard from last night, staring up at the apparition in the window.

"Listen," she says, handing me the headphones.

I put them on, and she presses *Play*. You can't make out our voices, just the occasional yell. The sound is mostly the roar of the wind and cracks of thunder.

"What is it? I don't..." I start to say, but Cris smirks and cranks up the volume.

"Listen closer," she says.

Singing. Beneath the thunder and wind and our excited, unintelligible chatter, there's singing. It's more like humming, really, a lilting and broken melody. And it's a tune I recognize.

"What... what is that?" I ask.

"Did either of you hear that last night?" she asks us.

Zeke takes the headphones from me and listens. I can barely shake my head *no*. My insides are melting.

"Creepy, right?" she says with a big grin.

"Yeah," I say, barely able to choke out the word.

"Dude," Zeke says, "That's that Iris Angel lady, humming some spooky-ass song."

"It's like a nursery rhyme or something, but I can't place it," Cris says.

"Yeah. Me neither," I tell them.

A lie.

"Hmm," Zeke says with a shrug. "Sounds kind of like the Itsy-Bitsy Spider."

***

Zeke and I step out into the sunlight, and it feels like when the lights come up at the strip club. I want to dash for the shadows and hide under something. Team members flit about the courtyard, waving EMF readers and other gadgets. I shield my eyes from the sun and wish I'd woken up in time for a greasy breakfast.

"You good?" Zeke asks. "'Cause you look like you just—"

"Don't."

"— had some bad sushi. I was going to say you look like you just ate some bad sushi."

"No, you weren't."

He grins. "Nah. I know that look."

"We met like three days ago," I tell him, looking around for something to change the conversation.

"I've seen that look before on lots of other folks. It's the look that says *oh shit, the world doesn't work the way I thought it did*. You're shook."

Oh, you know… There's a creepy old couple manipulating me and I don't know why and they're keeping secrets that maybe killed my friends and definitely ruined my life.

"I'm fine."

He reaches into his bag and shoves a hatchet into my hand. It's an old one, like you'd find in a grimy tool shed, but the handle is carved with holy symbols – ankhs, crucifixes, some Hebrew words.

"My favorite axe. His name is 'Iggy'. You can carry him. He'll make you feel better."

And strangely, it does. You ever have anxiety? Depression? Survivor's guilt? Maybe a growing fear that the world you live in is an illusion, and forces you can't comprehend are really the things in power? Carry an axe around, preferably one named after Iggy Pop.

"Now let's go into building six and put that thing in ghost bitch's face," he says. "Or one of those kids. I'm not picky."

Across the quad, building six sits, immovable. It's a monument to Soviet-era crudity, all steel and concrete. We keep our distance, circling the building until we can find a way in that doesn't face the quad. Elder locked the front door from the inside. The back doors are wrapped with thick chains, all shiny and new.

The path between building six and the brick wall to the property is narrow and littered with leaves. It's the kind of place kids like me would have gone to sneak cigarettes or read comic books instead of going to gym class.

And under a tree, there's a body curled up on a bench.

A sour taste rises in the back of my throat and every nerve ending buzzes. I find myself raising the hatchet. Zeke stops next to me. A steely calmness comes over him.

It's Rez.

"Oh God…" I say, barely a wheeze.

She sits up.

"Oh, come on! Can I just find one quiet place to take a nap?" she says.

The fear bottoms out and Zeke, and I exhale. I put my hands on my knees, trying to catch my breath.

"Damn, girl!" Zeke says.

"What?" she asks, sitting up.

"We thought you were dead!"

"No," she says, trying to make herself comfortable. "I just wish I was."

"Why are you out here?" I ask.

"That gym is gross," she says.

"So, you sleep out here? Like a hobo?" I ask.

"There are old beds in the dorms," Zeke says.

"What? So I can get some sort of raccoon parasite? No, thank you," she says, squirming on the bench. "What are you two dipshits doing? Wait. Why do you have an ax? Are you the killer?"

"We're gonna kill Iris Angel or maybe some of those kids," I say.

"Whichever we find first," Zeke says. "Have you seen any?"

"Not today. I've been trying my best to not be conscious. Now please go away," she says and rolls over.

We step a respectful distance away and turn our attention back to building six. There's a covered walkway between six and the building with the classrooms. Zeke sizes it up and looks over at me.

"Up the tree, across the top of the walkway, and over to that window?" he offers.

"Breaking and entering *and* climbing? You sure know how to show a girl a good time," I say.

Zeke bounds up the tree, moving with fluid grace. I struggle a bit more. After a few scrapes, splinters, and some creative language, I join him on top of the walkway. It sags a little in the center, so we tiptoe over to building six's only uncovered window.

After navigating around the busted pane of glass, we crawl into some sort of lab. There's a broken, beige monitor and a smashed keyboard on the floor, an old desk, and some equipment I can't identify. With its lenses, triggers, dangling wires, and exposed circuits, it could come from a machine shop or a steampunk dentist.

We sneak into the hallway. The building feels no different from the others – Spartan corridors and cell-like rooms that have been left to rot for decades.

"If we get caught? No money," I whisper.

"Coach is gonna flip his shit," Zeke says.

With his red bag slung over his shoulder, he leads the way. It's room after room of decay, illuminated only by cracks around plywood hammered over the windows. These rooms aren't beds or classrooms, though. These were stripped. A few of them hold the remains of obsolete technology – an old fax machine, a mashed rotary phone – along with stray, rotted boxes. Otherwise, this was the building they chose to clean out. The dorms and classrooms were mostly abandoned as they were, but not building six.

As we go deeper, the darkness thickens around us. I can feel myself slipping backward in time, like we turned a corner and found ourselves walking through twisting corridors of smashed plaster and cat piss. There's barely enough light to navigate, but a flashlight would give us away, so we continue on, groping our way through the shadows. My brain starts racing to draft reasons to leave.

I have to pee.
What if there's tetanus?
Is that black mold?

I choke them all back, my fingers flexing around the Iggy the axe. A hand falls on my shoulder, and everything in my body goes loose. I'm a millisecond from wetting my pants when I realize it's Zeke. He holds a finger to his lips, then points to his ear.

Sobbing.

Somewhere down one of these halls, someone is crying.

"Crying. Of course it's crying," I say to him, whispering.

"Would you prefer eerie laughter?" he asks, and motions for me to follow.

As we sneak, Zeke pulls one of his massive knives from his bag, and my heart starts to pound. I'm not scared of the knife, but of what it means. Before I realize it, I'm walking directly behind him, putting him between myself and whatever the hell is crying.

We descend a dark stairwell, using our hands to feel our way down. The crying is louder now, just down the hall. Zeke nods in that direction and continues before I can protest. Despite myself, I follow.

We pass more identical rooms, classrooms with old chalkboards and pastel-colored plastic chairs. These remains, they decided to leave. The sobbing grows louder with each step, and I'm watching Zeke's feet, trying to mimic how he steps so that I don't make a sound. As we get closer, another noise. The staccato scratching of someone writing on the chalkboard.

Zeke sets his bag down. We slide along the wall, inching toward the door where the sound is coming from. He readies his knife and holds up a closed fist, like we're Rainbow Six. The sobs are wet and ragged, not the pained wails of some tortured spirit, but of a man overcome. Zeke peeks.

Slowly, he pulls his head back and looks at me with an expression that can only be *Holy Shit*. He presses his finger to his lips and pulls me forward so I can see. I want to dig my heels in or curl up in a ball so he can't make me look, but I'm too scared of making noise to resist.

It's Elder, his face streaked with tears. A thin tendril of snot reaches down to his chin as he writes on the board.

Shalem kudd Pagru. Missakka Varuk shemt.
Kuthru gagynd. Kuthru chagoll.
Xal Diabonistes ak dru.

And then it clicks. It's *WitchTongue.* No one speaks WitchTongue, not in four-hundred years. I don't speak it, but I know a little, enough to understand that what he's writing is nothing taught in Sunday school.

I pull back so fast I nearly fall over. Zeke catches me and holds me still. We freeze. Inside, Elder has stopped writing. He's motionless, listening. Zeke and I wait for some sound, some signal that tells us we can breathe again.

Finally, Elder sniffs and takes a breath. Zeke turns me to face the other direction and gives me a quick push. He mouths *Go.*

We hustle, moving as fast as we dare. I round a corner into the lobby by the front doors. The daylight barely penetrates the murky glass to show us marble floors, old frames with faded pictures, and empty display cases. Where there were trophies and team photos, there's now broken glass and rodent nests.

"Hello?" Elder says from down the hall.

The granite baritone is gone. It's a question laced with fear and hope. A few heavy footsteps in our direction, then a pause.

Zeke points behind a reception desk, a half circle that faces the front doors. We duck behind it as Elder heads toward us. His footsteps are surer now. The boots echo with his military stride. He comes around the corner as we make ourselves small behind the desk.

Elder stops in front of it. He sniffles again and clears his throat. I can feel his presence, his gravity in the center of the lobby. I'm face to face with Zeke. He's frowning at me and wiggling the tip of the knife, a question. I shake my head *no.* His shrug is almost imperceptible.

My legs begin to cramp just as Elder turns and stalks away. It's a full minute after his footsteps have faded down the hall before we move. Zeke stretches. I put the hatchet down on the desk and take deep breaths to flush out the anxiety.

"All right. I admit," Zeke says as he peeks around the corner, "Maybe it is Scooby Doo, 'cause Coach is full-on crazy-pants."

"Right?!" I say.

"You see that wackadoo shit he was writing? What was that? Some kind of Satan-talk?"

"Yeah, actually it's WitchTongue."

"Say what?"

"WitchTongue. Or *Kammatu.* It's for summoning ancient entities, making pacts, curses. Real nasty, Lovecraft kind of shit. Most scholars don't even thin it's real. Last time I read anything about it, there are only two known examples of…"

He's not listening. A framed picture on the wall has his attention.

"What?" I ask. "What is it?"

He approaches like he's not sure he wants to touch it. Finally, he plucks it from the wall and blows off the dust.

"Yo," he says, and tosses me the photo. "Recognize anybody?"

It's a class picture, older than most of the others. Twenty kids, all lined up and staring into the camera without a single smile among them. They stand at attention. Looming over them with the black-eyed gaze of a raven is Iris Angel. Her lips are pursed into a tight knot. The sign in front of the class reads *Miss Angel's Fourth Grade Class– 1973.*

I hand it back to Zeke. "Yeah. She's creepy."

"Look again."

I take another look, scanning the faces of the children. Standing closest to Miss Iris is one with a familiar stare of cold iron.

"Holy shit. Is that Baby Elder?" I ask.

Before Zeke can answer, a cacophonous screech blasts from down the hallway. The glass plate slips from the frame and shatters on the floor. I grab the hatchet, but neither of us can move. The noise echoes across through the corridors, sounding like a giant bug trying to sing a song. The melody carries the jangly uncertainty of a child learning their first song on the piano. But it's not a piano and it's not a bug.

"Another one," I try to say, but it just comes out a choked wheeze.

"What the hell?" Zeke says and takes a few steps down the hall.

I reach out for Zeke, like I'm pulling him out of traffic. "No!"

"You okay?" he asks, but I can't hear him.

I can barely hear the shrieking sound over the roar of my blood. I can feel my lips moving, but no sounds come out. I can feel my feet moving, my lizard brain trying to drag me out of this place. My vision narrows to one spot on the wall above the desk.

We missed something. A faded image is painted on the concrete. The blue and yellow paint is chipped, but there's no mistaking the shape of the lighthouse and its giant eye.

CHAPTER FIFTEEN

The screaming in my brain extinguishes everything else. Sitting alone on the roof of the dorms, I can only take deep breaths. I don't know how long I've been up here. After seeing the Lighthouse, I fled, away from the noise, away from everyone. I squeeze my eyes shut. Elder has his own tape. Now he's punishing himself and the rest of us, letting loose that cacophony on the world.

Elder. The tapes. The Lazlos. The Lighthouse. Whatever happened to my team… it's all too much. Like reading WitchTongue, I know there's meaning there, but I can't make sense of it. The more I try, the more it all digs in, tearing bloody ruts through my brain.

The horizon is on fire with oranges, reds, and purples. It feels final. Every few minutes, another blast of notes comes from building six. The melodies, if you can call them that, are a little different each time as he keeps trying new ones, a higher pitch or a different time signature. They're different from the one at the original Lighthouse and different from this new cassette I've found, but it's all from the same songbook. One after another, he keeps playing them. Will one of them bring back Alan and the others? But hearing Turkmenistan again might be too much. I could pitch myself off the roof or go running off into the forest to face murderous ghost children or mountain lions or whatever the hell is out there. Better than that. Better than Turkmenistan.

Zeke's Walkman is in my hand. My finger hovers over the button. I don't understand the allure, the siren song that makes me want to hear it again, but it's there. It's the same compulsion that keeps Elder playing those tapes for the last few hours. He feels like if he just digs deep enough, if he can scrape away the dissonance, that there will be meaning there. He'll see his future in the tea leaves.

Then, as those sharp and shattered notes drift across the courtyard, I think I hear something else. In between them, amid the insectoid screams and the quasi-human jabbering is something familiar.

I take a look at the settings on Zeke's Walkman. *Play. Rewind. Fast-Forward. Stop. Fast Play. Slow Play.*

I press *Fast Play*. The screams wriggle and spasm like maggots in my ear. It's all I can do not to tear the headphones away. But the noises take shape as they're sped up. The utterances congeal into something like words.

WitchTongue.

The song in the night, the broken tunes I played at the Lighthouse and on the cassette I found in the office, they're not just noises. They're not just ear-splitting accidents or even the baying of the damned.

They're spells.

The words buried in tape are WitchTongue, like the words written on the chalkboard. I pull the homework papers from my jacket pocket. The phrases on the page aren't the same as the ones I'm hearing, but they're all from the same dialect. The crude symbols on each tape are the same as the symbols on the homework, and *those* are the same as the symbol on the door. Each sigil is a shorthand. It's the mark of the spell.

Or whatever the spell calls forth.

But spells don't work. They're not real. Spells are just words that desperate and lonely people want to use either to try to manipulate the world around them or to call to the world beyond. It's fantasy. It's sad and embarrassing and ridiculous.

And I'm terrified of it.

Some real *Evil Dead* shit. That's just great. I hurl the tape off the roof. It clatters against the bricks somewhere below.

Building six is another Lighthouse. I don't know what that means. After my friends vanished at the first one, I searched online for the logo, but found nothing. I don't know if it's a branch office or a church or some research facility. It sure as hell isn't a school. The Oswald Academy was just a front.

It wasn't coincidence that I was brought here. The Lazlos hired me because I was at the first location, but I don't know why. I can't ask Elder about the Lighthouse icon in the lobby. He'll know we were snooping. I'm here for a reason and it feels very sacrificial.

Below me, parked just by the gates, is the bus. I want the keys. To get them, I'd have to talk to Elder. I'd have to go back into that building. Even if the sounds were to stop, I don't think I could set foot in there.

The door to the roof opens, and my heart jumps into my throat until I realize it's just Zeke.

"You staying up here tonight?" he asks.

"I don't know, man."

"You should come down to the gym."

"What's up?"

"That girl, Rez? She ain't doing so hot."

***

Rez is curled up under a blanket, her skin clammy and pale. She shivers as Andi brushes the hair out of her eyes and applies a damp washcloth. Violet scurries around the cot, tying charms to the posts. A painted bird skull. A ribbon she found in the gutter. An origami dove made from a McDonald's wrapper. Nearby, a bowl of sage burns.

The atmosphere has changed. Maybe it's the sage or maybe it's the funk of twenty people, all hanging out in a poorly-ventilated gymnasium, but the atmosphere feels sick. It clings to me like a trip to a hospital or an airport.

I grin. "Come on. You're just hungover. If we get a greasy plate of enchiladas in you, you'll be just fine," I tell Rez.

She's the only one who laughs. "Yeah, this is one of those never-drinking-again moments. It's just yoga and smoothies forever. For real, I'm at the making-promises-to-God phase."

Andi and Violet don't crack a smile.

"What's wrong?" I ask.

"Don't tell me you can't feel it," Andi says.

I don't know what to say to that.

"Hers is a spiritual sickness," Violet says.

"What does that mean?" I ask. "Are you guys going to have to do some Benny Hinn faith healing? 'Cause I've always wanted to see that."

"Something's got to give, Clark," Andi says, "Or our lovely friend here will be dead by morning."

"Seriously?" I ask. "What in the hell are you talking about? Why didn't she leave when the police came?"

"The police never came, dear," Andi says.

"Yeah. And Elder never made dinner, either. I had to eat some cold hot dogs," Zeke says.

Rez's eyes are closed and she begins to twitch. Violet gets down on her knees and quietly prays.

"What in the hell is wrong with her?" I ask.

Before Andi can answer, Rez moans. She's fallen into a fever dream. Her lips move, uttering barely audible whispers. When I lean in, I recognize the blasphemies.

"Shalem kudd Pagru. Missakka Varuk shemt."

"It's Iris Angel," Andi says.

Rez sits bolt upright and gasps. Andi eases her back down onto the cot.

"Shit!" Rez says. "What happened? Was I asleep? Is the baby donkey here?"

"She also has a really high fever," Andi says.

"Iris Angel? Would you guys please cool it with this killer ghost nonsense? If she's sick, she needs a doctor, not some Gwyneth Paltrow bullshit," I say, not really believing the words as they come out of my mouth.

"Clark, darling, I assure you these aren't some fanciful antics," Andi says. "This is quite real and quite serious."

"Serious? Let me tell you about serious, Andi," I tell her. "Did you see Elder? He's coming unglued."

Andi looks at Zeke. "You two think Elder is the one behind this?"

Zeke holds up his hands. "I'm not saying it's *not* the ghost of Iris Angel, but the dude is legit kookaburra and if anyone here is a murderer, it's him."

Rez throws off her blanket. "I know how we can find out."

***

The four of us – Andi, Zeke, Rez, and myself – huddle around one of the small cafeteria tables, pretending to enjoy leftover hotdogs. Leftover hotdogs are kind of a staple of my diet, so it's not that much of a stretch for me. All of us steal glances at the kitchen. Blake guards the door. His nose is clownishly bruised from his fight with Zeke, making his narrow-eyed stares at us more comical than threatening.

"So Jojo's body is in the freezer?" Andi asks.

"As far as we know," I say.

"Elder could have turned him into an art installation or fed the dude to Iris," Zeke says.

Blake's a big guy, but nothing Zeke couldn't handle. "You want to just go whip his ass?" I ask Zeke.

"Aight," Zeke says, and wipes his mouth.

"Whoa. Whoa. Whoa," Andi says. "Boys, please. I swear, your testosterone is alarming."

Andi pushes away her untouched hotdog, stands, and winks at us. Blake crosses his arms as she sashays over to him. She puts a soft hand on his shoulder and leans in to whisper into his ear.

"You get more flies with honey, I guess," I mutter to the others as I try to stifle the twinges of jealousy.

The blood drains from Blake's face. His mouth flops open, and he backs away from Andi. "Get away. Don't you ever come near me again," he says.

He almost runs from the cafeteria, too afraid to take his eyes from her. Once he's through the doors and into the night, Andi turns back to us with a big smile. Stunned, we jump up to follow her into the kitchen.

"What in the hell did you say to him?" I ask.

"Do you really want to know?" she asks.

"No. No, I really don't," I say.

The kitchen is stainless steel, dirty white tile, and flickering fluorescent. It's not clean, but cleaner than the rest of the campus. No rodent nests or broken glass, just a bunch of 60s-era cafeteria appliances decaying in the greenish-glow. The walk-in freezer buzzes in the corner, an electric mausoleum. With my hand on the latch, I take a deep breath. "Everybody cool?" I ask.

Solemn nods. I open the door. We're hit with a blast of frigid air as we step inside. The wire shelves are empty except for a fistful of the cinnamon candy recovered from the scene. On the floor is a mound wrapped in plastic. It's irregularly shaped and wrapped thick enough that we can't see through it, but we all know what it is.

Zeke and I lift it and carry it out onto a metal table. No one speaks. Andi covers her mouth in horror. Rez leans on the table, trying to remain upright as her eyes droop and beads of sweat trickle from her brow.

I look to Zeke. He pulls out one of his knives and slices through the plastic. Jojo's skin is shock white. His clothes have stiffened, and his limbs are still twisted into unnatural angles. The blood has crystallized.

"Poor thing," Andi says, and puts a delicate hand on Rez's arm. "You sure you want to go down this road, sweetheart?"

Rez just nods. Under the pallid lighting, she looks little better than Jojo.

"So…" I ask. "Do we like light candles and hold hands or something?"

Andi scowls at me.

"I'm not being an asshole here. I don't know how this works."

"Just give her a moment, Clark," Andi says.

I look to Zeke. He gives me a reassuring nod, his hand gripping his knife. It takes the edge off, but even standing here over this corpse, I feel like I'm on the precipice of a pit. Behind me is my life as I understood it. Below is the inexplicable horror that comes next. With every moment, what I knew is eroding.

"Hey, dude. Wake up," Rez says to the corpse.

Nothing, just the buzzing of the freezer.

"We haven't met, but I'm Rez. These are my friends. I think you know some of them. Are you around?"

"Maybe he departed already," Zeke says.

"No," Andi says, and puts her arm around Rez to support her. "He's here."

Rez wipes the sweat from her brow and clears her throat. "Come on, Jojo. Don't be weird. I feel like shit and I need to lay down. Can you just come talk to us for a second?"

The lights flicker and dim, and a chill fills the room. My first thought is that I left the freezer open, but it's shut tight. I shove my hands into my pockets. Andi and Rez look above the table, into the air, expecting something.

Jojo opens his mouth. The jaw cracks. Bits of frost chip away. The sluggish tongue wiggles. He gasps. "Oh. Hello."

"Holy fucking shitballs!" I yell and stagger away from the corpse.

I knock into a table, nearly tipping it over.

"Dude, be cool!" Zeke says.

"Be cool? Jojo the undead pretzel is *fucking talking.*"

"Hey, Jojo. I'm Rez. I think you know the others."

The voice is strangled and dry. Jojo struggles to form the words with his blue lips. "Hello, everyone."

"Fuck you, Jojo!" I say. "This shit ain't right!"

"Jojo," Rez says, "I'll let you go in a second, but… I need to… I need to…"

One leg buckles. Andi catches her. Zeke rushes over to help.

"You good, buddy?" Zeke asks her.

Rez nods and continues. "Jojo, I know this is hard for you right now."

"Yeah… hurts. I'm tired," Jojo says.

Now it's my turn to slump to the floor. My legs won't work. The room spins.

"Who did this to you, Jojo?" Rez asks.

Jojo begins to cry, and as he does, I realize the voice isn't coming from his lips, but from the air around us. The sound bounces around the room. The light flickers.

"Jojo, honey," Andi says, "We want to help set this right."

"Please," Rez says, "Tell us who hurt… you…"

Rez's eyes flutter. She melts in Zeke and Andi's arms as the strength bleeds out of her.

Jojo's voice gets louder, and I can feel it in the air. "Sheeeee… did…"

The light pulses.

Darkness.

Andi gasps.

Light.

Rez collapses onto the floor. Zeke's got his knife ready.

Darkness.

A table is knocked over.

"I have her! I have her!" Andi yells.

Light.

Andi cradles Rez. A guttural voice crawls from Rez's throat.

"Shalem kudd Pagru. Missakka Varuk shemt. Shalem kudd Pagru. Missakka Varuk shemt."

Darkness.

The cracked voice of an old woman hums a broken tune. I crab walk away from the sound until my back hits the wall.

Light.

A hunched and grinning thing lurches over Rez. Long, stringy hair. Spindly limbs. Its withered fingers wrap around Rez's head.

"Zeke!" I yell.

He vaults over the table.

Darkness.

The lights come up, and I have to force myself not to shut my eyes. The thing is gone. Andi is on the floor with Rez. Zeke stands over them, a knife in one hand, the axe in the other. He scans the room.

The kitchen door flies open. Elder towers in the frame with Kyle close behind.

"See, Mr. Elder? Can you believe this?" Kyle says.

Elder hisses. "Drop the weapons, Silver."

"Oh, hell no," Zeke says, still looking around the room.

Knees bent, arms cocked, Zeke is ready for Iris.

Elder draws a gun from his belt, Rez's black 9mm. Kyle's face goes slack. He takes a step back as Elder chambers a bullet and points it at Zeke. Something is different about Elder. Cracks are showing in the stone façade. He's trying to choke back a quivering fervor, like the moment before Belloq looked into the Ark of the Covenant.

"Now, goddammit!" Elder says.

"Are you kidding me with this?" Zeke says, not backing down.

"Son, if you don't drop that knife, I'm going to drop *you*. Are we clear?" Elder says, aiming right at Zeke's head.

Zeke's face goes cold. He stares back.

"Zeke..." I say.

Zeke glances back at me and sets the weapons on the metal table.

Rez tries to sit up. "That's my gun, asshole. You can't just go through somebody's purse."

Elder tucks it back into his belt. "I've tolerated a lot of your abject stupidity over the last twenty-four hours, but I draw the line at desecration. On your feet. All of you."

122

CHAPTER SIXTEEN

Elder shoves us into a storage room in the back of the gym. It's crowded floor to ceiling with old AV equipment, deflated basketballs, and busted chairs too small for any of us to be comfortable.

"I'm sick and damn tired of your flagrant disobedience and outright rebellion. I told you it will not be tolerated, and I meant it," Elder says. He turns to Andi. "It's not a surprise from these three degenerates, but I expected better from you, Miss Thorn."

Andi, always sly, looks over her shoulder at us. "Like I've never been locked up before."

Elder ignores it. "You're to remain here for the duration of the investigation. We'll arrange for meals and bathroom breaks, but you won't be released until we leave tomorrow afternoon."

"A day? You're keeping us in here for an entire day?" I ask and motion to Rez. "Look at her, Elder. She needs a doctor."

Elder leans in. "You're lucky I don't whip your smart ass, Vandermeer."

"Listen," I say, trying to keep my voice from shaking. "Elder, please, walk away from those tapes. Burn them."

The f
ire crackles in Elder's eyes, and his face glows with fervor. The sound has been working on him.

"You don't know what you're talking about," he says, and his lips twitch into a mad grin.

He slams the door and locks it. Zeke and I lower Rez onto the floor. I collapse next to her. The smell in here is stale and the walls are too close and I can feel us sinking to the bottom of the ocean.

"Can you get us out of here?" I ask Zeke. "Please say yes. Please kung fu that door. I'm just going to run. I'm going to run until I reach civilization."

Zeke loosens up, getting ready to charge the door when Andi says, "Let's press *pause* on the martial artistry for a moment, shall we? Elder is unhinged. You kick that door, Zeke, and he's going to hear it. He'll come running with that gun."

"No, he won't," says a voice from the other side of the door.

Blake is in the window, grinning. He presses the gun to the glass.

"You try anything and Elder has given me permission to shoot you," he says, and laughs like his team just scored a touchdown.

"Permission to shoot somebody? This isn't the army, dumbass," I tell him.

Zeke's knuckles crack as his hands tighten into fists. Blake laughs again and disappears.

Andi kneels next to Rez and holds her hand. "Marianne won't last 'til tomorrow, boys," she says.

"That thing gonna kill her?" Zeke asks.

Andi nods. "And that's the easy part."

"What's the hard part?" I ask.

"Then she gets up, but she won't be Marianne anymore."

Zeke nods. "As it is, seems like Iris can only come into this world for brief moments. Even with that, she was strong enough to kill Jojo. But if she takes over Rez…"

"She'll be able to stay as long as she wants," Andi says.

Every thought on how to get out of here or how to help Rez is cut off by the image of Iris Angel, that *thing*, leering at me. My mind spins, reaching out for an explanation.

I'm still asleep and poisoned by nightmares from the screeching incantations on that tape.

I've had an aneurysm. Another one.

Schizophrenia.

I'm dead.

I prefer any of them to the truth that I can't get away from. Blood roars in my ears. I'm cold. I can't stop shaking.

"You all right there, cowboy?" Andi asks.

"Fine. I'm fine."

Zeke slaps me on the back. "Listen, we've got all of our bases covered. I got the muscle, Andi here's got the magic. Now we need you and your occult expertise, and we'll get Marianne and ourselves out of this mess, right?"

Andi looks away first, tending to Rez like she can't hear the conversation happening right beside her. It's a polite effort, but in this tiny room, I can't run from my shame. Andi knows the truth.

I pinch the bridge of my nose to try to quiet the roar in my head. Panic sounds like a freight train only you can hear.

"I'm not an expert, Zeke," I say. "Not in the occult or magic or demons or… or anything else, really."

"Nah. Don't be like that. We're still in the game. That's just the fear talking to you, riding shotgun. You've got to shove that bitch in the trunk," he says, and I want to believe him.

Deep breaths. Saying this out loud will probably hurt.

"I'm not an expert, Zeke," I say. "Like… at all."

Andi offers a slight smile, and her eyes glisten with pity. It's meant to help, to let me know it's okay, and she knows this is hard for me. But it doesn't help, not at all.

"What do you mean?" Zeke asks.

The words won't come. There's no way to arrange them, no polite euphemism that doesn't make me sound like an asshole.

"Clark knows more about the occult than most people. Don't let him sell himself short," Andi says to Zeke and pats me on the knee in a way that makes me feel even smaller.

It comes spilling out like blood from a wound. With lots of backtracking and interrupted thoughts, I tell him everything. I tell him about Horizons, the Cabrera family, and all my bullshit. By the time I'm done, Andi has rested her calming hand on the small of my back. I sit and await judgement.

Zeke nods, considering it like he's trying to decide between the enchiladas or the steak special. "So, you playing the occult guy on that show, that was just TV?"

"More or less," I say. "It didn't take them long to figure out I was full of shit. They fired me."

"And replaced you with the hot girl?"

"And replaced me with the hot girl."

Zeke nods again. Finally, he looks up at me and locks eyes. "So? Fake it 'til you make it. Well... you made it. Now this is it, the big show. No more faking it. It's time to step up."

"Yes. Marianne here is going to need all of us for what comes next," Andi says.

"Okay... Okay..." is all I can manage to say.

Andi starts looking around the room. "And I'm sorry, but we're running very short on time."

"Exorcism?" Zeke asks.

"Exorcism? Are you serious? I..." I say, but can't finish. Nothing makes sense anymore. Everything is on the table.

"More like a spiritual cleansing," Andi says. "We don't have much in here we can use."

"What do you need?" Zeke asks.

"Ideally, some sage, incense, candles, salt, a few sacred texts," she says as she searches the shelves.

Zeke hands her a box of white chalk. "There's some jump rope over here if we need to tie her up."

Andi takes the chalk. "Thank you, dear. The jump rope won't be necessary just yet, but this will have to do."

Andi starts to clear a space on the floor next to Rez. Zeke helps her, tossing boxes and an old volleyball net into the corner. I can only watch as I try to will myself to shrink until I'm nothing and gone. She draws an oblong circle on the floor and decorates the edges with symbols. I slide away from her.

"Clark, honey," she says, "Don't go anywhere. Marianne is going to need all of us for this next part."

I nod. "Yeah. Cool," I say, but no one is convinced.

Zeke crouches down next to me and puts a firm hand on my shoulder. "Yo, I know this is scary, bro, but you hired me to take care of shit, and you know what? I'm gonna take care of shit. We're in a bad spot, I ain't gonna lie, but let's let Andi here work her mojo. We fix our girl Rez, bust out of this cell, whip some ass, and then whip some more ass."

The pitch in my voice climbs with every syllable. "And we're just going to work some magic now? We're casting spells? Is that it?"

"I got you, brother."

I nod, take a few deep breaths, and close my eyes. "Yeah. Yeah. Okay. I'm sorry. I'm here. I got this."

There are hundreds of ghost hunting groups in the world. All of them are looking for something, but I know now that they really don't understand that *this* is what's waiting for them. I got what I wanted. I peeked behind the curtain. I guess now I have to deal with it.

When I open my eyes, Andi is finishing up the ceremonial space. The circle is lined with Enochian symbols, the language of the angels, and elaborate geometric patterns. When she finishes, she rifles through her purse, retrieving vial after vial of powders, grains, and herbs.

"No... no... not that one..."

"Are you carrying an entire spice rack?" I ask.

She holds one up and smiles, "There! Mugwort."

It looks like a tiny bottle of tea leaves. She drops a few pinches of it into a small, red bag. From her index finger, she slides off a ring set with glistening opal and drops it into the bag.

"Thank you, grandmother, for your wonderful taste in jewelry," Andi says with a smile, before leaning in close, her lips hovering next to Rez's ear. "Sorry about this, sweetheart."

She plucks a single, stray hair from Rez's scalp. Using her pinky, Andi curls it into a circle, adds it to the bag, and cinches it all closed.

"There," she says, dusting off her hands. "That will have to do."

She closes her eyes, clutches the bag to her chest, and whispers what sound like a brief prayer.

Zeke nods. "I don't much care for witchy shit, but you get props for resourcefulness, Andromeda."

"Oh, don't thank me yet, handsome. What comes next is going to be quite perilous."

"What now? Do we have to chant or something?" I ask.

"Or something," Andi says, and hands me a piece of the cinnamon candy.

"What's this for?"

"You eat it, dear," she says, and unwraps a piece.

Each of us gets one, even Rez.

"Marianne?" Andi says. "I'm going to put this on your tongue. Try not to choke on it, darling, alright?"

She slips the candy between Rez's lips. Rez, somewhat aware, closes her mouth around the candy and moans.

"Is this like a peyote thing? 'Cause I'm in no shape to trip balls right now," I say as I pop the lurid red lozenge into my mouth.

Before anyone can answer, the world gets fuzzy. I feel myself reeling backwards as everything tilts off its axis. I try to spit out the candy. Only a thin tendril of red smoke puffs from my lips. The air around me buzzes with opioid softness.

Zeke and Andi are standing over me. Zeke has a shining sword. Its blade is an impossible green.

"Where'd you get a sword?" I say, but my voice is coated in motor oil.

There's a rush of air and then a *pop*! And I'm back. We're in the storage room. I sit up and rub my face.

"It didn't work?" I ask.

Zeke holds up the sword. "Oh, it worked."

"Did you just find that in here?" I ask.

"I summoned it. With my chi," he says.

"Can you summon me one? One made of vibranium?" I ask.

Andi chuckles and helps me to my feet. "Come on, Clark. You're going to be just fine."

The chalk circle where Rez lays now emanates a purple glow, as if under blacklight. And here, in this liminal world, she looks… different. Her face is older, withered and not entirely her own. And her right arm has grown longer, the fingers twisted.

"What the hell is wrong with her?"

"It's worse than I thought," Andi says.

"Okay…" I say and put my hands on my knees. "Okay. This is… yeah…"

"Time is of the essence, gentlemen."

"Dude. I just found out ghosts were real like ten minutes ago and now apparently magic is a thing. I'm gonna need a second."

"I told you I was a witch, Clark," she says with a smile.

"I thought you said it for attention!"

"We've got to move, y'all," Zeke says.

The door is open. Blake is gone. As we step out into the back corridor behind the gymnasium, I notice that everything is lined with a purplish hue. It's all different now. Doors are in the wrong place. Hallways extend where there were none before, dozens of them, branching out like fractals.

"You know when you're dreaming that you're talking to your dad, but it's some other guy, but it's your dad? That's what this feels like," I say.

"Astral plane, bro," Zeke says, sword ready.

"It *is* a peyote thing!" I say, and my voice reverberates with a tinny sound.

We move quickly, Andi leading the way. Nothing I knew about the layout of the school matters anymore. A door that should have led us into the gymnasium instead puts us into another corridor. We're in the building with the classrooms. The halls twist and turn and double back on themselves. Some seem to stretch off into infinity. Everything is fresh and clean. Nothing is filthy. The lockers don't hang by their hinges, and the children's art on the walls doesn't peel with age. In the distance, I hear kids laughing and teachers talking.

We peek into classrooms as we walk. Some of them are full of students. They wear striped pants and turtleneck pullovers. It's the 1960s. I find myself reeling away from the rooms, the world spinning again. I can't catch my breath. Zeke grabs me by the arm.

"You gotta stay close, man," he says.

"Are we time traveling?" I ask.

"Kind of. Keep moving."

The next class, the kids are clad in bell-bottoms and plaid. The 70s. The white glow of fresh snow shines through the window, but the next window reveals the vibrant green of a Central Texas spring. Everything shifts out of focus as we pass. When I look back, the halls are different. It's all water through my fingers.

The bell rings, and the kids pour into the hallway. They laugh and chatter, unaware of us. Children from different years flood past. Kids from 1961 walk past 1973. They go through each other, ghost-like. Their voices are just echoes. I raise my hands, trying not to touch any of them. "You good, Clark?" Andi asks.

I can only nod.

"Zeke, stay ready. I can feel her," Andi says.

"Oh, I'm ready."

"She's close? Does she know we're here? Is she pissed?" I ask and look to Zeke. "Are you sure you can't summon me a sword? Or some sort of chi-powered shotgun?"

Zeke grins. "I'll teach you how some time."

Andi stops at an intersection. On the wall, gleaming with vibrant blue and yellow paint, is the Lighthouse icon.

"No, we can't go that way," I find myself saying before I realize it.

I turn around, but the classrooms are gone. The hallway is different again. No more lockers or announcements of parades or sporting events. Now it's the antiseptic white and beige of a clinic. There are men in lab coats, clipboards, and tasteful potted ferns.

"I don't think we have a choice," Zeke says.

We continue onward as the technicians buzz about. Their white coats have the Lighthouse logo embroidered on their lapel. Their conversation comes in bits and snippets. A man in horn-rimmed glasses from 1972 mutters about *positive results with the Edison phone.* A broad-shouldered woman in 1968 recommends *a lysergic acid drip.*

"Is this still the school?" Andi asks.

"Yeah," Zeke says. "I think we're in building six."

"What kind of shenanigans were they up to in here?" she says.

"Nothing good," I say, and as I peek into one of the rooms, I see a shaggy-haired kid in a Partridge Family t-shirt. White room. White table. A number of technicians are in the corner, their pens flying across their clipboards as they monitor the boy. In front of him is a Ouija board. As he stares at it, he giggles. The planchette is moving by itself.

The next one is similar. More technicians monitoring some kid with a crew cut and a nosebleed. He's focusing on a ball on the floor. The rubber ball sits on a line painted on the linoleum. The line is etched with measurements. The kid focuses. The technicians hold their breath.

One of them says, "Okay now, Terry. Relax and make it come to you."

The ball rolls about six inches and stops. The scientists all nod and write down the results. Terry, smiling, looks back at them.

"Yo," Zeke says and motions to me.

He and Andi are looking through a window into a larger room. Andi's jaw hangs open. There are kids in the room, standing in a circle under a single spotlight. Their hands are linked, and they're standing in a circle like some playground game. Their hair whips about in a phantom breeze. A lone child, a young boy, is in the center. His eyes are white and his mouth hangs open. He's floating. The other kids look up at him with solemn concentration.

Syn'arr et norr. Diabonistes gash. Qliphot kam vun.

The words drift from down the hall. It's a lilting voice, immediately parroted by a group of young voices. We follow it without speaking. Our steps are slowing, as if we all understand what we'll find.

Iris is there. She writes the profane words upon the board, and even here in this non-place they scour my brain. The WitchTongue finds purchase and digs in like splinters. The kids drone on, speaking the words back to her as she points to the board and enunciates. They're dead-eyed in their seats, all lined up at long tables in this room that is part classroom, part laboratory.

"Shalem kudd Pagru. Missakka Varuk shemt," she says with a smile. "We open our vessels to the wisdom of the Weeping King so that the powers of the Pagru will fill us up. Let go of your tainted core and allow the Outer Chaos to enrichen your feeble husks."

"Shalem kudd Pagru. Missakka Varuk shemt," the children repeat.

Iris turns her head to look at us. Her neck twists and extends as her face stretches out. She shows her serpentine fangs and spits at us.

"Drot mokk! Gul'dak kuhn!" she says.

The three of us stand in the doorway, frozen in place. Zeke raises the sword and snarls back at her. The sound of her voice crawls across my skin and curdles in my stomach. The words are heavy. They're anchors. I'm going to be stuck here as she hollows me out and fills my husk with her thick poison, and I have to move. I have to get out to get away to run down the hall until I can find a door and I can breathe again and I won't hear Alan screaming and I won't be screaming with him and these words I never want to hear again and I can find a long needle and jab it through my ears and—

"Clark!" Andi yells.

She's across the hall, but she's far away. I'm running, but I don't know where. There has to be a place where I can breathe. I'll know I'm safe when the air is fresh. I have to breathe. I have to get away from those words.

Andi is in the hallway, coming toward me like she's wading out into the ocean to save me.

I'm outside. The courtyard. There are no stars.

A howling crowd of people roils around me. They're moving as one, shouting and growling. They have flashlights and knives and guns. Their teeth gnash and spittle flies. I'm pulled along with them. In the center of the crowd is Iris Angel. Her lip is split and her eye is swollen. Her hair spins out of the tight bun, brushing over her mad eyes. She hisses at them and kicks as they drag her along. I'm pulled with the mob.

Somewhere, Andi yells my name. I can't tell where it's coming from.

We're inside. It's a theater. The stage is lit up and the red curtain glows like electric blood.

"Where's my boy?" A man with a .22 rifle yells.

"She's a damn Satanist!" someone else says.

I'm tossed through the crowd of flesh and sweat and fury. We tumble down the aisle, and I reach out for something, trying to stop myself. The mob spills onto the stage, and I hit face first. I want to stay there and try to hang onto the wooden stage to keep from flying off into the ether, into the darkness above. If don't hang on, I'll drift away into nothingness.

Above me, a lone rope drops from the darkness. There's a noose at the end. "Tell us what you've done with them!" A woman screams.

They beat Iris. They kick and stab her. She yowls in pain that twists into laughter. This makes them kick harder.

Between their feet, I can see out into the auditorium. The children are there. They're laughing and cheering. Some of them stand and clap, throwing things at the stage. In the middle of them is Iris Angel, sitting placidly, her good hand folded over her misshapen claw. Her satisfied smile lands on me.

"Burn the bitch!" a man screams.

When I raise my head, the mob is hoisting up the rope. The woman trapped in the noose flails, clawing at her neck as her face turns a dull purple.

It's not Iris.

It's Andi.

"No…" I try to say, but my voice comes out dry and broken.

I try to stand, but I'm knocked to the ground.

"Andi…"

Andi chokes. She wiggles at the end of the rope. Knives plunge into her abdomen. Her shirt is torn. They pull her hair and hoist her higher.

My legs won't work. I'm flopping on the stage, trying to escape the mass.

From the darkness of the theater comes Zeke. It's his eyes I see first, reflecting the green burn of the sword. He snarls and hurls it through the air. It flies end over end, over the heads of the children and up over the crowd, before dicing through the noose.

Andi drops. She hits the floor next to me and gasps for air. Blood trickles from her nose and lips.

"Spit it out," she says to me.

A half-dissolved chunk of cinnamon candy oozes from between her lips. It's sticky with blood and syrup.

There's a lump on my tongue. I wretch. The piece of candy slides out of my mouth. Cinnamon spit drips from between my teeth and out of my nose. My vision blurs with tears. I reach out to take Andi's hand. She squeezes back. Her fingers tremble. Zeke is there over us. I can barely make him out. He's roaring like a Viking gone berserk.

Darkness crowds my vision.

I'm falling through the stage. Into darkness. Into silence. I let go of Andi's hand.

Down there, swaddled in a tarp, are bones. Iris's decayed face, eyeless and leathery, looks back at me.

I sink deeper.

CHAPTER SEVENTEEN

My head swims. I wipe cinnamon slurry from my lips and look around. Zeke is awake, but wobbly. He's leaning over Andi. Andi is on her back, clutching at her stomach. She moans, her voice a wet rasp. Blood and sticky syrup froth around her lips.

"What? What's happening?" I ask.

"She got stabbed. What do you think happened?" Zeke says. He opens his mouth to yell but bites his lip. He shakes his head as he cradles Andi. "Clark, I know you were scared, but you were supposed to stay close to us. I had her. I had Iris. I was gonna finish this!"

In the center, the protective circle is empty. Rez is gone.

"Umm…" I say, but Zeke already sees it.

"Ah, shit."

Andi's eyes fly open. She coughs, trying to speak.

"It's okay. It's okay," Zeke says. "I got you."

She coughs again, red syrup bubbling onto her chin.

"I'm so sorry, Andi. God, I didn't know," I tell her, taking her hand.

"Run…"

"Nah, we're safe. We're back in the real world," Zeke says.

Andi points at the ceiling. "Run!"

Rez looms over us, floating in the air, one arm outstretched, long and mangled, the fingers ending in talons. She leers and her wrinkled face contorts with hate and the jaw opens like a python, the rows of teeth jagged with decay

"Damn!" Zeke shouts.

I stumble back and knock into a shelf of supplies. Half-inflated basketballs and gym shoes fall around me. The room is too small. Nowhere to run.

Zeke reaches down to scoop up Andi. Rez's malformed arm whips out and catches him in the chest. He flies off his feet. The crack when he hits the wall is so loud, I'm sure he's broken.

On the other side of the glass, Blake looks on, his mouth hanging open.

"Blake, open the door!" I shout. "Open the damn door!"

Blake runs.

The Rez-thing hisses as Andi struggles to her feet. It pounces on her. The claws hook into the meat of Andi's side, tear through the shirt, and plunge deep.

Andi whips her head back and screams.

"You'll get detention, children!" the Rez-things says.

With one quick jerk, it throws Andi. She hits the door hard enough to bash it from its hinges. Her smashed body tumbles across the tiles, side flayed open to show the yellow fat beneath.

"Andi!" I scream.

The thing grins at me, full of hate and glee. The neck jerks to the side and distends on the end of a noose we can't see.

Zeke staggers to his feet and raises his fists.

"Let's go then!" he says with a growl.

"Disobedience will result in corporal punishment," it says and begins to laugh.

The cackling is musical, laced with the discord of the tapes, channeling the WitchTongue from somewhere deep within.

The claws snap playfully at Zeke's face.

"Rez, if you're listening, I'm real sorry for what's about to go down," he says.

He watches the claws as the thing creeps closer. Zeke shuffles back, a half-step at a time, staying just out of reach. I back up with him, but there's nowhere to go.

At our feet, the chalk seal is spattered with Andi's blood.

Enochian symbols.

Enochian.

I *know* Enochian.

The monster swipes. Zeke whips his head back, narrowly avoiding getting his face sliced off. I dive under and slide toward the symbols.

The chalk is lost in the mess.

But blood works better. I swipe my hand across the puddle, wetting my fingers.

"The hell, bro?!" Zeke asks.

"Distract her! Distract her!"

Zeke lowers his shoulder and plows into the thing. It gasps. Bony limbs flail as Zeke tackles it.

With blood-slick fingers, I trace new symbols over the chalk, adding to them, embellishing.

"*Un, Graph, Ged, Gon, Fam.* In that order. Clockwise," I say to myself. "*Un, Graph, Ged, Gon, Fam.* That has to be right. Please be right."

Zeke and the Rez-thing grapple. It laughs with unhinged malice. Teeth snap at his face. With both hands, he struggles to keep the claws from his throat.

"*Un, Graph, Ged, Gon, Fam,*" I say, trying to remember exactly how the Enochian symbols look. "*Un, Graph, Ged, Gon, Fam.*"

I don't focus on the monster above me. I don't look at Andi's ruined body just past the doorway.

"*Un, Graph, Ged, Gon, Fam.*"

"Hurry," Zeke says. The claws hover closer.

"Hold her!" I shout.

A syphilitic tongue crawls from her mouth and worms across his cheek.

"Come see me, boys and girls. Come see Miss Iris," the voice says.

"Clark…" Zeke says.

The last of the blood smears into the final letter. "Holy guardians, I beseech you. With the wisdom of Abramelin as my key, I summon your light!"

It releases Zeke and jumps back in shock. A surprised croak crawls from its throat as it looks at the new bloody sigil that surrounds it. Zeke scurries back, taking care not to break the line.

The Rez-creature snarls at the symbol, then back up at me. The shriek is ear-splitting, casting out gobs of thick spittle and sending her stringy hair fluttering into a halo.

"Oh, she's pissed," I say.

"That worked? How the hell did you do that?" Zeke asks.

"I'm as surprised as you are."

Its body contorts as it floats in the center of the circle. The tips of its feet scrape the floor. One eye bulges from the socket, looking at the blood-seal. It pushes at the invisible barrier, poking and prodding with its deformed hand.

"What's it doing? What is that?"

"It's finding a way out," Zeke says. "We've got to go."

The revenant floats between us and the door. It hisses at the circle. It presses.

"It's time for your lessons children," it says.

The blood begins to sizzle. It boils away, throwing up thin tendrils of smoke.

"Oh shit. That's bad. That's bad, right?"

"It ain't good. I'm gonna hit her again. I'll hold her as long as I can. You run. Get everybody and go. You hear me?"

Zeke plants his feet and raises his hands like he's stepping into the ring.

"Are you crazy?" I ask.

Behind us, boxes topple over in the cluttered corner of the room. I scream. Zeke spins, fists ready, as a new shape emerges from the shadows. Violet pops out of a hole in the floor.

"Come on! This way!" she says, and ducks back into a trapdoor.

"Violet!?" I shout.

The Enochian symbols shrivel and char. The creature's tongue lolls out as she laughs. She pushes harder, closer.

Zeke growls and shoves me to the trapdoor. We drop down into a narrow, concrete passage. I take a last look as it reaches for us. It can't quite break free of the bindings. It unleashes another shriek of animal fury.

"Go! Go go go!" I say, and push Violet forward.

The sounds of rage follow us as we race down a dank and winding corridor that runs beneath the gym. There's just enough room to stand. Any second now, it will tear loose of the Enochian magic and come howling down the tunnel.

Violet's flashlight illuminates dust and sheets of cobwebs as we follow her.

"Sewer?" Zeke asks.

"Maintenance, it looks like," I say, but I'm just guessing.

I hope it's maintenance, but at this point, if Violet were to lead us to the abandoned underground lair of some undead blood-cult, I wouldn't be surprised. The tunnels branch off and split in every different direction. After a few turns, I'm lost, but Violet moves with confidence. We pass ventilation ducts and smaller tunnels and I realize this is how she's been making her way around campus the entire time.

Zeke keeps looking over his shoulder.

"We good?" I ask.

"For now," he says. "You want to tell me about you casting a damn spell back there?"

"Hell if I know. I used to read lots of weird shit. I didn't think it would actually work."

"It shouldn't have," Zeke says, and eyes me with suspicion.

"I'm unsurprised," Violet says.

She doesn't look back, doesn't slow down.

"Hey, Violet," I ask, "Can you slow down? I don't feel like chasing you again."

"Wasn't me that time."

Zeke looks at me and gives a knowing nod.

"Who was it?" I ask.

"Them," she says, as though it's the most obvious thing in the world.

"Them? Them who?" Zeke asks.

"The black-eyed kids. They're stuck here. They don't mean you harm."

"Can we help Rez?" I ask as I try to keep up.

I don't ask about Andi. I don't have to. It's written across Zeke's face.

Zeke shakes his head. "Might be too late for that. I hate to say it, but it seems like it's head-chopping time."

"We can't do that! Let's just find Elder, load up the bus, and GTFO."

"Nah, man. I liked Rez. We leave her like that? She suffers. Maybe forever. And who knows who else she'll hurt."

Violet shines her light up a rusty ladder. Above is a manhole, half-open to reveal a crescent of night sky. "This way," Violet whispers. Her alien eyes glint in the glow of the flashlight.

I climb. A memory surfaces with the sudden sting of an acid flashback. I'm descending into darkness as an eyeless corpse watches me drift down, down…

"Guys?" I say, halfway up the ladder. "What if I knew where they hid Iris's remains?"

CHAPTER EIGHTEEN

The cafeteria is dark and empty. I wasn't ready for the silence. You get used to the constant chug of the generator and when it goes silent, that absence is heavy.

"Generator," Zeke says. "Told you."

Even the freezer is quiet, Jojo's remains thawing and rotting inside. Somewhere close, in the hallways branching off from the gym, Iris roams. She hums to herself and mutters, interrupted by the occasional tortured scream. I don't know if the screams are hers.

"She's loose," Violet says.

"I guess the sheriff or whoever never came," I whisper. "Or Elder never called him."

"Or…" Zeke says as he cracks open the back door. "We're going to find his body strung up in the courtyard."

"You're not doing much to keep me from curling up in a ball and crying," I tell him.

Zeke turns to Violet. "Violet, get everybody together. Quick, all right? No messing around. Get them and get on the bus."

She nods once and scurries into the shadows like some ninja ferret.

I stick close to Zeke as we slip between the tables, heading out behind the cafeteria. The doors are cracked open and the sharp smell of gasoline lingers. On the patio outside, the generator has been eviscerated. It's a semi-portable thing on wheels, the kind you can get at a hardware store for a few hundred bucks. Gouges the shape of claws tear through its metal housing. Fuel bleeds out of the casing and onto the cracked pavement.

"Whoa…" I say, imagining those same wounds across Andi's torso.

Nearby is a cannister of gasoline. Zeke scoops it up and nods to a metal table. There's a haphazard stack of supplies. Hot dog buns, bags of potato chips, bottled water, and the like. I grab a big container of salt. Apparently, I'm going to fight an undead monster with a condiment. Before we head back to the gym, Zeke creeps over to a side door in the kitchen and presses a finger to his lips as he listens.

"Wait here," he whispers.

I shake my head and reach out to stop him, but he's gone, slipping off into the gymnasium. I stand there in the kind of silence you can feel on the back of your neck. Iris is still around. Her gibbering has faded, moving off into the distance, but I don't think she's gone far.

Or she's in here with me.

I turn around and scan the kitchen. We don't dare use flashlights, so I can only see by the moonlight coming through the cracked back door. I try to watch everything at once and wait for every shadow to move, to leap forward and eviscerate me. Each table is Iris. Each shadow is some undead fiend, waiting for just the right moment.

I open the door to the gym. It's just as dark, but twice as large. The shadows are bigger. The silence is heavier. Somewhere in the rows of cots and makeshift tents is Zeke. And maybe Iris.

"Zeke! Wait!" I whisper in a volume I hope ghosts can't hear.

I shuffle into the gym, doing a duck walk reserved for soldiers under fire or ghost hunters who have shit their pants. My footsteps are way too loud, echoing through the cavernous dark. Somewhere, a shuffling. I can't tell where.

"Zeke?" I ask again, but quiet enough that it barely passes my lips.

The lurid drapes of the Phantom League's den is the centerpiece of this camp of nerds. I crawl toward it, moving low, fast, and clumsy. From inside, I thought I heard...

On my hands and knees now. With every inch, I get lower to the ground. B the time I get to the fringe of the velvet curtain, I'm practically combat crawling on my belly. Inside, it's quiet, the quiet of someone waiting.

I wait there, feeling the seconds expand, trying to control my breath, wondering if it knows I'm here.

I whisper, "Zeke?"

The curtains part. Something bellows. A light blinds me.

I squirm, kicking and pushing across the gym floor. I lose the salt and gas cannister.

A hand latches onto my jacket and slams me hard into the floor.

Cold metal presses against the skin of my cheek. I slap it away and squint against the glare of the light.

Two shapes on the other side of the blinding light, one small, one large.

"Vandermeer?" one of them asks.

Before I can answer, a dark form moves out of nowhere. It smashes into the two standing over me, scattering them. The big one grunts. The small one squeals. Their flashlight hits the ground.

I know that squeal.

"Wait!" I shout.

The flashlight rolls along the floor and stops, catching a feral Zeke in a freezeframe. He holds Belinda in a headlock. Her arm is twisted up behind her Behind them both, Dominic thrusts out a crucifix. He waves it through the air like he's swatting away mosquitos.

"Let go of me!" Belinda says.

Zeke obliges. "What the hell you doing sneaking around in the dark?"

"What the hell are *you* doing? You just attacked me? You could have killed me, you psycho!" she says.

Dominic spins on his heels, still waving the shiny cross. "Are we safe? Is she here? What's happening?"

Zeke helps Belinda to her feet as I put my head between my knees and try not to faint.

"What's going on?" Belinda asks.

Dominic dabs his forehead with a pocket square. "The lights went out. There was screaming. Some sort of dirge, a hellish thing, a wail that spewed forth from the bowels of hell itself. Never have I heard such—"

"Shut-up," Zeke says.

Dominic's mouth hangs open, but he doesn't say another word.

"What was all the screaming about?" Belinda asks.

"Ghosts are real. They're trying to kill us. Now everybody get on the fucking bus," I say.

Belinda steps forward. "Wait. You saw an apparition? How would you classify it? Was it aggressive? Did it—"

I wave my hands, "Listen, this is a lot for me to deal with right now, so can we just talk about it later?"

"For real," Zeke says, "Me and my man here have got work to do. Now has anyone seen my red bag?"

"Oh!" Dominic says. He ducks back into his velvet brothel and emerges a moment later, proudly holding the bag in the air. "Here it is, your weapons of war, as it were."

Zeke takes it from him and examines it before glowering at the two of them. "Did you touch anything in here?"

Dominic starts. "Well, I—"

"Don't. This bag is sacred. I swear to Jesus Christ I will whip your Edward Cullen ass."

I scoop up the gasoline and the salt. "Yeah," I say, "I guess we're going to go fight a ghost."

Belinda's face glows with excitement. "You're going to confront it?"

"Put it to rest," Zeke says. "Clark thinks he knows where the remains are."

"I'm coming!" Belinda says. "Hang on!"

She disappears into the darkness before we can protest. Zeke looks at me, pain shadowing his face. Rez. We're going to put down Rez.

Dominic picks up the flashlight and shines it on his own face. "I will not be joining you. And I would like to humbly request an escort back to the bus."

"Are you serious right now?" Zeke asks.

"Dead serious, I'm afraid," Dominic says. "Please, Mr. Silver. I implore you. If there's any chance of encountering Iris Angel, I would very much like you to shepherd me to safety so that I can safely rejoin the rest of my clan."

Andi. And Rez.

My stomach curdles all over again.

"About your clan…" I say, but Belinda emerges from the shadows, weighted down with gear.

Audio recorder in one hand. EMF reader in the other. GoPro strapped to her forehead. Shotgun mic mounted on her shoulder.

I think of DJ and her unbreakable smile, playing with her toys before we found that goddamn door.

"Ready," Belinda says.

Zeke waves her off. "Maybe you should head back to the bus with Dominic."

"Don't gatekeep me," she says. "You want to play hero, that's fine, but I'm not missing this."

"Belinda," I say, "I don't think you understand—"

"Come on, Vandermeer. How bad could it be?"

"Bad. So bad. Real, real fucking bad."

Dominic waves his pocket square to get our attention. "Might I request that we please have this professional disagreement in closer proximity to our point of egress?"

"Point of egress?" Zeke asks and turns to me. "I kind of want to leave him here."

"He's right. Let's get the hell out of here," I say.

We follow Zeke out into the courtyard where everyone huddles inside the bus. Violet waits out front, perched on a rock like a crow on watch. Inside, heads bounce as excited whispers are passed back and forth.

Cris, Belinda's partner, has even more sharp edges than her girlfriend. She pops her head out the front door.

"Are we really just leaving?" Cris says.

Belinda shrugs and shows everyone her gear. "Occultex team claims they have something. I'm going to go document and—"

"No! We're leaving! Just get back on the bus! Please!"

Blake steps out of the bus, waving Rez's gun around. Everyone winces and ducks.

"It's all for real. That's what I've been trying to tell you. It was a monster. A really for real monster. I saw it!"

His voice cracks right along with his sanity. His face is whiter than the moon above, radiating panic.

Slow and sure, Zeke reaches out and slides the gun out of his grip. His stare stabs through Blake's boiling panic.

"I'm sorry," Blake says. "I'm sorry I ran."

"Uh huh," Zeke says

Without looking, Zeke dismantles the 9mm and tosses the pieces across the courtyard.

Blake's head sinks below his shoulders. He slinks back onto the bus. "I just want to go home."

Cris says, "But our readings are—"

"No one gives a shit about your readings, Cris," I tell her. "People are dead. Andi and Rez…"

Dominic turns to me. "What? Marianne and Andromeda? What happened to them?"

"Nothing good," Zeke says. "On the bus. Let's go."

I scan the faces. Violet climbs behind the wheel.

"Is that everyone?" I ask her.

One of the ParaSquad pipes up from the back. "Kyle wouldn't come. He said you were doing this for attention. We don't know where he went."

I shrug. "I'm good with that."

"I don't suppose anyone has the keys?" Dominic asks.

All the way in the back, his reedy frame folding in on itself, Simon removes his hat and clutches it to his chest. "Oh, may the Old Ones have mercy."

His panic ripples through the cabin. Whispers, hot with fear, ignite. I'm about to tell everyone we're sprinting back to the city when the engine grumbles to life.

Violet's hands twist wires beneath the steering column. She smiles at me. "YouTube."

She reaches for the gear shift when Zeke stops her.

"There's something we have to do first," he says.

"Shit. Are you sure about this?" I ask him and look back at the road leading to the school. Escape is *right there.*

Zeke nods. "You can go, man. I won't hold it against you. But if we can save her or stop her, I've got to try."

Somewhere on campus, Iris screams. But to me, it sounds like DJ. It sounds like Alan. It sounds like Melissa.

It's open! My God, it's open!

I try to swallow it down, but a current of white-hot fear rushes just beneath my skin. Maybe I'll die. Maybe that thing that was once Rez will slash me open or drag me to hell. But I can't go back to that couch. That's the slow death of nightmares and questions I can't answer. I can't leave Rez floating out there in the ether, lost to some unknowable thing like the rest of them.

Zeke takes the gas can from me and places the hatchet into my hand.

"Iggy," I say, marveling at the inscriptions on the handle.

"Damn right. You got this, brother," he says. He adjusts his red bag over his shoulder and smiles. "Let's go show old spooky that we don't tolerate this shit."

Everyone watches us as we step off the bus. Dominic grabs my arm. "We'll send back help," he says. "It's a noble sacrifice you're making for us to escape."

"What? Sacrifice?" I ask him. "No. You wait for us. You hear me? I'm serious."

"Oh…" he says. "Oh, yes. Of course."

***

I know this place, this theater, but I've never been here. Instead of a throng of murderous parents, it now only holds rot. The ceiling above sags, on the verge of collapse. The seats are vinyl and decimated with age. The red curtains hang like a flap of skin over the stage and I try to shake thoughts of Andi lying on the floor, broken and flayed.

"Man," I say, "I don't know if I can handle another dead body today. You go first."

Zeke raises a small crossbow I didn't know he had and scans the rows. We're alone.

"Why don't I get a crossbow?" I ask.

"You gotta earn crossbow privileges," he says.

Belinda takes the rear. She's just under six foot, broad shouldered, and carries herself like a line-backer or that dwarf from the Lord of the Rings movies. I try to avoid pissing her off. In the darkness of the theater, however, she looks small. Whatever courage I had withers. Seeing her afraid is like seeing your dad cry for the first time.

"You good?" Zeke asks.

"Sorry," she says. "I just… this is a once in a lifetime opportunity for research."

"Yeah," I say. "Getting butchered by an undead school teacher. Yay science."

Zeke holds open the red bag for her. "Want something? You pick."

She leans over and looks into the bag. "What would I do with that?"

"Kill shit?" Zeke says.

"I'm okay."

He shrugs and slings it back over his shoulder.

I nod to the front of the theater. "Up there. Under the stage."

We take our time. I'm trying to keep every corner illuminated with my flashlight while Zeke sweeps the room with his crossbow. Belinda follows. I look over my shoulder to see her camera jittering. I'm shaking, too.

We climb onto the stage and look around. Above us, the darkness is perfect. If I could pierce it with a needle, it would spill out, flood the theater, and drown us.

"There should be a trap door," I say, trying to ignore the shadows my light won't reach.

"Here," Zeke says, and kicks away debris.

Belinda runs her EMF reader across the floor, but it's silent. She just swallows and nods.

Zeke pulls a long blade from his boot. I have no idea how many weapons he has on him at any given time, but I imagine he doesn't fly often. He slides the blade into the crack and pries up the door.

Dust coughs out, and I bite my lip, every nerve ready to ignite. Zeke gets on his hands and knees and sticks his head into the hole.

"What? I wouldn't – Dude. Stop," I say.

He looks up. "It's here."

Whispers drift up to the stage. I spin around to see a sea of faces, watching us. The children are scattered throughout the seats, all of them gray-faced and dead-eyed.

"Oh…" Belinda says.

She turns her EMF back on and holds it out in their direction. The device, smaller than a cell phone, crackles softly and her breath catches in her throat.

"What are they doing?" she asks.

"I think they're just watching," I tell her, but I'm really waiting for them to hiss. Their jaws will unhinge and a crazy, wiggling tongue will lash out from between inhuman fangs. They'll swarm us.

"Hello," Belinda says, and her voice quavers more than her hands.

"Belinda," I say, "please don't talk to the killer ghost children right now."

"Sorry," she says.

Unperturbed, Zeke reaches down into the hole to fish out what he's found. I dare one of those little bastards to come up here. I'm not in the mood."

"Are you just gonna touch that?" I ask him.

He pulls out a decayed canvas tarp wrapped with duct tape and sets it down gently by the trapdoor. Gazing up through a tear in the material is an eyeless socket.

I gasp and step back.

Zeke grips the canvas and looks up at me. "It's about to get a whole lot worse. You ready?"

"Do it," I say.

He rips it open.

Iris Angel. She's in the fetal position, stuffed into the tarp. Rodents have had their way with her remains, but she's mostly intact. Blackened, leathery skin stretches over dry bones. There are stab wounds across her torso and gouges in her face. The remains of her clothes are charred, but there's still rope left around her neck. Her face is locked in a scream.

"That's... that's..." Belinda says, her voice heavy with sympathy.

Zeke looks at me. "You're up."

"Oh! Yeah," I say and fumble with the cannister of salt in my jacket.

All of my occult knowledge – the books I've read, the scrolls I've translated, and the pedantic weirdos I've had to talk to – all of it flies out the window. There are probably rites or incantations I should recite, or maybe I need to pour the salt into something resembling a holy symbol, but I can't remember anything but snippets of Hammer films and episodes of *Supernatural*.

"Do I say anything?" I ask.

Zeke shrugs. "Sorry, Iris. Be at peace," he says.

I pour the salt over her body, using about half of it to make an 'X'. Behind us, the kids whisper again. They lean to each other, their hands covering their mouths. I wonder what we don't know.

Zeke unscrews the gas cap.

"What in God's name do you think you're doing!?"

The three of us jump. I drop the salt and raise the hatchet. Belinda screams.

John Elder. He's at the front of the auditorium, baring his teeth. He marches toward us, his face twisted into a rictus grin of fury and madness.

"Elder..." I say, pointing at the black-eyed kids, but they're gone.

He lunges forward, grabs me by the leg, and yanks me off the stage. I hit the floor hard. Stars spark in my vision. I can't breathe.

"You do not touch her!" he yells. "Do you hear me?"

Zeke flies off the stage.

Elder's head snaps back with the force of Zeke's kick. Every movement is blur as Zeke unleashes on him. Elder tries to regain his balance, but Zeke comes at him like a dervish. The sound of the blows echoes through the hall. He's precise, brutal, and impossibly fast.

But Elder is hard. His training kicks in. He's still a soldier, and as the killer in him takes over, his face glows with zeal.

Blood from Elder's lips flecks across the floor. He uses the momentum, pulling Zeke in close and then past him. Zeke is thrown into the front row. Elder moves fast, driving a punch into Zeke's kidneys. Zeke sucks in a sharp breath and spins around, leading with his fist.

Elder goes low and takes out Zeke's right leg. The gun in Zeke's belt hits the floor and slides beneath the chairs. I lunge for it and slide across the filthy linoleum. My hands search through clots of dust and bug carcasses. I can't find the gun.

"Guys…" Belinda says.

She's staring at her EMF. The crackling is soft at first but getting louder. The needle twitches and begins to dance. We both back away from the bones.

Something plummets from the darkness above. It stops with a jerk, right next to us.

It's Iris, hanging from the rope. If Rez is in there, I can't see her. The bony arms jerk, fingers opening twitching. She shrieks, giddy and hungry. I stumble backward as the phantom rope severs.

She lashes out with her claws, right at Belinda. Belinda stands there, half her face cleaved from her skull, and looks at me, confused, not understanding that she's already dead. She goes down to her knees in a gout of blood and pitches forward into the trap door.

Iris opens her mouth wide, vomiting up wrapped pieces of red candy into the hole. She wipes her mouth with the back of her hand and turns her attention to me. Down she floats and erupts in a banshee scream.

Thwack! A crossbow bolt slams into her chest. She flies back like a sheet in the wind and tumbles across the floor.

Zeke, bloodied and swollen, looks over at me. He lowers the crossbow. Next to him is Elder, staring at Iris with the eyes of a child.

"Oh… Oh, Miss Iris. It's you. It's really you!" he says and begins to weep.

I grab Elder by the arm. "Run, you stupid bastard!"

He shakes me off and approaches Iris with reverence.

Rez is gone. She's gone. That's not Rez. Rez is gone.

I say it over and over to convince myself it's okay to run now. It's okay to leave this behind.

Zeke snatches up his bag. "I can—"

"Hell no! We're leaving!" I yell, trying to shove him down the aisle.

Iris's contorted body unwinds. She straightens, her neck uncurling until she's looming over Elder. Her misshapen eyes glow with a murderous fever.

In that tableau, I see something. On the back of Elder's neck is a symbol. It's scarred into the flesh, like it was branded long ago, but the outline is clear. It's the same marking that's on the cassette tape I found in the office, the inverted teardrop.

Elder holds his arms out wide. "Miss Iris, it's me. It's—"

She swats him hard. I hear the bones in his face crack as he flies off the ground. His body smashes into the first row, then flops end over end. He lays there draped across the seats like a cast-aside rag doll. Zeke and I scramble, tripping over each other in our frenzied rush for the door. Iris's frustrated, ear-splitting shriek chases us out the front doors.

As we race across the quad, I throw glances over my shoulder. She hasn't come out yet, but I don't know how ghosts work, not real ones. Maybe she can teleport. Maybe she can appear wherever she wants. Now that we have her attention, maybe running won't help. She might just murder us all on the bus or chase us all the way back to Austin.

Zeke staggers and holds an arm Elder nearly snapped close to his chest. A cut across his forehead bleeds freely down his face.

"You all right?" I ask.

He nods. "Fuck that guy."

"Indeed."

The bus is still there, engine idling. Everyone is crowded inside, waiting for us. The door swings open and as we climb aboard, there's a chorus of questions.

"What happened?"

"Are you okay?"

"Was it Iris?"

I shove people out of the way and yell, "Violet, drive!"

A gunshot.

The side mirror shatters next to my head. I spin out of the way, lose my balance, and fall to the ground. Everyone on the bus screams and dives behind seats.

Elder is coming. He marches forward with his own gun pointed at us.

"No one is going anywhere!" he says.

As he gets closer, I can make out his ruined face. She didn't claw him, but the force of her blow caved in his right cheek. His eye dangles from the fractured socket.

Zeke steps out of the bus, his face cold and hard.

"No one is leaving!" Elder yells again.

"Have you lost your mind, Elder? She's going to kill us!" I yell.

"This investigation has not yet finished. You will leave when I dismiss you!"

Zeke steps forward. "Alright, Coach. Why don't you drop the piece and play fair, huh?"

Elder fires a shot into the ground. Dead silence from the bus.

"Play? I'm done playing with you, Silver," he says. "If everyone doesn't get off the bus and get back to work, I will begin the executions. Starting with you."

No one moves.

"Get off of the goddamn bus!" he yells.

Violet steps off first. She's placid as ever with her elven eyes. Dominic follows and then the rest, their heads bowed like scorned children.

"Elder," I say, "No one here signed up for ghosts with sharp teeth. And there are a lot of ghosts with very sharp teeth. Let's leave. We'll even let you drive."

"The second bullet is for you, smart ass," he says.

Zeke takes another step to him, but Elder whips the gun around and puts it in his face.

"I will not be challenged," Elder says.

"Elder…" I start, but he turns the gun to me now.

"You. This is all on you. You're the fly in my fucking ointment, Vandermeer. Now get on your knees," he says. "Both of you!"

I kneel. Zeke just stares.

Elder says, "You haven't the slightest idea of what you're interfering with. Tonight is the culmination of an endeavor that will change the face of science and faith. This is the finale. This is what she was working towards. The lives of you ignorant degenerates pale in comparison to this decades long endeavor. Resources spent. Lives lost. Children. *Children* were placed upon the altar of this breakthrough, and you think I won't put a bullet in your head?"

"I'm sorry," Zeke says. "What were you saying? I was staring at your jacked-up eyeball."

"Have it your way," he presses the gun between Zeke's eyes and grits his teeth.

Zeke doesn't flinch.

"I have the tape!" I tell him.

Elder looks at me. "What did you say?"

"Those tapes you've been playing. I have the one you need," I say.

He lowers the gun. Zeke gives me a sidelong glance. He mouths *No.*

"If you're playing with me right now, boy…" he says.

"Let them go and I'll take you to it," I tell him.

He thinks on it, the one dangling eye staring at the dirt. The other eye bores right through me. Finally, he waves the gun at the others.

"Go," he says to them.

"Clark…" Violet says.

"Run," I tell her. "Go."

"You'd best listen to him, young lady, before I change my mind," Elder says.

The others file back onto the bus, casting sad glances over their shoulders. Elder guides Zeke and I with the gun.

"Lead the way. I don't think I need to tell you that I'm not in the mood for your bullshit," he says. "I'm still undecided if either of you are walking away from this."

CHAPTER NINETEEN

The gears on the bus grind and the engine fades into the night as we cross the courtyard. The silence descends around us. The buildings were ominous before when they were crawling with paranormal investigators. Now they're tombs encircling us, waiting.

Zeke and I walk like we're being led to the firing squad. In a way, we are. I have no idea what happened to the tape. I didn't really look to see where I threw it. It was kind of maybe in this direction. From the roof, it was probably destroyed. Or someone else picked it up. For all I know, one of the Wanderers is on the bus right now, wearing it around their neck. Zeke shoots me another glance that asks *What are you doing?*

I can only respond with a sheepish half smile. His sigh is almost inaudible.

"So, did you do that to his face?" I ask Zeke.

"No, but I was working up to that," he says.

"Enough chatter, girls," Elder says.

"Can you put on an eyepatch or something?" I ask. "I mean, it's super freaky."

Zeke says, "Do you see in two different directions like that?"

"Do you two really think I'm in any mood for your bullshit?"

I'm about to respond, but building six shuts me up. I find myself walking toward it. I don't know why. I can't roam around the campus forever. It won't be long until he figures out that I don't have the tape, that I'm just stalling. Might as well get it over with.

Why do I have to die in building six? No idea. It seems fitting. Maybe I'll die with something resembling an answer, but is it an answer I want? I don't know what was on the other side of the door at that first Lighthouse building. A Lovecraftian nightmare god? Elemental darkness? A Wal-Mart in New Jersey? Whatever it was made Alan scream, the kind of soul-abrading terror most people never have to hear. It would probably be better if I just lead Elder to the gym. Once everyone else is clear of this place and out of his reach, I could confess to him that I've got nothing and the tape was destroyed. Then he'd shoot us. That's better than going insane or getting devoured for all eternity by some unspeakable horror. But maybe joining Alan and the gang in whatever hell I damned them to on the other side of that first door is exactly what I deserve. I am the one who opened it, after all.

We give the theater a wide berth. All of us watch it as we pass, holding our collective breath. Iris doesn't come exploding through the doors. I imagine her slithering along the pavestones behind us or slinking alongside us, in the shadows, stalking. In every window, I think I see her face. She's on the rooftops. She's in the storm gutters.

Elder unlocks building six and shows us through. The first thing to greet us is the lighthouse symbol over the front desk. If the eye at the top blinked, I wouldn't be surprised. I don't even know if I'd be scared. Once your reality is upended, you have to look at every bit of madness that approaches you and say *Yeah. Sure. Why not?* Ghosts are real and they can kill you. What else? Vampires? Zombies? CHUDs? If I'm still alive when all of this is done, I'll have to look this in the face and acknowledge that this is the world I live in. I suppress a laugh, the kind of dizzy, light-headed cackle that comes with sleep deprivation or a complete mental breakdown. The only thing that keeps me moving right now is instinct. Well, that and the gun at my back. If I were given a second to breathe, to stop and think about the last twenty-four hours, my mind would splinter.

At the end of the hall is a set of doors Elder went through earlier, our final destination. My feet stop moving. Zeke stops, too.

"Where's the goddamn tape, Vandermeer?" Elder asks and presses the barrel into my spine.

I stammer. He can kill us. Shoot me right here. That's fine. I just don't want to go through those doors. I can't see the other door, the one with the symbol. Answers or not, I don't want to see it opened.

"Here," I say, fumbling for Zeke's Walkman. "It's right here."

Zeke hardens and shakes his head, like he doesn't agree with my choice.

I pull the cassette out and hand it to Elder.

He looks at it and narrows his good eye. "This?"

I say, "It's the one you want."

It's not. It's some metal band called Thunder Hag, whatever Zeke was listening to when I borrowed the player. I shoot a glance at Zeke, but he doesn't react.

"Where's the sigil?" Elder asks.

"It was on the case. I lost that. It was… it was a little teardrop looking thing. Had three stars inside," I say.

Elder regards the tape and nods. His lips quiver and for a second, he softens, overcome with longing. I can't look at anything but his caved-in face and his dangling eye. "Okay," he says. "Okay."

"So…" I say, "I guess we'll wait here while you do your thing? Give you some privacy. We don't mind."

"Don't be cute," he says. "Let's go."

"Wait!"

A scream from behind us. I yelp, jolted by the shock, while Zeke and Elder spin. Kyle comes running from behind the desk. He's covered in dust. His sculpted hair is mashed and matted over his bloodless, terrified face.

"It's me! It's just me!" he says as he runs up to us. "What's happening? Are we leaving? We need to leave!"

"Damn it, Foxwell," Elder growls, "I nearly killed you, son."

"We have to get out of here. We have to go right now," Kyle says.

"Kyle, leave," I tell him. "Just run. Get to the road and don't stop running. Everyone else has left."

"There's a monster," he says, and searches our face for an explanation.

"No shit," I say. "Just get the hell out of here."

"No," he says. "I can't go by myself. Please. Just let me stay with you."

"I really don't think you want to do that," Zeke says.

"Don't make me go back out there. I saw her. I saw Iris. She's real, man. She's real. I think she…" he stops, staring at Elder. "Your face. Mr. Elder. Oh God."

"We don't have time for this, kid," Elder says.

"Are you…" Kyle says, stuttering. "Are you undead? Are you a zombie?"

"Nah, he's just all fucked up," Zeke says.

Kyle doesn't understand.

"Have it your way, Foxwell," Elder says to him. "Come on."

Kyle sticks close. He keeps looking at the gun but doesn't want to ask any more questions.

The crazy old man steers us to the double-doors at the end of the hall. He tosses the keys into my chest and steps back.

"The one with its own ring," he says.

The keys jingle as my hands shake. I can see Zeke watching everything and assessing, waiting to make his move. I hope he has a move.

It's just another empty room. There's a tipped-over bookshelf, a filthy rug, and a collapsed foldout table. There are no windows and the low-ceiling suffocates me. Nowhere else to go. I don't see any door floating in the center of the room, no sound system, or bizarre sigils.

Elder grabs an LED lamp from the shelf and flicks it on. The cool white glow casts mad shadows across the room. He waves the gun at the floor. "The rug. Pull it up," he says.

Zeke and I exchange glances before he crouches and yanks the rug aside. In the linoleum is another trap door.

"Goddamn trapdoors. How many does this place have?" I ask.

"Open it," Elder says. "The small key."

I find the small key and bend to unlock it. The last trap door had a body inside. I don't know what could be worse, but I'm sure I'm about to find out.

Stone steps lead down into more darkness. I stand there at the verge before Elder nudges me forward with the barrel of the gun. "Go," he says.

Zeke goes in first, tensed and ready to swing. We descend into a basement. I try to move slow so that I don't step out of Elder's halo of light. Kyle has the same idea. He makes himself small and clings to Elder's belt. The room is musty, with motes of dust drifting through the flashlight's beam. I keep expecting rot or the coppery tang of blood. Instead, it just smells like an abandoned place, more so than the rest of campus.

Faces look back at us. Eyeless. Shriveled skin. Swaths of thick cobwebs stretch from skull to tiny skull. They're all lined up at three rows of foldout tables. It's Miss Iris's lost class, sitting in place like they're waiting for the lesson to begin.

Shalem kudd Pagru. Missakka Varuk shemt.

It's written on the blackboard.

We open our vessels to the wisdom of the Weeping King so that the powers of the Pagru will fill us up. Allow the Outer Chaos to enrichen your feeble husks.

At the back of the room is a door. It's probably a maintenance or coat closet, but that's no longer its purpose. A symbol is painted on the door in what looks like congealing blood. The blood's maybe a day old. It's the symbol on the back of Elder's neck.

The only sound is Kyle hyperventilating. Zeke's fists clench and unclench, wanting something to hit. I'm just trying to swallow, but my tongue doesn't work. If the symbol was different, if I changed it to the one I saw before, if Elder has the Turkmenistan tape, would it work? Could I undo it all?

Elder gets back to work. On a stool at the head of the class is a small tape player connected to two giant speakers. The speakers look like amps from an 80s rock concert. The dust has shaken off and collected on the floor, next to a box of cassette tapes.

It's not any box. It's *the* box, the one from the first Lighthouse. I can't understand it. It should be destroyed and paved over with concrete along with everything else. The tapes inside are all disorganized as Elder has gone through them one by one and cast them aside. He's tried all of them. What happened when he played *Turkmenistan*? Did his nose bleed? Were there screams?

"Clark," Zeke says and points to one of the bodies.

On the back of the kid's neck is the symbol, the same one as on Elder. The scar nearly glows in the dim light.

"Man, I've seen some wacky shit in my life..." Zeke says.

"She was priming them," I say. "She was getting them ready to be receptacles for whatever was going to come through that door."

Zeke's face hardens. He turns his snarl to Elder. "We weren't brought here to investigate anything."

"What do you mean?" I ask.

"This crazy punk ass is trying to summon something through that door. But it needs somewhere to go. If it didn't work with the kids…"

I look to Elder. "Us. We're the receptacles. That's why you brought us all here. Jesus, Elder…"

Elder looks up at us, his finger hovering over *Play*. "She was going to save us," he says. "Our parents had abandoned us here, but we found something better. We found *her*. We spent our time preparing our bodies to receive the silver light of the Weeping King. His glory was going to fill us up and we would spread his majesty all across this godforsaken shithole. We were to be his children on Earth. We would change this world. I've felt his power. It's real."

"What happened?" I ask.

Elder bows his head. "I was weak. I was scared, just a stupid kid. So, I ran. I hid in the woods. Then those other bastards came and they… they killed her while the rest of my class waited here. They waited and waited, and no one ever came for them. They're still waiting. I was shipped off and put into an institution. Every night, I begged Miss Iris to come for me. I begged for a second chance. Now I have it."

He fishes through his pocket and produces a fistful of the cinnamon candy. In each child's shriveled hand, he places a piece. The last three are saved for Kyle, Zeke, and me.

"Shalem kudd Pagru. Missakka Varuk shemt."

He presses *Play*.

For a moment, I think it *is* the right tape. Without the generator, the speakers are quiet. The only sound is a soft crackle from the tiny cassette player. From it comes a barrage of savage anger.

Then the thrashing guitar kicks in.

Elder steps back, like the tape has offended him.

"What? What is this?" he asks.

Zeke grins. "This is Thunder Hag. It's called *Banshee's Revenge*. It's from their first album. Wait 'til you get to the solo. It shreds, bro."

Here's the part where we die.

Elder shudders. Muscles in his neck go taut and a vein in his forehead pulsates. He ejects the cassette and crushes it in his hand. The broken plastic digs into his palm, sending rivulets of blood down his arm. Rabid, he bares his teeth at us. He points the gun at Zeke, then at me, then back at Zeke.

"You motherfuckers. You. Mother. *Fuckers*!"

"I have the tape!" Kyle says.

He holds one hand up to stop Elder. With his free hand, he fishes a cassette out of his back pocket. I don't have to see it to know that it's the one. Elder looks at him and doesn't believe it.

Kyle inches closer like he's surrendering his weapon in a hostage negotiation. "It's the one. It's got the mark, like on your neck. This is the one, right? I found it in the courtyard."

"Kyle, no," I say. "If there's one time in your life you really, really shouldn't be a stupid asshole, this is it, okay? Kyle—"

"Quiet!" Elder says.

Kyle hands him the tape and steps away. Beelitz, Germany, 1956. I can see the symbol, a detailed star pattern wrapped in an inverted teardrop. Elder examines it, sneers at me, and goes back to the player.

"Elder," I say as he inserts the cassette, "One of two things is going to happen. Nothing at all or something really, insanely horrible."

"Shalem kudd Pagru. Missakka Varuk shemt," he says again.

"Do not open that door, Elder," I say.

He presses *Play*. The screaming starts. It winds and undulates out of the speaker, an invisible worm. Mandibles spasm and open around a serrated maw. A fat, gibbering thing is slowly impaled on a spike that reaches up into a field of dying stars.

I cover my ears. Elder nods as tears drip from his good eye. Next to me, Zeke's jaw sets. He nudges me and motions to the door as he gets into a combat stance. Kyle screams and covers his ears, too.

The door shudders in its frame. The madness from the tape continues and I can feel it pawing at the door, trying to coax it open.

The knob turns.

Slowly, the door swings open on its own. Beyond is only darkness. No coat closet. No cleaning supplies. It's the same kind of black that was in the bottom of the pit. And from within, new screams join the chorus. I stumble until my back hits the blackboard. The noises steal my breath, and I can't focus, can't make my feet work.

Please be Alan.

If it's Alan, I'll scream.

Please don't be Alan.

Next to me, a body twitches. At first, I think I just bumped the table, but then, under the cry of the tape, I hear it. It sounds like rain on a tin roof. Bones rattle. Skin, dried and leathery, begins to crack. Dust erupts from fissures. Insects escape, scuttling for cover. Across the room, a head knocks to one side. Fingers dance. Teeth chatter.

Zeke backs toward the stairs and waves for me to follow. He doesn't have to tell me twice.

"Oh Jesus," Kyle says. "Please, Lord God Jesus Christ Almighty, protect me."

I grab him by the arm and shove him up the steps. One of the corpse children stands. The pits of its eyes are filled with jet black nothing. Others follow as the old limbs loosen. Their jaws open and close. Then they begin to keen. The noise from the tape comes crying out of their rotten guts.

Elder chants in WitchTongue. He shoves the gun into his pants and holds his arms out wide. His voice sings out, booming with ecstasy.

Arbatta Guk! Muhalot. Merr. Akka!

The class of dead kids surges forward. They swarm him in a wave of desiccated skin, claws, and teeth. I'm halfway up the stairs when I hear him scream.

***

"What's happening?!" Kyle says. "What's happening right now?"

"We're running, asshole," Zeke says. "Run faster."

The noise behind us roils, sounding like a swarm of metallic locusts dumped into a wood-chipper. We're halfway across the yard when one of the doors to building six bursts open.

The children scurry out. They cling to the walls and lope along the ground, twitching and squalling. They're hunting, a tide of sharp teeth and hate.

"My bag!" Zeke yells as we pass the theater.

He breaks right before I can protest.

"Come on!" I yell to Kyle.

Kyle shakes his head, tripping over himself as he runs in the opposite direction. His arms flail as he blindly sprints across the quad. They're going to at him.

I race into the theater after Zeke. "Have you forgotten about the zombie witch lady?"

Near the stage, Zeke scoops up his bag and pulls out a short, straight-edged sword. My hatchet isn't far away. I must have lost it in the chaos. Up on the stage is the open trap door. A smear of Belinda's blood leads right up to the edge. I hope to hell that she doesn't rise up to chomp on us, but I'm not ruling it out.

"They'll find us," I tell Zeke.

He's facing the front doors, fingers wrapped around the handle of his sword.

"Let 'em," he says.

"How many of these little bastards do you think you can kill?"

"Oh, I can take down ten-year-olds all day long, son."

The front doors fly open. They come for us, scuttling down the aisles and over the chairs. Some scamper up the walls and into the shadows of the ceiling high above. I stand next to Zeke and raise Iggy the axe.

"Not gonna lie," Zeke says. "I've been waiting for this all weekend."

The first one leaps. Zeke sidesteps and brings the blade down through its torso. Withered organs tumble out. The halves go flying, but don't stop moving. Another thing scurries from under the seats. Its fanged maw opens wide for my leg. I kick out on instinct. Its head whips back. It tumbles, gets back on all fours, and launches at me again.

Zeke spins and skewers it through the skull. It kicks and claws at him. Another one comes bounding from behind us, off the stage. With a twist, Zeke hurls the one at the end of his blade. They crash into each other. Just as I turn, Zeke snarls and staggers.

The upper half of the first one drags itself to him and latches onto his leg. Teeth shred his pants and lacerate the flesh beneath. He kicks it loose and takes out another one with a backhand.

There are too many.

Zeke stabs one and five more take its place. He cuts them in half, and they keep coming for us. In seconds, they're flying at us from every direction. Leading with the hatchet, I windmill my arms, trying hit anything and everything. Claws tear at my jacket and slice my skin.

One clings to my arm like a damn spider-monkey and sinks its teeth in. I drop Iggy and throw my weight into the stage, pinning the bastard. It wiggles and lets go. On the stage is the cannister of salt.

I grab it and wildly fling a trail of it into the air. The children hiss and recoil, their screeches turning to pained cries. They hold their clawed hands up to cover their faces before surging in again.

I toss more of the salt in a wide arc. The little fuckers kick and thrash like they've been pepper sprayed. Zeke drives them back with broad slashes. I swipe the hatchet into one that snaps at my wrist. It clips off the thing's nose. It shudders and thrashes as a tendril of green smoke sizzles from the wound.

"Your magic hatchet is working!" I yell.

"Gas!" he says. "Get the gas!"

The gas cannister sits on the stage next to the bag of Iris's remains. We can finish this. I squirm onto the stage, kicking loose from the throng. I fumble with the cap and drop the cannister.

Three of them leap onto the stage. I snatch up the gas can. They pounce. Claws fly. A barrage of rotten fangs snaps in my face. I stumble back and hot pain erupts in my calf. Teeth sink into my arm. All of it is drowned out by their jagged keening. Somehow, I shake them loose. The scent of gasoline stings my eyes.

It's spilled. The puddle creeps across the stage, soaking the red curtain.

"Lighter!" I yell.

In one graceful leap, Zeke clears the lip of the stage and decapitates one of the children advancing on me. He whips out a Zippo, flicks it, and tosses it down on the floor.

The flame races across the stage and engulfs the curtain. The children recoil. Zeke doesn't relent. I catch my breath. Next to me, the headless thing is still moving. Its tiny taloned hands grab at me. I punt it into the curtain. The thing squeals. It spins and seizes, tossing fiery bits of flesh and clothing all around.

Burning chunks of rotting curtain rain down on the stage. As the flame eats through, I see a backstage door.

"Come on!" I say.

Zeke follows. He grabs a fistful of curtain and with a hard jerk, pulls the whole thing down. The blazing sheet collapses onto the hungry mass of the little bastards. We run.

"Please don't be locked. Please don't be locked," I say as we race to the door.

Zeke doesn't try the knob and doesn't slow down. With his shoulder, he hits the door and smashes it open. Black smoke belches out into an alley behind the theater. We spill into the cool night.

I turn and slam the door, cutting off the din. "You okay?" I ask.

Away from the fight, Zeke slumps against the wall. "I'm good," he says, but his bloody, shredded clothes tell me otherwise.

There's a chunk of skin missing from his right bicep and two, long gouges are dug into the scalp near his mohawk. I'm not much better. I don't even want to look at the wound on my calf. I can feel the blood running hot into my Chuck Taylors.

"We just fought zombie monster kids. Holy shit! Zombie monster kids! And we're going to have to get tetanus shots," I tell him.

We turn to stumble out into the courtyard when we hear it and stop. It's barely audible, a faint tune on the fall breeze. Iris, humming her broken melody. I stick my head out of the alley. She's floating across the brick, drifting in aimless, lazy circles. Her head lolls on her stretched neck.

"Come, children. It's time to sleep. Let the King's majesty take control. You are his, once again. *Da Dee Dee Dee Da Dee Dee.* Did you do your homework?"

We slip into the side door of the building with the classrooms. Zeke still has his sword. I've still got Iggy.

"Man, my favorite nunchucks were in that bag," he says. "I had them blessed and everything."

"When we get paid, I'll take you to the mall and buy you all the nunchucks you want."

"Deal."

We stop to catch our breaths. Neither of us wants to acknowledge our wounds. The adrenaline ebbs and the world starts to wobble. I lean on the wall and hope it's not from blood loss. Through the crack in the door, I peek out to keep an eye on Iris. She glides around the courtyard, babbling.

"What's the plan?" Zeke asks.

"The road isn't far."

"We running?"

We'd have to cross the courtyard to get to the road. She'd spot us.

"Hell yes, we're running, but not that way," I say. "Out the back. Hop the fence. Run through the trees. We'll find the road eventually."

"You want to go into the woods?"

"We can't stay here."

Our whispers skitter off down the dark hallway. I take one last look through the door and my insides go cold. Iris is gone.

"Shh!" I tell Zeke, but there's nothing to hear. She's silent.

Zeke pushes me down the hall. "Stay low. Stay quiet."

We creep along. Moonlight filters in through broken, dirty windows and is occluded by plumes of smoke. I can smell the theater burning, but the flames haven't spread yet. I hope it devours this entire damned place.

In the shadowed corridor behind us, a sound. Iris's song.

Zeke grabs me by the collar and yanks me into an alcove. We hold our breaths and listen to her warble.

"*Doo doo dee dee doo*," she sings, and then pauses. "Ooh. What's this?"

We watch around the corner as she finds something on the floor. It's a spotted trail of our blood. I look down and see the bloody footprints and fat drops, black in the moonlight, that lead right to us. Her long, distended hand reaches out to touch the smear. She holds stained fingers to her lips and a bloated tongue laps at them.

"You've got to be fucking kidding me," I say.

Iris bends. Her body contorts. In a second, she's slithering along the floor, floating just inches above it, but moving and twisting like a snake. Her tongue leads the way, mopping up our trail.

Zeke jerks his head toward a stair well leading up. We ascend, taking careful steps around the cast aside chairs that choke the passage.

"Mmm. Yes. Yes yes yes. Detention for you. Detention. Stand in the corner. Your parents will not be notified. You will be eaten. Yes."

We move as fast as we dare, trying not to make a sound. I stop to wipe away some blood, but only end up smearing it around. Zeke drags me along for a few feet, then slumps over onto a desk askew in the hallway. The corridor is lined with rooms, but each of them is a dead-end. Her voice gets closer, coming up the stairs behind us. I throw his arm over my shoulders and pull him into a room.

The door is stuck. Iris drifts into the hall. Her high-pitched, gravelly voice leads the way. "Come out. It's time for class. Yes. *Groos akka mon shudd.* ABCDEFG."

We press ourselves to the wall behind the open door. The swath of blood on the linoleum will take her right to us. Zeke stands up straight and grips the sword.

"What's this? What's this?" Iris says, close now.

Her clawed hand extends past the threshold and into the room. I kick the door as hard as I can. It slams shut on her arm.

Her cry is ear-splitting.

"BAD CHILDREN BAD!"

Zeke spins out of hiding, all of his wounds forgotten. I kick the door again and drive it into her withered forearm. Iris hurls herself against the door. The glass window cracks. Her ruined face presses up against it.

"Zam kot! Vuul lanachem!"

I back away from the door, looking for something to defend myself with.

Zeke whispers to himself. *"Om visvaaya naam gandharvalochni naami lousatikarnai tasmai vishwaya swaha."*

He repeats it over and over. Spittle flies from his lips. He focuses on the door.

Iris stops. I can't see her through the glass.

"Dude," I say. "You gotta teach me those words. Is that a Kali prayer? That shit totally worked!"

Iris passes *through* the door. She's grinning.

Oh yeah. *Ghost.*

"Dat dat dee dee dat—"

Zeke leaps. His sword flashes. Iris's mangled arm falls to the floor. It squirms and immediately begins to sizzle and rot. Iris's jaw distends. Her milky eyes roll. She yowls and roars around the room faster than I can follow. Desks and chairs scatter and bounce as she knocks them aside. Zeke staggers to the center of the room, trying to get a bead on her.

With a furious shriek, she rockets into him, knocking him off his feet. They hit the window. It shatters.

And they're gone.

I rush to the window. Smoke clouds the courtyard, obscuring the moon. Two floors below, I can make out Zeke's motionless body, lying on the bricks.

CHAPTER TWENTY

The smoke is a churning knot of thorns in my lungs. The flames dance from the roof of the theater, and the roar of the fire is all I can hear.

By the time I get to Zeke, he's trying to push himself upright.

"Holy hell. You're alive," I say.

"Bitch threw me out a window," he says. "Where's my blade?"

I look around as he coughs a spray of blood onto the pavestones.

"Just stay—"

Iris is there. She's across the quad, floating in place. The smoke swirls around her and eddies in black spirals. And her arm has grown back. She tilts her head at me.

"*Kashaaaaa. Rok azthul.* Take your seats. Turn to page seventeen."

Zeke inhales with a sharp hiss as he uses my leg to pull himself up. From his belt, he draws another hidden blade, this one long and black.

The theater is a bonfire. We're far away, but the wall of heat is unrelenting.

"Wait," I say. "The fire should burn up her body, right? The bones? So… we're good?"

Zeke shakes his head. "She's got Rez as an anchor now. The connection is too strong. She's practically invincible on the physical plane."

Iris pirouettes around the courtyard. Every *la de da dee* draws her closer to us. She stops in mid spin. Her body racks with spasms as he disgorges a spray of slimy cinnamon candy, still in the wrapper, onto the ground. She starts spinning again, softly humming to herself, getting closer and closer.

"You run," Zeke says, readying his blade. "I'll hold her off as long as I can."

I feel the candy Elder gave me in the pocket of my jacket and an idea takes shape.

"Yeah. Keep her busy!"

I turn and run.

Zeke looks surprised. "What? Really? You're just gonna leave me?"

I yell over my shoulder. "Just give me a few minutes!"

***

I limp along as fast as I can, leaving moonlight-blackened streaks of blood across the gym floor. I ignore the shadows. They can't be worse than what's out there. Ghost hunting gear is scattered. Cots are knocked over. Clothes and

161

personal belongings are tossed around from everyone leaving in a hurry. I race through the camp and try not to think about what comes next, what surely won't work.

More blood streaks the back corridor behind the gym. Andi's body is gone. The only thing left is the busted storage room door and the thickening pool of crimson. I stop and what little breath is left in my lungs escapes. It's almost worse than seeing her actual remains. Thoughts of Iris devouring her whole try to push their way inside, but I shake them off and run to the storage room where Elder locked us up.

I fall to my knees and sweep away the old gym equipment littering the floor. The Enochian wards are charred and illegible. Iris burned her way through them to escape. Beneath them are what remains of Andi's original chalk portal, the arrangement of arcane marks and symbols that dragged us into the astral plane.

If there's anything I remember of insane shit like this from all of the grimoires I pretended to understand, it's that blood is better than chalk. Andi's blood is all used up, so I slide my palm across the blade of the hatchet. It parts the skin so smoothly I'm not even sure if it cut me. When the blood escapes the wound, a giggling voice in the back of my mind asks if my tetanus shots are up to date.

I run my fingers through the blood as it spatters onto the floor, retracing Andi's symbols, but the room is dark and the chalk is obscured with cooked blood.

"*Graupha, Tal, Machls*? Is that right?"

I wipe away the symbol for Tal and reverse it.

"*Pal*? Was it *Pal*? Oh, fuck me!"

"Right words, wrong order, cowboy."

I scream and tumble ass over tea kettle away from the voice. The hunched silhouette in the doorway doesn't flinch as I present the axe like a crucifix.

"Fuck! Fuck!"

"It's *Tal, Graupha, Machls*. So close."

Andi.

She slumps down in the doorway, clutching at the shredded flesh of her abdomen.

"Jesus! Andi!"

I jump to my feet and try to help her up. She waves me off and rolls over onto her back.

"You were close. *Tal* first. Then *Graupha* and *Machls*."

"We thought you were dead."

She laughs. "No, honey. I've had hangovers worse than this. Now be a dear and let's finish this little spell, shall we?"

She's lying. Her side is torn open and her leg is snapped clean at the shin, bending in an unnatural direction.

"Andi…"

"Do hurry, Clark. *Tal, Graupha,* and *Machls.* You know the symbols. Come now."

I finish the symbols. She reaches over and adds a few flourishes, arcane squiggles and scratches drawn with the blood from her wound.

"That will work quite well, I think," she says and gestures to a pile of boxes gym shirts shoved next to the wall.

"My conjure bag," she says, and barely gets the words out before slipping into a furious coughing fit.

I grab the bag.

She fights off the coughing and wipes the blood from her lips. "I trust you have the candy?"

I hold it up. "Should I just…?"

"Eat up," she says.

"You can't come with me?" I ask.

She laughs, but it's weak and thick with blood in the back of her throat. "Afraid not, handsome. But remember that hatchet. You'll need it."

***

I'm standing in the center of the circle, the soft purple glow lining everything. This time, I can see my body.

My own body.

It's lying there in the circle, not far from Andi.

My fucking body.

My dead body, right there on the floor. This didn't happen before. Now there's darkness lurking all around. Endless seas of it, threatening to wash in with a black tide and sweep everything away. All the purple lines of this slice of unreality shimmer and flicker, and I feel myself slipping away from it. Shadows bleed in around the edges.

"Clark," Andi says as she stares up at the ceiling. Her voice is distant and tinny, like through an old radio. "I won't be able to hear you, but you can hear me. Focus on my voice. I know this is scary right now, but you've got to hurry. Find Marianne. Set her free. Go."

"How? How do I set her free?"

Andi's eyes flutter closed.

"Andi? Andi!"

She doesn't stir. I hover over her, just some disembodied thing floating in the astral plane. Her chest rises and falls, almost imperceptibly.

I step over her and out into the corridor behind the gymnasium. It's all *Cabinet of Dr. Caligari*. The walls bend in unreal ways, connecting with ceilings that stretch off into infinity. Angles that don't make sense. Lights that shift and bend around corners, everything still draped in gauzy purple.

I move through the halls and into the gym proper. The ceiling is gone. The walls stretch up into shadows and the shadows give way to another vast gulf. I look forward, trying not to give it my attention. If I look at it, it will look back. It will suck me up into it or I'll float away and the sensation of floating is already all too real. I don't move so much as the floor moves beneath me. I think of Zeke, of getting to him in time. Of Marianne.

"Clark…" a voice says from the shadows.

It's a sharp whisper, both next to my ear and a mile away.

I stop in the middle of the gymnasium floor. The walls are just the *idea* of walls, a representation, like a high school play.

"Clark, please…"

It's just a shadow in the corner of the room, but that shadow is infinite. It cuts deep through the wall and through reality, into an endless night with no bottom and no end. A wave of purple vertigo grips me and I'm not touching anything. I'm not even here. I'm not anywhere. In that shadow are four shapes.

Alan stands there, his gangly frame hunched with the weight of a man lost in the desert. I can't make out his face, but I know it's him. DJ is behind him. Melissa. Travis. They stand like wraiths, flickering and floating, there, but not there.

"Clark, you've come for us," he says far away, but so clear.

"Alan?"

"It's not a void out here, Clark. It's an ocean. Come swim with us."

I can't see his face. It's a blur, an Alan-shaped fog.

The walls are fading, just the memories of a dream.

DJ waves at me. Her smile is big but the eyes… I can't see her eyes.

In my hand is something heavy. It sends off sparks, an iridescent charge that dances from my fingers and up to my shoulder.

It's Iggy. The symbols carved into the handle – Aramaic, ankhs, Hebrew – gleam like electric emerald.

"Clark…" Alan says again.

I can feel the floor again. It's beneath me. The walls, they're around me.

And outside is Zeke. I can help him. And maybe I can help Rez.

I look at the hatchet in my hand and when I look up, Alan and the others are gone.

I'm solid again. I'm rooted.

I move.

The doors don't open for me. I just find myself on the other side of them, in the courtyard. No stars overhead. The courtyard exists separate from everything else, an island floating in the nether.

A shriek draws my attention.

I look up, expecting to see Iris.

But it's Rez. The angry and frustrated cry comes from her mouth, but her face is slack. Her eyes are dark and her head rolls on her shoulders. Her body floats through the air as her arms reach out, jerking and bouncing like a marionette.

She sweeps down. Zeke dives and skids across the bricks. He moans and staggers to his feet. The knife in his hand is slick with blood. His own blood soaks his ragged clothes. Eyes glazed, he stumbles, moving forward through force of will.

"Yo, Rez," he says through bloodied lips, "if you're in there, cut me some slack. I need a little time-out. Just for a second."

She swoops down again, her body puppeted by forces unseen. A ghostly green illusion envelops her. I can see it now, the shape of Iris Angel, trapping Rez in a phantom shell. It's not Rez's claws that slash into Zeke's back, but the false skin, the mangled arm of Iris.

Zeke hits the ground again as the fresh wounds gush. Immediately, he struggles to rise. His thick arms tremble and blood trickles from between his gritted teeth.

"Zeke!" I shout.

He doesn't hear me.

But Rez does. Groggy, her eyes open. Her lips tremble.

"Clark…" she says.

Her fingers slide up to her neck. Feeble, they brush against the rope around her throat.

The noose.

Her head lolls to the side again and the eyes go blank. I drift across the courtyard and follow the noose. It trails back behind her, snaking along the courtyard bricks, past the bell and rusty benches, all the way to the other side. There it curls up around the leg, up the torso, and around the neck of Iris Angel, a cackling crone standing in the corner, playing puppet master to Rez. On one end of the noose is Rez. At the other, Iris.

Iris sees me and leers. She jerks the rope with her clawed hand. The howl that comes from her mouth is echoed from Rez's lips. Rez jumps at the command, dropping out of the air at Zeke again. She's playing with him, batting him about like a cat with a toy.

"There are no excuses for tardiness, class."

I slash the hatchet down hard across the rope.

A current blasts through me like I've grabbed a livewire. Iris howls, but it's cut short by a green shockwave that erupts from where the axe cleaved through. The noose withers, a spent fuse. Everything is noise and light. The darkness turns white.

The tide roars in to tear it all away.

***

I awake with a gasp, muscles rigid, teeth grinding, blind with pain, and choking on cinnamon slurry. The nuclear charge through my veins wanes and I roll over to gag. Syrup drips from my nose and lips, mixed with blood and vomit.

A soft hand brushes against mine. Fingers lightly squeeze my wrist.

"I'd offer a clever *bon mot*, sweetheart, but all I've got right now is *hell yeah*," Andi says.

"Did I do it? Is it over?"

I feel my jacket and touch the floor, afraid that if I don't focus on it, I'll just drift away.

She laughs, just a breath escaping her perfect teeth. "You did. Go see to our friends. And perhaps seek some medical attention. I'm afraid I'm bleeding to death."

I squeeze her hand. "I'll be back."

"I know."

***

Smoke fills the courtyard as the theater fire rages. Flames have leapt to the adjacent buildings. They're going up fast. Mingling with the smoke is the scent of ozone and charred meat.

"Zeke!" I shout.

"Over here!" he yells, leading me through the smoke.

I find him next to the bell post, digging through a wet carcass. His clothes are shredded and beneath that, his flesh. Torn skin bleeds freely, but the face beneath the soot and blood is all rage. He pulls at soggy sheathes of meat. It drips with white sludge, but Zeke fights it, trying to penetrate the hide like he's devouring a cooked chicken.

"What the hell is that?"

"Help me!" he says.

I curl my nose and try to dig. The goo is sticky and reeks of shit and death.

I gag. "Sweet Christmas, what in the hell…"

It's Iris. Her bloated and torn body is hunched over, bent and twisted on the gravestones. And Zeke is burrowing into it.

"What the fuck?! Is this some kind of warrior thing? Are you going to eat her heart? Please wait for me to leave if that's the plan."

A slimy hand bursts out of Iris' back.

I scream and raise the hatchet.

The hand gropes, reaching and tearing, trying to push through the mottled and slimy hide. Zeke grabs it and pulls.

"Help me!" he says.

I groan, drop the hatchet, and grab a big flap of the meat. It's tough and sticky, like a Hot Pocket forgotten in the oven.

Rez's face appears through a birth canal of gristle and slime. She takes a deep, gasping breath.

"Oh, fuck me this is so gross!" she says.

"What the shit?!"

"Pull, damn it!" Zeke says.

He tears her loose from the Iris husk. They both fall back onto the bricks. Zeke pulls her close and wipes the ooze from her eyes. She coughs up chunks of it and retches.

"Oh God. I swallowed ectoplasm. So nasty!" she says.

Zeke starts laughing. He slips onto his back as the black smoke thickens and billows over us. Rez laughs along with him as she digs it out of every crack – her ears, her hair, and nose.

"At least I'm not naked," she says.

Their laughter turns to coughing as another cloud of smoke rolls over us.

"We need to get out of here," I say.

Zeke holds up a hand. I grab him and lift him to his feet.

Pain erupts in my ankle, like a knife scraping the bone.

"Shit!"

"Class isn't dismissed!"

The voice is scorched earth and broken glass. It's shattered bones stuck in a child's throat.

The husk of Iris digs her talons into my ankle. The rotting, eyeless face looks up at me and hisses. She yanks hard and pulls me to the ground. My head cracks on the bricks and the world spins.

Rez screams.

Zeke rolls around, groping for his knife.

Iris pulls me close. A swollen tongue unfurls from her maw. Pustules erupt on its tip as thumb-sized maggots writhe from the empty sockets. She vomits candy. The cherry-red wrappers tumble down on top of me. They smell of cinnamon and puke.

Rez stands. She stumbles past, dodging Iris's other hand.

The bell begins to ring. Over the roaring of the fire and Iris's banshee howl it's frantic and loud. Rez yanks the rope, over and over, screaming back at Iris as tears cut through the grime on her face.

From within the heart of the fire come screams. Howling children, hungry and furious, answer the call. Burning, they tear through the flames. A parade of flaming demon kids. Some missing limbs or entire chunks of their bodies.

Iris releases me. Her body pops and snaps as she stands up straight. She floats up into the air.

"My babies. My children. Please take your seats!" she says and opens her arms wide.

I jump to my feet. Rez and I lift up Zeke.

The hoard hits Iris.

They bite and claw, flames licking and spreading, jumping from them to her. Iris wails with shock. She thrashes. They latch on with pit bull tenacity, piling on her as she attempts to float.

She rises up, up above the courtyard and the bell, up above the smoke.

As we stagger away, it's a flaming, teeming mass floating in front of the moon.

The wind brings another surge of black smoke. It wipes them away, but her screams carry and we still hear the gnashing of teeth.

The bell keeps ringing.

In the smoke, we see the ghosts of the children, not the demonic, toothy things chomping on Iris, but the pale souls of the kids. No black eyes. No wail of the damned. While their bodies are inhabited by unknowable terrors, ripping Iris to pieces, these quiet spirits line up in the smoke, watching us leave. When the wind whips up another cloud, they're gone.

We run.

***

The smoke crawls through the woods and across the road, turning everything around us into a dark, preternatural fairy tale. Behind us, the flames devour the campus. It lights up the countryside. Jagged shadows dance around us. I jump at every one of them.

My eyes sting. I squint through it as I try to drag Zeke along. Rez struggles to push a metal dish cart down the road. Andi rests atop it, moaning on her makeshift gurney. Darkness starts to cloud the corners of my vision. The inside of my shoe is filled with blood and I can feel wounds on my arm opening and closing as we stumble.

I stop. From the shadows on the side of the road, there's a lilting sound. Weeping. Zeke reaches down and pulls a four-inch blade from his boot. He puts it into my hand.

"Go for the heart."

"Oh, not now," Rez says.

I lower Zeke to the ground. We should run, but if Iris is still coming, she's going to catch us.

But the sobbing sounds familiar.

"Kyle?" I ask.

Kyle's head pops up out of the bushes. His face is ruddy, streaked with tears and ash.

"Clark?" he says.

"Go for the heart," Zeke says again.

"Kyle," I say, "we've gotta go, man. Now."

"But…" he says, looking up and down the road.

"I'm serious, dude. Come on."

He looks at me and I see the heart-broken kid behind the black t-shirt and hair gel. "But I pissed my pants," he says.

I start to laugh. It comes out weak at first, but gathers momentum, turning into something unhinged. I can't stop. Zeke, lying in the dirt, laughs, too. Rez doubles over. Even Andi snickers.

"It's not funny, you assholes!" Kyle says.

I collapse next to Zeke. We cackle, staring up at the smoky night sky.

"Fuck you, Kyle," I say in between peals of laughter. "Fuck you."

Kyle steps into the road. The dark stain on his crotch and down his legs makes us roll. It's not even funny, but we can't stop.

"It hurts," Zeke says. "Oh damn. Stop. It hurts too much."

"Something's coming," Kyle says.

A grinding squall in the distance coming from the other direction, away from the school, getting closer. It's the sound of metal-on-metal and a coughing growl. Kyle ducks back into the trees. The rest of us can't find the strength.

White lights. I squint and shield my eyes.

"It's the bus!" I yell.

Kyle darts from his hiding place and runs straight for it. The brakes scream, and they swerve to keep from hitting him. He bounces along outside, trying to flag them down. It rolls to a stop next to us and the door flies open.

From behind the wheel, Violet gives us a lopsided grin. "That's a pretty fire."

CHAPTER TWENTY-ONE

"When we come back to Gold Mine, we're gonna dive right into the Gold Rush stage! Stay with us!"

Did they know?

A commercial for Keebler Tater Skins.

Was it all part of their plan?

A commercial for Shakey's Pizza.

Leave. Call the police. Post it to social media. Burn the house down.

A teaser for the five o'clock news in Gary, Indiana.

I'm hypnotized by the relentless inoffensiveness of daytime television. Tracking lines fuzz across the image as the unshakeable grin of the game show host ushers us into the next round. It's not the same tape as last time, and I think that maybe the Lazlos must have an entire collection of these.

Through it all, I grind my teeth, rehearsing my *I'm mad as hell* speech. People are dead. Monsters are real. My bank account is empty. And the Lazlos knew. They had to have known. Sending a group of misfits out to a haunted school was just some ruse, a part of their grand experiment. All I have now are nightmares. And debt. They're going to foreclose on my condo. I'll have to live in my car, and I can't fathom anything that will leave me feeling more vulnerable than sleeping in the back of a Honda Civic while things like Iris Angel stalk the night.

Another gameshow, this one called *Super Shock!*, starts and I'm ready to flip over the daybed and throw the old television out the window. I've been here in the parlor for at least half an hour. I think the TV is trying to brainwash me. I'm listening for secret messages buried in the audio of the VHS tape when the doors open, and Kitty and Rupert Lazlo come in.

Their yellow-toothed smiles are like daytime television.

"There he is!" Kitty says, wheeling her motorized cart into the room.

"There he is indeed!" Rupert says.

They're still dressed like rodeo clowns. Their pancake makeup cracks around their lips and eyes. Before, I wanted to laugh. After this weekend, I want to set them on fire and run screaming from whatever the hell is going on in this house.

"Kitty made a delicious cherry pie just for you, Clark!"

"Fresh cherries, right from the farmer's market!" she says.

What happened to Alan and my team?

What is the Lighthouse?

Did you know Elder was involved in batshit crazy sorcery?

"I'm good," I say.

"You sure?" Rupert asks, playfully punching my arm. I bite back the pain and hope my stitches don't rupture.

"It's double cherry and you know what that means!"

"Doubly delicious!" Kitty says, and they laugh together.

"No, thank you."

"Well, you had a tough weekend, friend," Rupert says.

Both of their smiles turn into exaggerated frowns fit for children's theater. If a rascally puppet appeared, I wouldn't bat an eye.

"Yeah," I say. "It was… something."

They hold hands and nod. "Yes, yes. We never anticipated that this could happen," Kitty says.

"Such a horrible shame," Rupert says. "Those poor kids."

"And Mr. Elder, just such a troubled individual. I wish we'd been able to get him the help he needed. Sometimes, you just never know about people," she says.

"No. You really don't."

I stare at them, trying to see past their platitudes and cartoonish expressions. Is what happened at the Academy just *de rigueur* for them? Until yesterday, I thought they were flamboyant frauds. They'd bilked hundreds of families out of money for decades, and if they were going to pay me, then I'd take it and run. But now…

"*Tsk tsk*," Kitty says, shaking her head. "These are the perils when you deal with the restless dead."

"Yup," Rupert says. "Those foul spirits preyed upon his mind and took advantage of his trauma and weakness. I imagine he was possessed by the demons at that school the moment he set foot on campus. That must be what happened, ain't that right, sister?"

"They do take advantage of the spiritually sick, brother. Such a darn shame."

"Yeah," I say, my words tangling in my throat. "Can we…?"

Rupert grins again. "A man who likes to get to the point! I respect that!"

He hands me a small stack of papers and a pen.

"If we can just get your John Hancock right there, we'll get all of this sorted and get you paid, buddy!" he says.

I take the papers and try to find my words. "But you wanted proof. We didn't…"

Rupert slaps my leg. "Good enough for government work. Let's just get this out of the way so we can make you a little richer. What do you say?"

I start signing blanks without thinking, trying to go through the pages as fast as I can. Then I realize that these are non-disclosure agreements.

Deaths related to fire…
Rupert and Kitty Lazlo are not culpable…
No discussion with any parties not listed in this document, including press, law enforcement…
Fines exceeding one million dollars…
Sensing my apprehension, Rupert says, "Oh, that's just the regular business nonsense we've got to get out of the way. You understand."

"But… you don't want to say anything? You don't want to tell people what happened?"

"Oh no, dear," Kitty says. "We've found that the authorities tend to want to blame the living when something like this happens."

"They just can't deal with the truth, Clark. Not like you and me," Rupert says.

"But this…" I say. "What happened… it changes everything. It… it's all real."

They nod, squeezing each other's hand. "And you can't tell a soul," Kitty says.

"No," I say, setting down the pen. "No, people have to know. I… Kyle has footage. The Scientific Anomalies team, they've got the cameras they set up. We can cut it together and take it to… I don't know… put it up online or something."

And you knew. Say it.

"I just don't think that would be appropriate, Clark," Rupert says while Kitty shakes her head.

I look down at the papers. "I can't…"

"Well, son," Rupert says, "we're going to need you to sign that. And I mean dot every 'I' and cross every 'T'."

"So we can give you the money," Kitty says.

"An electrical fire, huh?" I ask.

The lie is a shard of glass that sticks in my brain.

"It's just such a gosh darn shame," Rupert says.

"A darn shame, yeah…" I say.

I sign the papers.

Kitty pulls an envelope out of her vest.

"You did such a fine job, honey. Rupert and I expect to have a lot more work for you in the future. We could use somebody who truly understands what we do. And we could get you some walkin' around money."

We trade. Inside are two checks.

"One for you," Rupert says. "And one for your friend, Ezekiel."

"And a little bonus for each of you," Kitty says, batting her maudlin eyes. "You've earned it. And there's more coming."

"Heck yeah. We've got a genuine Specter Scout as part of the family now!"

I stand. Boneless. Bloodless. I swallow hard. My words come out thick and heavy. "My friends… you said you were going to help me find them."

"Oh sure! Sure!" Rupert says. "We're asking about your pals, this Lighthouse business you were talking about, and the doors and whatnot. Not a lot coming up just yet, but we'll keep poking around for you. That's a Lazlo guarantee."

I want to punch him right in his giant fucking yellow dentures.

"The tapes," I say, the words spilling out before I can stop them. "Elder had a box of them. The same box from that place out east of town, where my friends… disappeared. Where'd he get them?"

Kitty and Rupert exchange puzzled looks. A lie is coming.

Kitty bats her thick, fake lashes. "Well, we wouldn't have the slightest, hon."

"Like we were saying, he was a sick, sick fella. Probably fooling around with black magic," Rupert says. "Best to let that one go."

Kitty shakes her head again, "Mr. Elder was a mysterious man. But if we learn something about your friends, sweetheart, you'll be the first to know."

My lip quivers and my fists clench. Icy sweat dribbles down my spine. "One of the tapes came from you, from your organization."

"Oh, Clark," Kitty says, "We've been doing this all over the world for so long there's really no telling. You know, all sorts of people used to work for us and if they sent a tape somewhere then—"

Rupert rests his hand on hers, quieting her. His smile is gone, and I see how deep his eyes are sunken into his face, just two black pits staring back at me.

"Son, you've been through a lot these past couple of days. Like I promised, a bunch of your questions have been answered, ain't they?"

My fingernails dig into my palms.

"But take it from me and Kitty, this line of work can be a real son of a gun. And those tapes are bad business. You keep poking around in that darkness, something's liable to reach out and snatch you right up. Best to keep on truckin' past this one."

Kitty clucks her tongue. "Yes, sirree."

He stands and grips my shoulder with a cold, withered hand. "We like you, Clark. It'd break our hearts if something were to happen to you."

There's no air in the room. Just the smell of his rancid breath and the acrid bite of Kitty's perfume.

"Thank you," I manage to say, and turn to leave.

Over Kitty's shoulder, in between a Hummel figurine and a plastic plant, is a photo on a shelf. My heart stutters when I see it. And it sees me. The

Lighthouse logo. The Eye of Providence. The Lazlos stand in front of it, smiling for the camera.

Their daytime television smiles return. I can feel them on me all the way out to my car.

EPILOGUE

Zeke stands in my doorway with a bag over his shoulder and a box full of books in his arm. His face is all stitched up and the other arm is in a sling. Then I see bags two and three at his feet.

"You gonna let me in?"

"Uhh. Yeah. Come in," I step aside and say. "What's all this?"

"My stuff."

"And?"

"You need a roommate."

"I don't—"

"You. Need. A roommate," he says and looks around my condo.

Fast food wrappers. Empty soda bottles. My shredded and bloody clothes in a pile on the living room floor.

"This shit is sad," he says and drops the box of books on my coffee table. "Besides. I've been living in my car. I'm kinda sick of it."

"Why do you live in your car? You're homeless?"

"Yeah. This monster-hunting gig? It doesn't pay so well."

I fish his check out of my back pocket and hand it to him. "Except for today."

He takes in the numbers, looks up at me, and smiles. "Fifteen thousand dollars. All I had to do was get chewed on by little goblin bastards and thrown out a window."

"What's with the books?" I ask, nodding to the box.

He sits on the couch and levels his gaze at me. "That's everything I've got on ghosts, the occult, monsters, and other spooky shit. This is the real business. You can't order this from Amazon. It's kept me alive this long. If we're going to do this, you've got some homework."

The box is water-stained and torn. The books inside are just as weathered, some dog-eared, some leather-bound and cracked with age.

Malleus Daemonium

Houses of the Eight Archons

Killing Cryptids

"Can these help find my friends?"

"If not, somebody out there knows. And I can be pretty persuasive."

I sit next to him. "Good. Now show me everything you've got on Rupert and Kitty Lazlo."

THE END

AFTERWORD

It took a long time to get here. Thanks for waiting. After my first novel, *the Black Goat Motorcycle Club*, there were a lot of false starts. Novels written. Novels discarded. Screenplays. Podcasts. YouTube. Many of those aborted efforts were nascent versions of what you see here. But now, we're finally out of the gates. There's a long, weird road ahead for Clark and the rest of the crew, a road full of tacos, nunchucks, and yes, werewolves. Sign up for my newsletter at www.jasonsmurphy.com.

The Occult Technologies, Incorporated gang returns in Occultex Book Two; *Necromancers On Drugs.*

ABOUT THE AUTHOR

Jason Murphy lives in Texas and spends most of his time writing novels, screenplays, video games, narrative podcasts, and comics. When not researching or writing about tradecraft, the occult, or the fantastic, he can be found spending time with his family, reading, or watching movies. He collects records, PEZ dispensers, Star Wars stuff, and Conan comics. He can occasionally be lured out of his lair with the promise of barbecue/tacos and good conversation.

Printed in Great Britain
by Amazon